GETTING GREEDY

A DOC WHITE ADVENTURE

B.R. SNOW

Copyright © 2019 B.R. Snow
ISBN: 978-1-942691-62-4

Website: www.brsnow.net
Twitter: @BernSnow
Facebook: facebook.com/bernsnow
Cover Design: Reggie Cullen

Other Books by B.R. Snow

The Thousand Islands Doggy Inn Mysteries

- The Case of the Abandoned Aussie
- The Case of the Brokenhearted Bulldog
- The Case of the Caged Cockers
- The Case of the Dapper Dandie Dinmont
- The Case of the Eccentric Elkhound
- The Case of the Faithful Frenchie
- The Case of the Graceful Goldens
- The Case of the Hurricane Hounds
- The Case of the Itinerant Ibizan
- The Case of the Jaded Jack Russell
- The Case of the Klutz King Charles
- The Case of the Lovable Labs
- The Case of the Mellow Maltese
- The Case of the Natty Newfie
- The Case of the Overdue Otterhound
- The Case of the Prescient Poodle
- The Case of the Quizzical Queens Beagle
- The Case of the Reliable Russian Spaniels
- The Case of the Salubrious Soft Coated Wheaten
- The Case of Italian Indigestion (A Josie and Chef Claire Sojourn)
- The Case of the Tenacious Tibetan
- The Case of the Unfettered Utonagan
- The Case of the Valiant Vizsla

The Whiskey Run Chronicles

- The Whiskey Run Chronicles – The Complete Volume 1
- The Whiskey Run Chronicles – The Complete Volume 2

The Damaged Posse

- American Midnight
- Larrikin Gene
- Sneaker World
- Summerman
- The Duplicates

Other Books

- Divorce Hotel
- Either Ore
- Get Off Your Duff and Write the Book

To the St. Croix Writer's Circle

CHAPTER 1

I woke with a start when the rooster, the local cock of the walk, loudly announced his presence. The bird, a magnificent black strutter with scarlet comb and wattle was thick through the chest and, based on his inability to keep his mouth shut in the early morning, living on borrowed time. Several other roosters joined the chorus and began their daily ritual of saying hello to their brethren along with the rest of the neighborhood.

I waited out an extended round of crowing then relaxed into my pillow and closed my eyes. The tick of the overhead fan lulled me back to sleep, but a soft spatter of rain kicked in. The tin roof began playing a syncopated rhythm that reminded me of a steel drum band attempting to play jazz. My cell phone buzzed and I glanced at the clock that read 5:10. I grabbed my reading glasses and struggled to identify the idiot calling so early in the morning.

"Merlin?" I said, sitting up in bed.

"What's up, Doc?"

"Me, if you must know," I said, stifling a yawn. "Why the hell are you calling me at five in the morning?"

"It's five there?" Merlin said. "Oh, yeah. That's right. It's only ten here."

"How's Hawaii?"

"I'm leaving today," Merlin said. "It's too…paradisiacal."

"Yeah, I've heard that about the place," I said, managing a small smile. "Where are you headed?"

"I'm going to D.C. for a few days. Then we'll see from there."

"Back into the belly of the beast, huh? I repeat. Why are you calling at five in the morning?"

"I had dinner with one of our old friends tonight, and he told me this crazy tale about how you had decided to move to the Virgin Islands."

"Who was it?" I said, rubbing sleep out of my eyes.

"I won't mention his name. Just in case anybody happens to be listening. And if you are, you guys really need to get a life." Merlin chuckled softly. "It was our old friend from Budapest."

"Budapest?" I said, searching my memory bank. "Okay, I got it. How's he looking these days?"

"Like death warmed over," Merlin said.

"So, about the same?"

"Yeah," Merlin said. "What's the deal, Doc? What the hell are you doing in the Virgin Islands?"

"Relaxing. Trying to enjoy retirement," I said, lighting a cigarette then coughing loudly when I took my first drag.

"Those things are gonna kill you," Merlin said. "Where are you?"

"St. Croix. Christiansted to be exact."

"What the hell are you doing down there, Doc?"

"Like I said, relaxing."

"Yeah, and I'm training to be a ballerina," Merlin said. "Well, I know you're not working." Merlin paused before continuing. "You're not working, right?"

"No, those days are over."

"Then it has to be a woman."

"Maybe," I said, finally giving up all hope of getting back to sleep and climbing out of bed.

"Well, I know it's not your ex-wife. That ship sailed and sunk a long time ago."

"No kidding," I said, laughing. "Try again."

Merlin fell silent, obviously giving it some thought.

"The Russian blonde you fell for in Helsinki?"

"Olga?"

"Yeah, that's the one."

"She's dead, Merlin."

"Oh, that's right," Merlin said. "What happened to her?"

"I shot her."

"Oops. Sorry, I completely forgot. Well, since she was about to shoot you, I guess you didn't have much choice."

"Yeah."

I waited out another long silence.

"Well, the only other woman I can think of that would you make you chase your tail halfway around the world is Elle. But it can't be her."

I went silent as I headed to the kitchen to make coffee. Merlin picked up on it and pressed the issue.

"Elle? Please tell me it's not her, Doc."

"I wish I could."

"You're such a glutton for punishment."

"She's in the middle of a nasty divorce. According to the rumors, the question of who gets their place down here is a major bone of contention."

"People are so stupid," Merlin said. "Fighting over crap."

"Hey, Sylvia and I spent two months arguing about who was going to get a box of CDs."

"Regardless, it's just a house."

"And only one of three," I said. "Both of them have moved in to convince the lawyers how much they love the place."

"Lovely," Merlin said, laughing.

"They've apparently got some sort of War of the Roses thing going on at the moment."

"Good movie," Merlin said. "Albeit, a dark, cautionary tale. How's she doing?"

"I haven't seen her yet," I said, staring at the coffeemaker and willing it to completion.

"What's your plan?"

"I thought I'd figure out a way to bump into her," I said. "I need some closure."

"So, you're going to stalk her?"

"No, I'm not going to be stalking her. It's a small island. It's only logical that at some point we'll run into each other."

"Geez, Doc. What the hell are we going to do with you?"

I could almost see my diminutive friend's disparaging stare.

"What are you working on?" I said, desperate for a new topic.

"Not much," Merlin said. "Our friend from Budapest needs a little help, and I owe him a favor. But I'm done with the other stuff. I've used up my nine lives, and I think it's time to quit pushing my luck."

"Smart."

"What about you? How are you going to stay busy?"

"I'm setting up shop as a PI."

Merlin fell silent, then laughed loudly.

"You're joking, right?"

"No. I'm not."

"Doc White is going to become a private investigator?"

"That's the plan," I said. "I got my business cards yesterday."

"Why on earth would you do that, Doc?"

Good question. A question I'd been asking myself since the idea first hit me on the flight to St. Croix.

"It's a way for me to stay sharp without having to deal with the stress of our former life," I said.

"Like getting shot or tortured?" Merlin said, laughing again.

"Yeah, stress like that."

"You're going to spend your time on the lookout for cheating spouses and guys who are behind on their child support?"

"I guess I'll be doing whatever people hire me to do," I said.

"You're not going to tell them about your old job, right?"

"Only when I have to," I said. "As far as anybody down here knows, I'm a retired cop from a small town in Vermont who's looking to escape the winters."

"Who also happens to be looking for the lost love of his life."

"Like I said, Merlin, it's about closure," I said, pouring a mug of coffee. "You should come down when you get a chance. I've got lots of room."

"Maybe I'll do that," Merlin said. "Did you buy a place down there?"

"I've got an option on it, but I'm going to hold off for a while."

"That's probably smart," Merlin said. "After you two reconnect, you'll probably want to get your own love nest."

"Don't start, Merlin. It's too early."

"Well, I'd say you're nuts, but you already know that."

"Yeah. And thanks for the vote of confidence."

7

"Glad I could help," Merlin said, laughing. "Okay, Doc. I'll let you go back to bed. Keep it loose."

"Will do," Doc said, then sipped coffee. "And next time, check the clock first."

"You got it," Merlin said. "Later."

He hung up and I tossed my phone on the kitchen counter. Coffee mug in hand, I headed for the wraparound gallery that fronted the house. I glanced over the edge and spotted the rooster strutting his stuff up and down the driveway. When he saw me, he puffed his chest out and let loose with three high-pitched squawks.

"Hey, big mouth, don't push your luck."

The rooster ignored me and resumed his strut.

I looked out over the harbor where a blanket of rain was making its inexorable march across the choppy water. Appreciating the early warning, I walked back inside to close some windows then headed for my office. I stopped in the middle of the room and glanced around at the stacks of boxes that still needed to be unpacked and put away. Dreading the prospect of starting my day that way, I sat down at the desk and turned my laptop on. I sipped coffee while waiting for it to boot up then punched in the address of a local website. Since the latest island news was a good place to look for potential clients, I began scrolling down the page but stopped when the banner headline caught my attention.

"Jump Up?" I whispered to the screen. I read the article then sat back, intrigued by the idea of costumed devotees of an ancient spirit called the Moko Jumbie walking on stilts. "Could be fun."

Walking on stilts? Isn't life hard enough already?

I shook my head at the voice. After making a return appearance several weeks ago, it was becoming all too frequent and increasingly annoying.

I'm only here to help.

I sighed and considered going back to bed. But as the rooster kept reminding me, the day had officially begun and I, while still two cups of coffee from alert, was wide awake.

CHAPTER 2

I dawdled for an hour as I waited the rain out. I worked my way through email, deleted most of it unopened, then tidied up before showering. Deciding a long walk in a soft drizzle didn't sound bad, I grabbed a container from the fridge and made the short walk across the lawn to my neighbor's house. As I always did, I scanned the exterior and fought the urge to have Sebastian's house painted.

I made my way toward the front porch and stopped when I heard the scratching of nails on wood vying for traction followed by ferocious barking designed to scare the crap out of potential intruders. The dog hit every other step on his way down to the lawn and made a beeline for me. Then recognition registered and he stopped at my feet and wagged his tail.

"Hey, Samson," I said, kneeling down to pet the dog.

The dog, a thick-chested Crucian mutt with a lot of pit bull in him, rolled over onto the wet grass for a belly-rub. I laughed at the expectant look the dog was giving me and complied with his request before continuing toward the house. Samson led the way but paused on the top step to shake off a torrent of water and grass. I knocked and looked out over the harbor as I waited.

"Good morning. Is that you, Doc?"

"Good morning, Sebastian," I said, opening the screen door. "I brought you some soup."

The old man grinned as he shook my hand then focused on the container. He struggled with the lid but managed to get it open. He held it close to his face and took a long whiff.

"That's very kind. Thank you, Doc," he said. "Fish chowder?"

"It used to be," I said with a shrug. "But you seemed to have a tough time getting the last batch down. So, I ran it through the blender."

"So, it's a soupy soup?" he said, his eyes twinkling at his joke.

"There you go," I said. "I'm heading into town to have some breakfast. Do you need anything?"

"No, I don't believe so," he said. "Are you taking Samson with you?"

"I thought I would. I didn't get a chance to walk him yesterday."

"Yes," he said, giving the dog a sad smile. "I'm afraid I'm failing as a pet owner."

"It's not a problem, Sebastian. I'm happy to do it." I focused on the dog. "You ready to go for a walk?"

The dog bounced in place then rested its front paws on my thigh.

"I think he likes the idea," Sebastian said, the sadness in his eyes impossible to miss.

"Do you need help with anything before we go?"

"No, I'll be fine," he said, peering out over the gallery. "I love the rain. Did I ever tell you about how we loved to run around in it when I was a boy?"

"Yes, I think you might have," I said, unwilling to remind him he'd told me the story at least a dozen times.

"Oh," he said, his lips pursed. "I must have forgotten." He leaned forward to rub the dog's head. "Okay, enjoy your walk."

He headed inside then returned with the dog's leash. I attached it to the dog's collar, and Samson immediately tightened the slack. I waved to the old man as we headed down the steps onto the lawn, a wave of melancholy washing over me until Sebastian's stark, daily reminder of my own mortality began to fade. Samson led the way and stopped as he always did when we reached the pothole tying the driveway and street together. The dog stared down at the massive hole, about four feet across and at least two feet deep, now half-filled with rainwater.

"Don't even think about it," I said with a laugh when I realized the dog was seriously considering an early morning dip.

I gently tugged the lead and Samson continued down the hill that would take us to Gallows Bay. As we walked, I looked out at the harbor and the morning boat traffic, a combination of commercial and pleasure craft crisscrossing their way in and out. When we reached Café Nirvana, I sat down at an outside table and waited for the dog to settle. I waved to an ex-pat couple I recognized then studied the menu. Moments later, my waitress strolled over, saw the dog and immediately knelt down to pet him.

"Good morning," she said, glancing up. "What's his name?"

"Good morning. His name is Samson."

"Appropriate," she said, nodding. "Where did you get him?"

"He belongs to my neighbor," I said, studying her closely. She was Crucian and somewhere in her thirties. Her hair, a gorgeous chocolate brown was stacked on her head in a tight bun. "You're new, right?"

"I started yesterday," she said, getting to her feet. "I needed a reason to get out of the house and Grams said she needed the help." She glanced around the now empty gallery and shrugged. "But between you and me, she doesn't."

"Grams? Mrs. Smith is your grandmother?"

"She is. I'm Felicia."

"It's nice to meet you. I'm Doc."

"Doc," she said softly as if trying the name on for size. "What can I get you?"

"Coffee, please. And I'd like a stack of pancakes with a side of bacon," I said, wondering why I'd even bothered to look at the menu. "And could you bring a side order of sausage for Samson?"

"He doesn't do his own hunting?" Felicia said with a grin.

"I'm trying to break him of that," I said, grinning back.

"Let me put your order in," she said, strolling away.

I did my best not to stare as she walked away then grabbed the newspaper from the empty table next to me. Halfway through, I shook my head and tossed it aside.

"The world is a mess, Samson," I said, glancing under the table at the dog now curled up at my feet.

The dog thumped his tail in agreement then placed his head on my foot and dozed off. I sipped coffee as I waited for my food. When Felicia returned carrying a tray, Samson went on point and crept out from underneath the table.

"Settle," I said in a low tone. "You know the deal, Samson. Half now. The rest of it when I finish eating."

The dog cocked his head then gently accepted the piece of sausage I was holding.

"He's a good dog," Felicia said. "Who's your neighbor?"

"Sebastian Anders," I said.

"I know Sebastian," she said. "Do you mind if I sit?"

"Not at all. As long as you won't get in trouble with your grandmother."

"Let's call it my morning break," Felicia said, reaching under the table to pet Samson. "Are you one who bought the Matthews' place?"

"I didn't buy it," I said. "But I have an option on it."

"Oh," she said. "I must have gotten bad information." She caught the look I was giving her and shrugged it off. "It's a small island, Doc."

"As I'm learning," I said, digging into my stack. "Would you like some?"

"Thank you, but no. How's Sebastian doing?"

"He's…hanging in there."

"The last time I saw him, he was struggling," Felicia said.

"Struggling? With what?" I said, setting my fork down.

"Getting old," she said softly. "He must be ninety."

"Ninety-one."

"A good run by any definition," she said without emotion.

"When did you see him?"

"A couple of years ago," she said. "I was following up on a report he filed about an intruder."

"You were?" I said, surprised. "You're a cop?"

"I was. And a good one," she said, staring out at the street. "When I went out to follow up on the complaint, I jokingly suggested to Sebastian he get a dog. I had no idea he'd take me seriously."

"And now you're a waitress?" I said, placing both elbows on the table and leaning forward.

"Not by choice," she said, sliding into an effortless laugh. "And I don't like my chances."

"What happened? To your career as a cop?"

"I was unceremoniously driven off the force," she said, her eyes boring into mine. "I had the audacity to file a complaint."

"About what?"

"The roaming hands of several of my colleagues," she said.

"Geez," I said, sitting back in my chair. "That sucks."

"That's what I thought," she said. "I tried to hang on, but after I filed the complaint, things got worse. I'm surprised you haven't heard the story."

"I only recently moved here," I said.

She nodded and again stared out at the street.

"It was quite an ordeal," she said. "Eventually, it was either get out or cave and become the department's regular punch. But…I'm nobody's chew toy."

I sat in silence toying with my pancakes.

"Your breakfast is going to get cold," she said, nodding at my plate.

"It's okay," I said softly. "When did you leave the force?"

"Six months ago. The department and I eventually came to an understanding."

"They wrote you a check to walk away?"

"Oh, so you have heard the story," she said, again laughing easily. "I spent the first four months on Gram's couch feeling sorry for myself. And the last two trying to figure out what the hell I'm going to do with the rest of my life. Being a cop is all I've ever wanted to do."

"Nothing against waitressing, but I can't imagine you're going to be happy doing it for very long."

"I've been here two days, and I'm already miserable," she said, noticing my empty cup. "But duty calls, let me warm up your coffee."

"No, thanks," I said. "Half a gallon a day is my limit."

"What brings you to St. Croix, Doc?"

"I thought I was ready to slide into retirement," I said, glancing down when Samson nudged my leg. I broke off a piece of sausage and held it under the table.

"You're a little young to retire, wouldn't you say?"

"In my line of work, it's not the years, it's the mileage."

"What did you do for work?"

"I was a small-town cop in Vermont," I said with a shrug.

She studied my face then shook her head.

"Sorry, Doc. I'm not buying it."

"Really?" I said, surprised.

"No. You're too…worldly to have been a small-town cop. But I think you might have worked in law enforcement. FBI, maybe." She sat back in her chair but maintained her stare. "I'm right, aren't I?"

"No, I didn't work for the Feebs," I said, put back on my heels by her directness. "I bet you were a good cop."

"I was," she said, still closely studying my reaction. "Not the FBI, huh? Well, it was something like that."

"Maybe," I said, sliding a forkful of pancake into my mouth.

"How are you enjoying retirement?"

"Actually, I've already started working again," I said. "I'm a newly minted PI."

"Good choice," she said, nodding. "There's a lot of people down here who can use your services."

"Why do you say that?" I said, again setting my fork down.

"Because there's a lot of people who can't get squat out of the local cops," she said. "Do you intimidate easily, Doc?"

"No," I said immediately. "Why do you ask?"

"Because the cops will hate you snooping around into things they might want ignored," Felicia said.

"It's that corrupt?"

"They have their moments," she said as she placed a hand on her head to tighten the bun. "And they hate people shoving it back into their face about how corrupt they can be. Especially by someone like you."

I frowned at her comment and let it roll around in my head.

"You mean, a white guy?"

"You're a quick study, Doc," she said.

An idea floated to the surface, and it was my turn to stare off into the street. I fed Samson another piece of sausage without looking as I ran the pros and cons through my head.

"I smell something burning," she said eventually.

"What?" I said, making eye contact and spotting the grin she was wearing. "Sorry. I drifted off for a sec."

It's kind of a nice break in the day, huh?

I ignored the voice and focused on the dog. I fed Samson what was left of the sausage then wiped my hands. I glanced across the table and couldn't miss the fact Felicia was still studying my expression with a coy smile.

"I was just wondering about something," I said.

"It happens to the best of us," she said. "Are you going to share it?"

"I was just wondering if you'd like to come work for me. I mean, with me."

She sat back in her chair without taking her eyes off me. But her expression had darkened.

"Is this your way of taking pity on the down on her luck Crucian girl, Doc?"

"I don't do pity," I said, shaking my head.

"Good to know," she said, still on edge. "So, what is it then?"

"It's simply a job offer."

"An offer too good to refuse?" she said. "Maybe an offer designed to get me horizontal?"

Struck by her bluntness, I sat back and spotted Samson staring up at me with an expectant look. I rubbed the dog's head to buy some time then sat back and draped a leg over my knee.

"No, that's not part of the job," I said. "Any decisions about getting horizontal will be strictly up to you."

I wouldn't mind having a vote.

"Good answer," she said, finally breaking the tension at the table. "What would I be doing?"

"I'm new to the PI business, but I imagine it would be anything that comes up based on what the client needs," I said, then felt the need to clarify. "Within reason, of course."

"Why don't I believe you?" she said.

It sounded like a legitimate question I needed to answer.

"Probably because you used to be a cop," I said with a shrug. "And there's that horizontal thing hanging over us."

She laughed loudly, startling Samson. The dog poked his head out from under the table and looked back and forth at us before settling back down.

"I'm a little gun shy these days," she said. "Tell me more."

"I don't really know much more at this point, Felicia. But we'll figure it out."

"Just like that?" she said, still unsure.

"Pretty much," I said. "But it's not a pity offer. I'll need help getting clients, and you're a local who used to be a cop down here. I imagine a lot of people trust you."

"They do. Will I get a chance to stick it to the cops?"

"Every chance we get," I said, laughing.

"What about money?"

"More than you'll make as a waitress," I said. "And a whole lot more than you will laying on your grandmother's couch."

She sat back and Samson draped his head in her lap. She stroked the dog's head for several moments before focusing on me.

"I'm going to need to think about it, Doc."

"That's not a problem."

"When do you need to know?"

"There's no hurry."

"Okay," she said, nodding. "I do miss the work. But I have no idea who you are."

"Then let's start with an easy one," I said.

"How so?"

"Are you planning on going to Jump Up?"

"I never miss them," she said.

"Then go with me," I said. "We can get to know each other a bit. You can show me the sights. Explain some of the history. Stuff like that."

"I suppose I could do that."

"And you should feel comfortable being there with me," I said.

"Why's that?" she said, raising an eyebrow.

"Well, as far as I can tell, it's a vertical event."

CHAPTER 3

I checked in on Sebastian and Samson before making the short drive into town. I got lucky and found street parking then walked up Hill to Queens Cross and headed for balter. The crowd was building, a blend of locals and tourists all determined to have a good time, and I kept glancing around for signs of the stilt walkers. Deciding it must be too early for their appearance, I paused at the front door to take a final look around the crowded streets then entered.

"Good evening," the hostess said. "Are you here for dinner?"

"Good evening. No, I'm just meeting someone for drinks."

"No problem," she said, gesturing toward the bar. "Enjoy your evening."

I sat down at the small bar, ordered a Presidente then glanced around the upscale establishment that would have been right at home in any mainland city. I was halfway through my beer when Felicia entered and spotted me sitting a few feet away. She was dressed for comfort, and her hair was again wrapped tight on top of her head.

"Good evening," she said, sliding into the seat next to me. "Am I late?"

"Good evening," I said, raising my hand to get the bartender's attention. "Not at all. I just got here. What are you having?"

"A glass of wine, please," she said, smiling at the man behind the bar. "Pinot Grigio."

She sat back in her chair and glanced around the dining room, waving to someone she recognized. Then she focused on me.

"How was the rest of your day?"

"It was good. Quiet."

"Quiet is good," she said. "And very underrated."

"Delight in meditation and solitude," I said softly.

"Who said that?" Felicia said, pausing mid-sip.

"I thought I did."

"So, you're a comedian, too?" she said, sliding into what appeared to be her trademark laugh.

"It's a Buddhist sentiment."

"Maybe I should give the Buddha a shot," she said, swirling the wine in her glass.

Something about the way she said it caught my attention; contemplative yet tinged with a trace of self-pity.

"Because your faith has been severely tested?"

She stared at me then nodded before taking another sip.

"Yeah, you could say that."

"Can I ask you a question?" I said.

"Are you going to try to slow-walk me toward enlightenment, Doc?" she said through a playful grin.

"No, I decided a long time ago that wasn't in the cards until I figured it out for myself."

"A man without all the answers," she said. "How refreshing."

It was my turn to laugh.

"So, what's your question?" she said.

"I'm just wondering if that hurts," I said, pointing at the bun on top of her head. "It's wrapped so tight."

"What a weird question. You really are an odd duck," she said, gently pressing her hair. "No, it doesn't hurt. Don't you like it?"

"I have a feeling it wouldn't matter what you did with it," I said. "Have you given any thought to my offer?"

"It's all I've been thinking about all day," Felicia said, taking a long sip.

"And?"

"I'm still thinking," she said without emotion.

"Take all the time you need."

"I will," she said. "But there was one thing you said that bothered me."

I silently replayed our conversation at the restaurant as I took a couple of sips but came up empty. I sat back in my chair and waited.

"You made a comment about being a white guy," she said eventually.

"And that bothered you?"

"The context bothered me," Felicia said. "You inferred some sort of racial overtones about living down here."

"I did," I said, nodding. "What about it?"

"You seemed to be saying black people have a problem with whites."

"I was referring to initial reactions," I said. "The first hurdle."

"I see," she said. "It's okay if you don't want to talk about it. It's a difficult topic."

"No, I'm very comfortable having the conversation. If we can't talk about it, how the hell are we ever going to fix it?" I said. "There's an initial mistrust that only goes away over time. From both sides. And depending on the individuals involved, maybe not even then. It's unspoken and often obscured by the friendly nature of the people who

27

live here. But it's there. And to deny it is…well, quite frankly, less than honest."

"It cuts both ways," Felicia said.

"Of course, it does," I said. "And given what's been perpetrated on the world by my so-called brethren, if I were of…darker persuasion, I'd feel exactly the same way."

"Interesting. So, it's all about overcoming an initial mistrust?" she said, giving it some serious thought.

"It is for me," I said, reaching for my beer.

"Okay," she said, nodding. "It just seemed like an odd comment to make."

"It's an observation. Not a philosophy."

"Good to know," she said, then glanced out the window. "It looks like a big turnout."

"You about ready to go?" I said.

"We have plenty of time," she said. "By now, you must be familiar with the concept of island time."

"I am," I said. "It's called being fashionably late where I come from."

"And where exactly is that, Doc?" she said, grinning at me. "Vermont, right?"

"I've been there," I said, deflecting the question. "It's nice. But cold in the winter."

"It doesn't matter," she said. "You'll tell me when you're ready."

"Maintaining a little mystery is a good thing," I said.

"Another observation?"

"No, actually, that one is more of a philosophy," I said, laughing.

She took a small sip then set the half-filled glass down and stared at it.

"I should probably slow down," Felicia said. "It's going down way too easy."

"I have to watch it myself," I said. "It's a drinking culture."

"It is," she said, nodding. "Among other things." Then she fixed a hard stare on me. "Why did you move here, Doc?"

"You mean, of all the gin joints in all the towns in all the world?" I said.

"Sure," she said, laughing loudly. "If you feel the need to go all Bogie on me."

That laugh is going to be a problem for us.

I nodded to the voice and decided to be honest with her.

"I came here because of a woman."

Surprised by my response, she flinched but quickly recovered. Probably reading too much into her reaction, I took it as a good sign.

"I see," Felicia said. "Where is she?"

"I imagine she and her husband are at their house on the north shore," I said.

"Ouch," she whispered.

"No, it's okay. It's been a long time. All that remains are questions."

"And you thought moving here was a good way to get them answered?" Felicia said, reaching for her wine.

"That's what I thought. Now, I'm not so sure why I even bothered."

"Have you seen her?"

"No, I haven't," I said. "But like you said, it's a small island. It's bound to happen. I suppose it's possible they're here tonight."

"Unrequited love, huh?" she said, again giving me her best cop stare. "The one that got away?"

"It was more of a slow drift apart. As opposed to an escape, if that's what you're asking."

"I'm just being nosy," she said, again swirling the wine in her glass. "What happened? Did you guys end up cheating on each other?"

"No. As far as I know."

"Was it about money?"

"I'm sure that had something to do with it," I said. "He's got a ton. And that was before I made mine."

"And she couldn't handle the winters in Vermont, right?" she said, again tormenting me with her laugh.

"You're tenacious," I said, laughing along.

"All the good cops are."

"There was a lot more to it than just money," I said. "Have you ever been in a relationship that could only get so far until it hit the wall?"

"You see a ring on this finger?" she said, flashing her left hand. "What do you think?"

"I had a therapist who loved to say that there's a very thin line between love and hate," I said, glancing off into the dining room as I flashed back to the memory.

"Sure, I get that," Felicia said, nodding.

"Unfortunately, Elle and I were always daring each other to step across it."

She laughed again then drained the last of her wine.

"So, how did you make your money, Doc?"

"I stole most of it," I said with a shrug.

"Probably not the smartest thing to say to an ex-cop."

"Good luck catching me," I said with another shrug. "And the people I stole it from will never miss it."

"Because?"

"Because they're either dead or in prison," I said. "If it helps, they were all scumbags."

Felicia sat back in her chair, deep in thought.

"You're not joking, are you?" she said eventually.

"No."

"I'm going to need to hear a lot more about that," she said.

"I'm sure you will," I said. "Eventually."

"As long as I'm working for you, right?"

"Or if we're dating," I said, deciding it was time to put one of my cards on the bar.

"I see," she said, now wary. "You got a preference?"

"I don't know," I said. "Maybe we can do both."

"Workplace romances are tough," Felicia said. "You ever tried it?"

"Yeah. Once in particular. It didn't end well," I said.

"What happened?"

"I shot her," I said, then caught the look of shock in her eyes. "In self-defense, of course."

"Of course," she said, raising an eyebrow. "That pesky thin line, right?"

"They don't come much thinner," I said, finishing the last of my beer.

"You stole all your money and shot your ex-girlfriend," she said, relaxing a bit. "So much for maintaining an air of mystery."

"Trust me, there's a lot more where that came from," I said.

"I believe you," she said. "But I have to say, that's quite a recruiting pitch you've got there, Doc."

"Thanks," I said, grinning at her. "I've been working on it all day."

"How about we go check out the party?"

"Sounds good," I said, tossing money on the bar before sliding out of my chair. "I could use the walk. Let's go find the vertical ones."

"Don't take this the wrong way, Doc, but you're a very strange man."

"The word you're looking for is damaged," I said, holding the door open for her.

"Aren't we all," she said, heading outside to the sights and smells that immediately overwhelmed us.

CHAPTER 4

We came to a stop at the corner just outside the restaurant. The crowd had continued to build, and the best description I could come up with for what stretched out in front of me was a scene of relaxed-festivity. Felicia tugged my arm and nodded for me to follow her. We headed down Company past several shops that were still open, many with their wares on display outside. A food truck throwing off copious amounts of meat-flavored smoke made my stomach rumble as we walked past. I came to a stop to take a closer look at what they were grilling and glanced at Felicia who had her eyes on the half-chickens sizzling on one section of the large grill.

"You want to eat now?" I said.

"Let's wait," she said, again gently tugging my arm as she continued down the street.

Moments later, I heard the unmistakable sound of a steel-drum band, and we were soon standing in front of a dozen teenagers dressed identically in khaki shorts and bright blue polo shirts. The boys, all doing their best to look composed and cool, were playing oversized drums in the back row. The young women were less reserved and wore huge smiles as they handled the higher octaves on smaller drums that glistened in what was left of the sunlight. I listened to the multi-part arrangement, nodding as I tapped my foot.

"They're good," I said. "And young."

"They're sponsored by one of the local churches," she said, waving to one of the band members who beamed back at her.

"Tell me about the Moko Jumbies," I said, glancing around for signs of the stilt walkers.

"The original slaves from Africa brought the tradition with them," Felicia said, sitting down on a set of steps. She waved to a couple as they passed then focused on me. "Many of the slaves' traditional practices weren't allowed by their owners, but that one managed to survive."

I flinched at her mention of owners but continued to pay close attention.

"The Moko Jumbies are seen as cultural symbols of our heritage. And their presence is considered a blessing."

"Okay," I said. "I get it. But what does the term mean?"

"It depends," Felicia said. "To many people, Moko means healer. Jumbie is a term for spirit. Or ghost."

"So, they're considered some sort of protector?"

"Basically, yes," she said. "And in costume, they are no longer human. They have become Moko Jumbies."

"Do the stilts have some sort of religious significance?" I said, again scanning the crowd for signs of the walkers.

"Yes," she said. "To some, their height is a tribute to the power of God. Other people had more practical beliefs. They believed the Moko Jumbies were capable of seeing danger before it arrived in the village and were able to warn other members of the tribe. It probably sounds odd to you."

"Not any stranger than a lot of other religious practices," I said. "If I'm not careful, I'm liable to come back as a cockroach."

"You're really a practicing Buddhist?" Felicia said, surprised. "I thought you might be joking."

"Practicing is the operative word," I said with a laugh. "But yes, I am. I'm drawn to the idea of being able to keep coming back until I get it right. But don't worry, I'll be around for a while."

She laughed and shook her head.

"Yes, from what I've seen so far, Doc, you've definitely got work left to do. Come. Let's walk."

We strolled back up Company, and the crowd grew as we got closer to balter. We made a right and headed in the direction of the boardwalk that fronted the harbor. We came to a stop in front of another band, this one a five-piece playing an energetic style of reggae-tinged funk. I immediately began tapping my foot as I studied the rhythm section.

"These guys are good," I said, then did my best to not stare at Felicia as she swayed to the music.

"They are," she said, grabbing my hand. "Dance with me."

"I don't dance."

"Really?" she said, surprised. "How unfortunate."

"I barely balter," I said, gently pulling back against the tug she was giving my arm.

"Balter?" she said, raising an eyebrow as she let go of my hand. "Like the restaurant?"

"To dance clumsily," I said, staring off into the distance.

"I did not know that," she said, then continued her solo dance.

My eyes went back and forth between her and the stilt-walkers who were slowly making their way up the hill from the Boardwalk. There were six of them, and their effortless, inexorable march up the inclined street was soon my sole focus. Felicia also studied them while she continued to sway back and forth to the pulsating funk.

"Impressive," I said.

"What?" she shouted over the music.

"I said they're impressive."

"They are."

"They've gotta be fifteen feet tall," I said, studying the stilt walker at the front of the pack.

Dressed in a bright red floral costume, his or her face covered by what looked like a hospital mask, the walker's expertise was evident. The band finished the song to loud applause, and Felicia brushed sweat off her forehead. I handed her a bottle of water, and she took a long swallow as she continued to watch the elaborately costumed walkers.

"How do they learn to do that?" I said.

"There's a training school on the island," she said, then tossed the empty bottle into a nearby trash bin.

"Keeping the tradition alive?"

"Exactly. I tried it once when I was a kid," she said. "It didn't go well. After I did a face-plant, I decided some people are better off at ground level."

"I had a similar experience when I was trying to learn how to waterski barefoot," I said, shaking my head at the memory.

"How so?"

"I asked the guy who was teaching me what I was supposed to do," I said. "He said, the second time, you want to lean back as far as you can. I said, what about the first time?"

"And he said, don't worry about the first time?" Felicia said with a grin.

"Exactly. Face-plant at forty miles an hour," I said. "Not a pleasant experience."

We watched the stint walkers continue to head straight for us. The band launched into another up-tempo song, the volume amped up even louder. I tapped my foot as I stared at the walkers. All six were clearly visible, and I got my first good look at their ornate costumes that were tailored to each individual. The drums and bass thumped loudly as the keyboard player began an intricate solo, but the walkers maintained their focus as they walked past the band.

Then the red-clad Moku Jumbie appeared to stumble and lose balance. The walker's steps increased in frequency and stride in a desperate attempt to remain upright but was soon out of control and heading directly for us. I stepped in front of Felicia when I realized the walker was about to fall and, moments later, he crashed into me. I ended up flat on my back with the Moku Jumbie on top of me, and apart from a labored attempt to get control of his breathing, he wasn't moving.

"Are you okay?" I said, staring up directly into the mask the walker was wearing.

"Are you all right, Doc?" Felicia said, kneeling down over both of us.

"Yeah, I'm fine," I said, gently holding the Moku Jumbie by the shoulders and rolling him over onto his back. "But I think this guy hurt himself."

"Are you sure you're okay?" she said, gently touching my chest.

"Yeah. Why do you ask?"

"Because of all the blood," she said, glancing at the stint walker sprawled out on the ground. "If it's not yours, then it has to be his."

I sat up and examined the Moko Jumbie. Despite the red costume, it was impossible to miss the blood surging out of his chest.

"What the hell?" I said, rolling over onto my knees. "He's been shot."

Felicia tore away the upper portion of the walker's costume and grimaced when she spotted the seeping wound.

"Oh, no," she said, pressing both hands against the walker's chest. "Give me a hand, Doc."

I did as instructed and we worked in tandem to stem the flow of blood. A crowd had formed in a circle around us, and I glanced up and spotted the other Moku Jumbies staring down from above at their fallen colleague. Moments later, we heard the walker exhale loudly then fall silent. I stared down at my blood-soaked hands then shook my head and slowly got to my feet. Felicia held two fingers against the walker's neck then extended a hand. I helped her up and we stared at each other in disbelief.

"He's gone," Felicia whispered.

"Did you hear a gunshot?" I said, my eyes scanning the immediate area.

"Not over the music," she said, shaking her head. She knelt down and slid the mask off the walker's face. "Geez. Not Willy."

"You know the guy?"

"I do," she said as tears began streaming down her face. "His mom is a friend of mine."

"Why would anybody want to shoot him?"

"I have no idea," she said, then addressed the stunned, yet rubbernecking, crowd. "Please, stand back a bit. The police will be here soon."

At the mention of the police, most of the people moved back, and I couldn't miss the fact that several others were beginning to make themselves scarce. I took another look around the immediate area then my eyes drifted up. I nudged Felicia's arm and she followed my stare.

"Second floor," she said, nodding. "The trajectory angle works."

"It does," I said, scanning the windows and the flat roof of one of the buildings overlooking the street. "Easy shot from up there. You got any ideas?"

"No," she said, wiping her hands on her blouse. "Just a whole bunch of questions."

The onlookers began to part like the Red Sea as two uniformed cops appeared. They both nodded at Felicia then knelt down over the body. They shared a brief, hushed conversation then got to their feet.

"We're going to need to speak with all of you," one of the cops said in a loud voice. "So, please, remain where you are."

The other cop wandered over toward us and gave Felicia a small wave.

"Good evening, Felicia," he said, then glanced at me.

"Good evening, Tony," she said with a nod while keeping a close eye on the other cop who was again kneeling down over the dead Moko Jumbie.

"It's been a long time," the cop said. "You're looking good."

"Thanks," Felicia whispered, then tensed up when the other cop got to his feet and headed our way.

"I should have known," the cop said in a mocking tone. "Whenever there's trouble, Felicia can't be far away."

"Screw you, Walt," Felicia said as she again wiped her hands on her blouse.

Then he noticed my dark stare and gave me the once-over.

"You have a problem, sir?" he said.

"I guess that remains to be seen," I said.

"I imagine you're right," he said, his eyes narrowed. "Judging from the blood on you, am I correct assuming you found the body?"

"He lost his balance and fell on me after he got shot," I said softly.

"How do you know he was shot?" the cop named Walt said.

"Well, the exit wound in his chest was my first clue," I deadpanned.

He thought about responding to my tone, then shrugged it off.

"We'll need to speak with both of you," Walt said. "But first, I need to get a few things organized around here." He gave me a cold stare. "So, stay close." He snapped his fingers at the other cop. "Let's go, Tony. You're on crowd control."

Felicia's dark expression didn't change as we watched them head off.

"Let me guess. They're part of the wandering hands gang?" I said.

"Tony's okay," Felicia said. "But Walt's a pig."

"Good to know," I said, taking another look around. "What do you think?"

"I'd need to get up there and take a closer look," she said, glancing up at the roof. "But the shot had to come from above."

"Yeah," I whispered. "Geez, the poor kid couldn't have been out of his teens."

"No, he wasn't," Felicia said, then focused on the two cops who were now chatting with several other colleagues who'd arrived at the scene. She glowered at several of the policemen then shook her head and walked to the other side of the street.

"What are the chances they'll catch whoever did it?" I said, studying her expression.

"It depends," she said.

"On what?"

"On who they think shot him," she said, glancing over at me.

I thought about the cryptic nature of her comment as I continued to study the immediate area. When I looked back at her, Felicia was in full cop mode as she scanned our surroundings through narrowed eyes.

"You got any thoughts on a motive?" I said.

"No," she said. "I haven't seen Willy since I arrested him several years ago."

"Several years ago?" I said, confused. "A kid-criminal?"

"Willy started early," Felicia said. "But I thought he'd cleaned up his act. This is gonna kill his mom."

"Yeah, I'm sure it will," I said, taking another look around. "I've got a whole bunch of questions."

"Me too," she said as she followed my eyes to the second floor of the building directly across the street from us. "Doc?"

"Yeah."

"I'll take the job."

CHAPTER 5

Dupree Perkins studied the article in the Avis then closed the newspaper and slid it to one side. The paper fluttered in the breeze and Dupree drained the last of his beer and set the bottle on top of it. He stretched his long legs out, crossed at the ankles, as he leaned back against the picnic table.

"Man, that poor kid," Dupree said softly as he studied the boats coming in and out of the harbor. "What a way to go."

"Hey, he was warned. No freelancing."

"Yeah, I know. But still, he was a good kid." Dupree glanced over at his associate, Harry Wilder, and watched as he examined his sunburnt arms. "You need to start using sunblock and lotion," Dupree said, shaking his head. "Or you're gonna end up looking like a lizard."

"I'm fine," Harry said, scratching his forearms and throwing off a torrent of dead skin. "I just need to build up a base."

Dupree chuckled as he reached into his shirt pocket. He lit a joint and took a long hit as he continued to stare out at the water.

"What are you doing?" Harry said.

"I'm having a smoke," Dupree said, exhaling. "What does it look like?"

"Out here? What if somebody sees you?"

Dupree glanced over his shoulder at the stretch of empty picnic tables between them and the entrance to the Nauti Bar. He took another hit then held it out to Harry.

"I'll take my chances," Dupree said, exhaling smoke again.

"Nah, I better not," Harry said. "We're working tonight."

"Not until nine," Dupree said as he continued to hold the joint out.

"Maybe just one," Harry said, taking a long hit before handing it back. "Here comes the St. Thomas ferry," he said in a smoky-squeak. "You think the shooter was on it this morning?"

"If he knows what's good for him, he was. But I imagine he left the island last night," Dupree said, taking a final hit before extinguishing the joint and slipping it back into his pocket. "I still can't believe he had the kid shot."

"He doesn't like surprises," Harry said.

"Then let's hope he doesn't find out what we're up to," Dupree said, then flinched when the music began blaring from the outside speakers. "Really? Country? Did you ask the bartender to play that crap?"

"It's a brilliant American art form," Harry said.

"Let me ask you a question, Harry," Dupree said, glancing over. "How does a Julliard graduate end up playing country music?"

"It's about storytelling," Harry said, immediately defensive. "You wouldn't understand."

"How many stories about beer and trucks can there be?"

"It's about a lot more than beer and trucks, and you know it," Harry said.

"Okay, whatever you say, Harry. It's not worth fighting about. You keep listening to your country crap. I'll stick with jazz."

"Jazz," Harry said with a snort. "The music of pseudo-intellectuals everywhere."

"I'm not going to waste my time trying to explain it to you," Dupree said. "Man, that's good weed."

"I played jazz for years."

"Really?" Dupree said. "I didn't know that."

"Yeah," Harry said, staring out at the harbor. "Three sets a night in front of maybe two dozen people. All of them convinced they were smarter than everybody else just because they liked jazz. Or at least did their best to convince others they liked it."

"Well, I love it," Dupree said. "Now that's the truly great American art form."

"It's fun to play," Harry said. "But I finally figured out, for most people, jazz is just too much work to listen to."

"You played jazz guitar?" Dupree said, studying his associate's expression.

"I was playing piano back then," Harry said, shaking his head. "For fifty bucks a night. What a waste of time."

"And you gave it up to write hillbilly schlock?"

"See, that's exactly what I'm talking about," Harry snapped. "Typical jazz snob."

Dupree laughed and placed a hand on Harry's shoulder.

"Don't take it personal, my man. I get it. Listening can be hard work. Especially when country music is blaring through the speakers."

"Go screw yourself, Dupree," Harry said, then glanced over at Dupree. "I've been working on a new song."

"Cool. Lay it on me," Dupree said, turning toward Harry and draping a leg over his knee.

"I'm still working on the verses, but I finished the chorus," Harry said.

"Let's hear what you got," Dupree said.

"It's called It Sucks Getting Old."

"You'll get no argument from me," Dupree said.

Harry sat straight up and recited from memory.

"When the truth is finally told, after all those years being bought and sold. You find yourself out in the cold. No hands on the gold. Or the centerfold. If I may be so bold, there's not much beauty to behold. So, before I go, the truth must be told…it sucks getting old."

Harry leaned back against the picnic table and waited for Dupree's response.

"Well?" he said after a long pause.

"I assume you'll be working beer and trucks into the verses, right?" Dupree deadpanned.

"Why do I even bother?"

"Relax, man. I like it," Dupree said, nodding. "It's good. It's got that common man quality. You know, working your butt off for years before you finally figure some stuff out. Hopefully, before you're too old to put it to good use. It sucks getting old. Can't argue with that. Yeah, good stuff. I like it."

"Thanks. You want another beer?"

"Yeah, maybe a traveler for the road," Dupree said, then grinned at Harry. "You know, for the truck ride."

"Go screw yourself, Dupree."

"Relax, I'm just busting your chops. It's good. I hope you sell it and make a million bucks."

"It ain't about the money," Harry said.

"Harry, let me tell you something I've learned over the years," Dupree said. "It's always about the money."

"Maybe," Harry said, staring out at the water. Then he nudged Dupree with his elbow. "Look who's here."

They watched as the luxury sailboat slowly made its way into the harbor and approached the long dock.

"Beautiful boat," Dupree said.

"Yeah," Harry said without taking his eyes off the massive vessel. "How much does something like that go for?"

"If you have to ask, you can't afford it," Dupree said. "It's gotta be a hundred feet. Maybe more. And I'm sure it's all tricked out inside."

"I'm sure it is," Harry said. "The guy has to have the best of everything."

"You'll get no argument from me," Dupree said, nodding at the woman who had left the boat and was now standing on the dock waving goodbye. "Take a look at her."

"She's blonde," Harry said. "The one he dropped off last week was black."

"Yeah," Dupree said. "The man gets around."

"Why do you think he always drops them off here?" Harry said.

"Well, the man is going through a divorce," Dupree said, watching the woman stroll down the dock. "It's not like he can be dropping his chippies off at the yacht club. Too close to his house."

"Yeah, makes sense," Harry said. "I still can't figure out why the man needs more than his missus. She's something else."

"She is," Dupree said, staring out at the boat that had left the dock and was raising its mainsail. "Maybe he got bored with her. Or he just sleeps around because he can."

"Maybe she'll get the boat in the divorce," Harry said. "I'd love to take a ride on it."

"I wouldn't get your hopes up, Harry. Even if she did, the only chance we'd have to get on it would be as bartenders."

"Yeah, you're probably right," Harry said, nodding. "So, how much do you think he paid for it?"

"I heard he bought it used," Dupree said. "Probably fifteen, maybe twenty million."

"For a used boat?"

"Better than paying fifty for a new one," Dupree said with a shrug.

"Life ain't fair," Harry said.

"Hey, there's the title of your next song," Dupree said with a laugh. "You can do a whole album on that theme."

"I'm sure I could," Harry said. "You ready to go?"

"Yeah," Dupree said, slapping his thighs before getting to his feet. "Come on. Let's go steal something."

CHAPTER 6

I gave the enormous pothole a wide berth as I slowed down then came to a stop at the entrance to the driveway. Unable to see a path around it without running the risk of doing damage to the bottom of the vehicle, I put the car in park and left it running before I hopped out to examine the pothole that seemed to be getting bigger by the day. Felicia also climbed out and stood next to me as I stared down at the ground.

"I didn't know you were putting in a pool," she deadpanned.

"Funny," I said. "But it's a problem. What do I need to do to get it fixed?"

"Give me two hundred bucks."

"Does that include the cost of materials?" I said, glancing over at her.

"You idiot," she said, laughing. "We just need to get you moved up to the top of the list."

"Okay," I said, frowning.

"I know the guy who heads one of the maintenance crews," Felicia said. "And two hundred will get him out here. Make it three hundred, and he'll have a crew out here tomorrow morning."

"Do you know everybody on this island?" I said.

"Most of them," she said with a shrug then climbed back in the passenger seat.

I hopped back in and did my best to inch the car around the pothole. But one of my back wheels dropped, and I heard the frame scrape against the edge. I shook my head in frustration then picked up speed as I drove up the driveway to the house. We walked inside and headed straight for my office. Felicia sat down on the couch and made the call. I listened to her side of the short conversation then she tossed her phone on the coffee table.

"He'll have a crew out here as soon as he can," she said.

"Money talks, huh?" I said, firing up my laptop. "I thought we'd go shopping later to get you a desk."

"Sounds good," Felicia said. "What are you doing?"

"I've been working on an ad," I said, studying my computer screen. "You know, to drum up some clients."

She got off the couch and studied the ad over my shoulder.

"Island Probes?" Felicia said. "Catchy."

"I couldn't come up with a better name," I said, glancing up at her. "I've been looking for a follow-up story on the murder. But it's gone quiet."

"Yeah, the cops are slow-walking this one," she said, heading back to the couch.

"Because?"

"I spoke to Willy's mom yesterday," Felicia said. "The cops are already trying to convince her to move on."

"What?" I said, getting up from my desk and sitting down in an armchair across from the couch.

"No suspects, no clues, no real witnesses," she said.

"So, instead of digging in, they just let it go?"

"Pretty much," she said with a shrug.

"Why on earth would they do that?" I said, baffled by the lack of basic follow-through.

"Why don't we let her try to explain it?" Felicia said, glancing out the window at the car heading up the driveway and coming to a stop next to my SUV.

"She's here?" I said, getting to my feet to look out the window.

"That's her," Felicia said, heading for the door.

I remained in the office and listened to the muffled conversation the two women were having by the front door. Then they entered the office. Felicia led a woman to the couch, and she sat erect with both hands on the purse perched on her lap. She was somewhere in her fifties and obviously still in shock at the loss of her son. She gave me a blank stare then glanced at Felicia who had sat down next to her.

"Doc, this is Mildred Johnson," Felicia said. "Millie, this is the man I was telling you about. Doc White."

"It's nice to meet you, Mr. White," she said, then sighed.

"The pleasure is mine, Mrs. Johnson," I said. "I'm so sorry for your loss."

She took a few deep breaths and managed a small nod.

"How can we help you?" I said, taking a seat across from them.

"I'd like you to find the person who killed my son," she said softly.

"I see," I said, glancing at Felicia. "I give you my word that I'll do my best."

"Oh, with all due respect, I'm not here because of you, Mr. White," she said, her blank stare unchanged. "I'm here because of Felicia."

"Okay," I said softly.

"I wouldn't know you from Adam," Mrs. Johnson said. "But Felicia tells me I can trust you. And that's enough for me." Then she made solid eye contact with me. "I'm afraid I don't have much money, Mr. White."

"Mrs. Johnson, you have enough to worry about at the moment," I said. "Let's not add money to the list."

She raised an eyebrow at me then glanced at Felicia.

"I told you," Felicia said, gently patting the woman's knee.

"People who offer to work for free make me suspicious," Mrs. Johnson said.

"Me too," I said with a shrug. "But let's call it an investment Felicia and I are making in our new business. You know, as a way to start building our reputation."

Mrs. Johnson glanced back and forth at us then managed a small shrug. She sat back on the couch but continued to clutch her purse with both hands.

"Tell me a bit about your son," I said.

"I thought Willy had turned the corner," she said after a long pause. "But I knew he had been up to something the past few months."

"Such as?" I said.

"I really don't know," she said. "Whenever I tried to press him, he would always say I worried too much. But I knew he was doing some things he shouldn't have."

"How did you know that?" I said, gently probing.

"Odd hours. Missing work. Late night phone calls," she said. "There were a lot of things, Mr. White. A mother knows."

I nodded and filed the information away for additional follow-up.

"What have the police told you?" I said.

"You didn't tell him?" she said, doing a half-turn toward Felicia.

"I thought he should hear it from you," Felicia said, again patting the woman's knee.

"The police want the whole situation to go away," she said softly.

"I don't understand," I said, leaning forward in my chair. "That is their job, right?"

"How well do you know the island, Mr. White?"

"Not well," I said. "I've only been here a short time."

"I'm afraid there are times when the police can't be counted on," Mrs. Johnson said.

"Because they're corrupt?" I said, watching her closely.

"I'm sure that's part of the equation at times," she said.

I frowned at her cryptic nature of the comment but waited for her to continue.

"But the main problem is that some of the police are scared," she said.

"Scared? Of what?"

"Retribution," Mrs. Johnson said.

I sat back in my chair deep in thought.

"The police are worried about what might happen to them if they dig too deep into your son's murder?" I said.

"Yes. But I imagine they're most worried about what might happen to their families."

I sat quietly staring out the window as I processed what she'd just told me.

"Gangs," I said eventually. "You're talking about gangs."

"Very good, Mr. White."

"The local gangs know where the cops and their family members live, right?" I said, glancing at Felicia for confirmation.

"It's a small island, Mr. White," Mrs. Johnson said.

"And you think Willy was involved with one of them?"

"I didn't," she said. "Until I talked to the police. It's pretty clear they think he was."

"Okay," I said. "That gives us something to start with. Was Willy still attending the stilt walking school?"

"He was," she said.

"I know the owner," Felicia said.

"Now, there's a surprise," I said, flashing her a grin before refocusing on the grieving mother. "Were you at Jump Up the other night?"

"I was," she said, her eyes brightening for the first time since she'd arrived. "I never missed one of Willy's performances."

An idea bubbled to the surface.

"You didn't happen to get it on video, did you?"

"Actually, I did," she said, again reaching into her purse and removing her phone. "I was standing on the corner next to the restaurant the whole time."

"Balter?" I said.

"Yes, that's the one," Mrs. Johnson said. "I replayed what I recorded once. But I couldn't bring myself to watch it again."

"Did you show it to the police?" I said.

"I did. The cop took one look at it then gave me my phone back. He said there was nothing useful on it."

"That's odd. Would you mind sending the video to me?" I said, handing her one of my business cards. "The email address is on the card."

"Of course," she said, tapping the keypad on her phone as she glanced down at the business card. "There you go."

"Thank you," I said, anxious to get a look at the video. "Did Willy have any personal items on him the night he was killed?"

"Just his wallet," she said, digging through her purse. "The cop returned it yesterday."

"May I take a look?" I said.

She handed me the wallet, and I flipped through it. Then I removed a business card and read it.

"Son of a gun," I whispered.

"What is it?" Felicia said. "You know the person?"

"Not directly," I said, handing her the card.

"Brewster Greedy," Felicia said. "He's got a place down here somewhere. He's rich, right?"

"Extremely," I said, then focused on Mrs. Johnson. "Would you mind if I kept this card?"

"No," she whispered. "Do you think you can find the person who killed my son?"

"I have no doubt, Mrs. Johnson," I said.

"How can you be so sure?" she said, cocking her head.

"It's what I do," I said, slipping the card into my pocket.

"You'll let me know if you find something?" she said, getting to her feet.

"We will," Felicia said, also standing to give the woman a long hug. "Hang in there, Millie."

"What choice do I have?" she whispered, then extended her hand to me. "It was nice meeting you, Mr. White. And thank you. Please find my son's killer."

"We will," I said, clasping her hand with both of mine.

Felicia led her out to her car and returned a few minutes later. She again sprawled out on the couch and stared at me.

"Why did you do that?" she said.

"Do what?"

"Promise her you'd find the guy who killed Willy."

"Because we will," I said, grabbing a pen and pad and jotting down some notes.

"Just like that?"

"Well, we've got some work to do. But yeah, just like that," I said. "This is an easy one."

"Okay, Doc, whatever you say," she said, shaking her head at me. "Let's take a look at that video."

I connected my laptop to the large screen television attached to the wall behind my desk. I sat down next to her on the couch and pressed the play button on the remote.

"Our first time at the movies," Felicia deadpanned as she tucked her legs underneath her. "Should I make popcorn?"

"And you call me strange," I said, focusing on the screen.

We watched in silence at the scene playing out. The audio was a muffled mess of street sounds, but the video was clear. Moments later, we spotted ourselves in the crowd. Felicia was swaying and dancing to the funk band. I was tracking her movements closely.

"You were staring at my butt," she said, glancing over at me.

"Was not," I said. "I thought I recognized somebody in the crowd."

"Okay, Doc," she said, laughing as she refocused on the screen. "The second floor is cut off."

"Yeah, from where she was standing, she'd be shooting down at an angle. That's too bad."

We continued to watch the scene play out. When the costumed Willy made his way up the street, his mother focused solely on him for several seconds before pulling back to reveal more of the crowd. When the stilt walker began to stumble, I saw myself step in front of Felicia then watched as Willy fell and crashed into me. The video captured the initial swell of the crowd surrounding Willy then ended soon after.

"I hate to say it, but I think the cops were right," Felicia said. "It doesn't look like there's much there."

"Let's watch it again," I said, grabbing the remote.

Halfway through the second viewing, something caught my eye, and I hit the pause button.

"What's the matter?" Felicia said.

"I think I saw something," I said, rewinding the video and putting it on slow motion. I leaned forward and concentrated hard on the screen. "There," I said, freezing the image on display.

"You lost me," Felicia said with a frown.

"Look at the Moku Jumbie behind Willy," I said, climbing off the couch. I went to the screen and pointed. "Right there."

"The one in yellow?"

"Yeah, what do you see?"

"A big canary on stilts," Felicia said with a shrug.

"Watch it play out," I said, clicking the remote.

We watched in silence then Felicia gasped.

"His arm," she said. "He's raising his arm."

"He certainly is," I said, again freezing the image. "I can't see it clearly, but I'm pretty sure he's got something in his hand."

"I think you're right," she said, getting up and approaching the screen. "Go forward a couple of frames. Wow. Did you see that?"

"The quick flash near his hand?" I said.

"Yeah. Something reflected the light."

"Something metal."

"Son of a gun," she said, sitting down on the desktop and swinging her legs back and forth. "He got shot by one of the Moku Jumbies?"

"That's my best guess at the moment," I said, replaying the same section of video several times. "The guy in yellow couldn't have been more than fifteen feet behind Willy."

"Easy shot," Felicia said. "And he didn't have to move his arm much."

"No, he didn't."

"I wonder who else shot video," she said.

"There have to be others," I said. "Hopefully, we won't need to try to track them down. That would be a major pain."

"We need to pay Albert a visit," she said, hopping off the desk.

"Is he the guy who runs the stilt walker school?"

"That's him," she said, sprawling back out on the couch. "So, how do you want to do this?"

"Well, we definitely want to start by talking to the guy who runs the training school. And we'll need to speak with the chief of police."

"I'll let you handle that one on your own," Felicia said, scowling.

"I can do that," I said. "After that, we'll go have a little chat with Mr. Brewster Greedy."

"The business card in Willy's wallet," she said, nodding. "How do you know the guy?"

"He's Elle's husband," I said.

"Your ex-girlfriend? That oughta be an interesting conversation," Felicia said, laughing. "You think he's involved in Willy's murder?"

"Oh, I sure hope so."

CHAPTER 7

We ate lunch on the gallery accompanied by
Samson who had sniffed out the chicken we were eating.
Felicia offered to do the dishes while I escorted the dog
next door and checked in on Sebastian. We talked briefly
and I gave him a plate of food, cut into bite-sized pieces,
before heading back to the house. As I waited for Felicia to
join me, I noticed my back tire that had developed a slow
leak.

"What's the matter?" Felicia said as she strolled
toward the SUV.

"I think the pothole has claimed another victim," I
said, studying the tire.

"There's a tire place on the way to the training school.
Is it okay to drive on it?"

"We're gonna find out," I said, climbing into the car.
"It's too hot to deal with changing it."

"How's Sebastian doing?"

"Not well," I said. "I think he's running out of gas."

We headed west, and ten minutes later I spotted the
handwritten sign and pulled into the parking lot of the tire
repair shop. I spoke with the owner, decided to just get a

69

new tire, then sat down on a bench next to Felicia who was scrolling through her phone.

"It'll be about half an hour," I said, glancing around at the handful of cars parked nearby.

"No problem," she said without looking up.

I sat quietly and let my mind wander over the case. Anxious to talk to the owner of the training school, I checked my watch several times before Felicia finally spotted my impatience.

"Relax, Doc," she said as she continued to scroll through her messages. "Island time, remember?"

"Yeah, I should probably work on that."

"It couldn't hurt," she said, then glanced up at me. "And thank you, Doc."

"For what?"

"For making me feel like I'm making a contribution again," she said softly.

"Don't mention it," I said. "I don't think I could do this without your help."

She gave my comment some thought then shrugged.

"I'm sure you could. But it would be a lot harder."

Twenty minutes later, we pulled off the highway, and I parked in front of a small, rundown building that appeared

70

to be a converted house. A man came outside when he heard us arrive and greeted Felicia with a warm embrace.

"Good afternoon, Felicia. It's been too long."

"Good afternoon, Albert. You're looking good. Is Maria here?"

"She's inside sewing," he said with a chuckle. "As always." Then he gave me the once-over before extending his hand. "Good afternoon. I'm Albert."

"Good afternoon. I'm Doc. Doc White," I said, returning his handshake. "I'm a private investigator."

"Is this about Willy?" he said, glancing at Felicia before focusing on me with a blank stare.

"It is," Felicia said.

"I don't know anything about it," Albert said. "Just what I read in the paper."

He maintained his expressionless stare.

"It's okay, Albert," Felicia said. "He's cool."

"You two are working together?" Albert said.

"We are," Felicia said.

"Okay, come on inside," he said as he wheeled around and led the way.

The inside of the building was cramped, and I could hear the intermittent whir of a sewing machine coming

71

from the back of the building. Albert motioned for us to sit down, but he remained on his feet.

"What do you need to know?"

"We have some questions about one of your stilt-walkers," I said.

"Good afternoon, Felicia."

"Good afternoon, Maria," Felicia said as she got to her feet to embrace the large woman who had shuffled into the room. "How are you?"

"Busy," she said with a laugh before focusing on me. "Good afternoon. I'm Maria."

"Good afternoon. I'm Doc."

"They have some questions about what happened to Willy," Albert said.

"Ah, Willy," she said through a heavy sigh. "Who could do something like that?"

"That's what we're trying to figure out," Felicia said.

"Willy was a regular at your school?" I said.

"He's been training with us for years," Albert said. "But his attendance lately was spotty."

"How so?" Felicia said.

"We never knew if he was going to show up for practice," Albert said.

"But he never missed a performance," Maria said.

72

"No, he didn't," Albert said softly. "Willy was a good kid. But he had his problems."

"Were they gang-related?" I said.

The couple looked at each other before responding. Eventually, Albert shrugged.

"It's certainly possible," he said. "The thought had crossed our minds."

"Do you know any of the people he was hanging out with?" Felicia said.

"Apart from the other kids in the school, no," Maria said. "He didn't talk much about his life. But he was great on stilts."

"One of the best," Albert said.

"Were you at Jump Up the other night?" Felicia said.

"No, we had a family commitment," Maria said. "I couldn't believe it when I heard the news."

"I'd like to show you a photo of one of your stilt-walkers," I said, reaching for my phone. "This was taken at the time Willy was shot." I let the video play then froze the image I was looking for and held my phone up.

"Willy wore the red costume," Maria said with a sad smile. "It was his favorite."

"You made it?" I said.

"I make all of them," Maria said.

"Who's the person in the yellow costume?" I said.

Maria and Albert stared at the image then frowned at each other.

"I have no idea," Maria said.

"How is that possible, Maria?" Felicia said. "There were only a half dozen Moku Jumbies. How could you not know who it was?"

"That's not one of my costumes," she said, shaking her head.

"What?" Felicia said.

"I didn't make that costume," she said. "Do you see the flower pattern?"

"I do," Felicia said.

"I never use flowers," Maria said. "Isn't that right, Albert?"

"It is," he said, studying the image. "No, that's definitely not one of our students."

"You're positive?" I said, baffled by the news.

"Unless one of our students was wearing a costume made by someone else," Albert said.

"Is that possible?" I said.

"Highly unlikely," Maria said. "We're quite strict about that."

"Are there other schools on the island?" I said.

"You're new around here, right?" Albert said with a chuckle. "No, sir, we're the only game in town."

"Is it possible someone decided to join the other Moku Jumbies?" I said.

"Sure, I suppose," Albert said, glancing at his wife.

"It would be an odd thing to do," Maria said. "Do you think that's the person who shot Willy?"

"We think it's a possibility," Felicia said. "Do you keep a roster of all the kids who've trained here?"

"Of course," Albert said.

"How many students have you had?" Felicia said.

"Over the years?" Albert said, glancing at his wife. "It must be at least a couple hundred, right?"

"Probably more," Maria said. "Where did you put the notebook?"

"I think it's in the sewing room," Albert said.

They both headed off to the back room.

"Well, that's too bad," I said, sitting back down. "I thought we'd gotten lucky."

"You still think it's going to be an easy case?" Felicia said with a grin.

"It's just a temporary setback," I said, reaching for my phone.

"Who are you calling?"

"Brewster Greedy."

CHAPTER 8

My stomach churned as I turned off the highway. I squeezed the steering wheel tight with both hands then noticed Felicia studying me with a bemused look.

"What is it?" I said, slowing down to navigate the winding road that led up to the house.

"This is the first time I've seen you out of your comfort zone," she said. "You know…edgy."

"What makes you think I'm on edge?"

"Let's call it a combination of cop and female intuition."

"I'm fine."

"When was the last time you saw her?"

"It's been a long time," I said. "Look, it's no big deal. I'm fine."

"Is that going to be today's mantra?" Felicia said with a laugh. "I'm fine?"

"Yeah, I suppose it is," I said, managing a small smile.

"The Buddha would be proud," she said, then glanced out the window. "I always wondered what this place was like. It's incredible."

It was. The massive house was white, perched on a hill overlooking the ocean and undoubtedly offered panoramic views from all directions. I drove past the front of the house on the circular drive that fronted the property and parked. We climbed the steps onto the wraparound gallery, and I rang the bell. As we waited, I looked out over the ocean and shook my head.

"Geez," Felicia grunted as she scanned the property. "So, this is how rich people live, huh?"

Before I could respond, the front door opened halfway and her head appeared. When she caught my eye, she pulled the door wide open and stared at me in disbelief. Her hair was a few shades lighter and cut shorter than I remembered, but the piercing glare of her blue eyes was still intact. But the one thing that struck and stayed with me was that the enormous gulf between us had remained unchanged since the last time we'd seen each other.

Strangers with shared history.

She put her hands on her hips and cocked her head. Like me, I was sure she was desperately trying to come up with an adequate response. In the end, she opted for the obvious.

"Doc? What the hell are you doing here?"

"Hi, Elle," I said, extending both arms.

She slowly leaned in and we shared a brief, awkward hug. Her familiar smell wafted over me and brought back a flood of memories. Then Elle took a step back and fixed her eyes on me again. Then she realized Felicia was standing next to me and extended her hand.

"Good afternoon. I'm Elle Greedy."

"Good afternoon. I'm Felicia."

"Pleased to meet you."

Their handshake was also brief but not nearly as awkward as the hug.

"Why are you here, Doc?"

"We're here to speak with your husband," I managed eventually. "I called yesterday. Didn't he mention it?"

"I haven't spoken to him in three days," Elle said, finally taking a step back from the doorway and waving us inside.

I glanced around the massive foyer, dominated by marble and mahogany, then my eyes landed back on her. She was wearing a long tee shirt over what I assumed to be a bathing suit, and she began twirling a pair of swim goggles in her fingers.

"You have a beautiful home," Felicia said.

"Actually, it's just a house," Elle said. "But thank you."

Elle and I continued to stare at each other. Eventually, Felicia cleared her throat, and we both glanced at her.

"I'll give you two a chance to catch up," Felicia said. "Is there somewhere I could wait?"

"The sunroom is down the hall on your right," Elle said, pointing without taking her eyes off me.

"Thanks. Take your time," Felicia said, grinning at me as she headed off.

"Who's that?" Elle said, nodding in Felicia's direction.

"She's my partner," I said, then felt the need to clarify. "My business partner."

"She's quite stunning," Elle said. "Especially for a spy."

"No," I said, shaking my head. "I gave that up years ago."

"I see," she said, chewing her bottom lip. "Now you're selling door to door?"

I chuckled, did my best to relax, but felt my stomach churn again.

"I'm a private investigator."

"You're joking, right?" she said, raising an eyebrow. "Here on St. Croix?"

"Yeah."

"Why?" she said, giving me her best no-nonsense stare.

"Because retirement bored the crap out of me," I said with a shrug. "How are you doing, Elle?"

"I'll be fine as soon as I get through this divorce," she said, finally softening a bit. "So, you're here to see Brewster. What the hell did he do now?"

"Nothing," I said. "His name came up on a case I'm working. I just need to have a quick chat with him before crossing him off the list."

"That didn't take long," she said, twirling the goggles faster.

"What?"

"I ask a question, you tell me a lie," she said softly. "Brewster is probably out on the back patio. I'm going for my swim."

"Maybe we can chat after," I said.

"Doubtful," she said, fixing another hard stare on me. "But it was nice seeing you, Doc."

She wheeled around and strolled down the marble hall. I watched until she disappeared from sight then headed in the same direction. I poked my head into several rooms on my way then eventually found Felicia inside an enormous room dominated by floor to ceiling windows.

"Well, you're not bleeding," Felicia deadpanned as she gave me a quick once-over.

"I think it's all internal," I said. "You ready to do this?"

"Lead the way."

A few moments later, we passed what appeared to be an office and something caught Felicia's eye. She came to a stop in the doorway.

"What is it?" I said, peering over her shoulder.

"He's got a Basquiat," Felicia said, entering the room.

"Is that some sort of weird dog breed?" I said, following her.

"No, you idiot," she said, laughing as she pointed at a large canvas on the wall. "The painting. It was done by Jean-Michel Basquiat."

"Never heard of him," I said, staring at the painting, a distorted, multi-colored portrait of a human head.

"American. Haitian descent, I think," Felicia said, concentrating hard on the painting. "Lived in New York but died of a heroin overdose."

"The heroin explains a lot," I said, doing my best to make sense of the abstract portrait.

"Philistine," she said, laughing. "One of his paintings recently sold for a hundred and ten million."

"I need to pick up a brush," I said, glancing around the room. "Holy crap. He has a lot of paintings."

Felicia stepped back to take a look around the room. Her eyes went wide, and she began to slowly make her way through the collection on display.

"Unbelievable," she said, shaking her head. "That's a Hirst. That one's a Richter." She came to a stop directly in front of a painting that looked vaguely familiar. "And that…is a Gauguin," she whispered in a reverent tone.

"Now him I've heard of," I said, studying the painting.

"There's gotta be fifty million worth of art hanging in this room. Maybe even more," she said, taking another look around. "What does this guy do for a living?"

"Finance, I think," I said. "I never really wanted to know much about him."

"I gotta meet this guy," she said, tugging my hand.

We eventually made our way through the first floor to a large flagstone patio. Off to one side, about a hundred feet away, was a large swimming pool where Elle was churning laps. Stretched out on a lounge chair, completely ignoring the woman in the pool, was a man reading a document with a glass of juice in one hand. When he heard us approach, he set both down then got to his feet. He was short and barefoot and dressed in baggy shorts and a tee shirt. But it was obvious he kept himself in good shape, and he studied both of us with a small smile and extended his hand.

"Good afternoon. Mr. White?" he said, executing a perfect handshake.

"Good afternoon, Mr. Greedy. Please call me, Doc," I said. "This is my partner Felicia."

"Good afternoon. It's wonderful to meet you," he said, taking her in with a look that put Felicia on edge. "Please, have a seat."

We got settled in at a table, and he poured juice for both of us without asking. Then he sat back in his chair and gave me a long once-over.

"So, you're the famous Doc White," he said.

"Guilty," I said, taking a sip. "This is good."

"Papaya and mango," he said, raising his glass in salute. "I'm so glad to finally have the chance to meet you, Doc."

"Why's that?" I said, frowning.

"Because of our shared history," he said, nodding at the pool. "My wife hates talking about her past." Then he flashed a conspiratorial grin. "But you already know that about her, right?"

"She can be very private," I said, nodding.

"Indeed," he said. "I believe you two first met while working on a technology project."

"We did," I said, nodding.

"Tell me, Doc," Brewster said. "Was my wife any good?"

"I beg your pardon?" I said, feeling my neck flush.

"No, I'm not talking about that," Brewster said, laughing. "We both know the answer to that question. I'm referring to her work abilities."

"She was great," I said with a shrug. "Incredibly smart and she's worked very hard."

"I'm sure she did. She is tenacious," he said, then took a long sip of juice. "And now you've left the tech world to become a private investigator. That's quite a career shift."

"Yes, it is," I said, glancing at Felicia. "But you gotta eat, right?"

"Absolutely," he said, nodding. "Speaking of which, would you like a snack?"

"No, we're fine," Felicia said. "But thanks."

"It's no problem at all," Brewster said, glancing at his watch. "But it's the staff's day off, so I'm afraid you'll need to help yourself."

"I'm sorry," Felicia said, confused.

"My morning window of kitchen access has closed," he said. "It's one of the rather bizarre aspects of our pending divorce settlement."

"You're only allowed in the kitchen at certain times during the day?" Felicia said.

"We have a lot of rules," he said, laughing. "She and her lawyer are convinced I'm going to eventually blink and cave. But they're dead wrong."

"I can see why you love the house," I said, glancing around.

"It's okay," Brewster said. "But control of this property is more about the principle involved."

"Good luck with that," Felicia said, frowning. "On the way in, I spotted the Basquiat in your office. I hope you don't mind we went in and took a look."

"Not at all," Brewster said. "That's why they're hanging on the wall. I took a flyer on the Basquiat several years ago. Turns out I was right about him."

"He was an amazing artist," Felicia said.

"You really think so?" Brewster said, raising an eyebrow at her. "I always thought his work was rather pedestrian. Almost infantile. But I imagine all that heroin didn't help."

"You don't like it?" she said, surprised.

"It doesn't matter what I think," he said. "What matters is that other people like it. Actually, I've been thinking about unloading it. After that idiot in Japan paid over a hundred million for his, I figure the timing is perfect to sell it."

"What about the Gauguin?" Felicia said.

"That one is a different story," he said with a grin. "That painting is my pride and joy."

"I imagine it is. It's worth a fortune," Felicia said.

"Oh, it's not about the money, Felicia," he said. "Pretty name. Felicia. No, that painting, for me, is all about life choices."

"The search for meaning and a better life in Tahiti to escape what he considered artificial. An escape from the conventional," I said softly.

"Very good, Doc," Brewster said. "My wife's former interest in you begins to make some sense."

I flinched but let his comment pass without a response.

"You said over the phone you needed to speak with me about a case you're working on," Brewster said, leaning back in his chair and getting down to business.

"Yes. Willy Johnson," I said.

"Willy Johnson?" he said, staring out at the ocean. "Why does that name sound familiar?"

"He died a couple of nights ago," Felicia said.

"Oh, of course," Brewster said, nodding. "The young stilt-walker who got shot at Jump Up. I read about that in the paper. Tragic." He refilled our glasses then relaxed back into his chair. "Why do you need to speak with me about it?"

"Your business card was found in his wallet," I said.

"My business card?" he said, genuinely surprised.

"Yes," I said.

"How is that possible?" Brewster said, glancing back and forth at us. "I wouldn't know the young man if I fell over him."

"We were wondering if someone who works for you might have given it to him," I said.

"What did the young man do for work?"

"We're not sure," I said. "Why do you ask?"

"I have been looking for a new gardener," Brewster said. "And I asked my staff to keep an eye out for potential candidates."

"That probably explains it," I said, glancing at Felicia. "Do you remember who you asked?"

"All of them, I think," Brewster said, rubbing his chin. "I can't remember at the moment, but I will certainly find out and get back to you."

"Thank you," I said, sliding one of my cards across the table. "We'd appreciate it."

"Not a problem," Brewster said, deep in thought. Then he brightened. "Tell you what, I'm having my annual barbecue tomorrow night here at the house. It's always quite a party. You should both come. I'll do my best to have some information for you by then."

I glanced at Felicia who was giving me a sly grin. I scowled at her then focused on Greedy.

"I don't know if that's such a good idea," I said, nodding at the pool where Elle continued to pound laps. "You know, given all the history."

"All the more reason to come," he said, enjoying the idea way too much. "And it will give you two a chance to catch up. Now that the initial shock of seeing each other again has worn off, right?"

"We'll have to think about it," I said.

"It sounds wonderful," Felicia said. "What time should we be here?"

"Anytime after seven," Brewster said, beaming at her. "Perfect. Let me walk you out."

"No, that's okay, Mr. Greedy," Felicia said. "You relax. We'll find our way out."

"You must call me, Brew," he said, extending his hand toward her. "I look forward to seeing you again, Felicia. What a beautiful name. Felicia."

"Yes, I like it too," she said, pulling her hand back.

"Doc, it was a pleasure meeting you," he said. "I just picked up a case of Black Pearl. Remind me tomorrow night to open a bottle. You do enjoy a good cognac, right?"

"Actually, I do," I said, remembering I still had a couple of bottles at the house.

"Of course," Brewster said. "You're obviously a man who enjoys the finer things life has to offer." Then he nodded at the pool with a grin. "Or at least believes he does until they prove otherwise."

We departed with a wave and made the long walk through the house back outside where my SUV was baking in the sun. I climbed in and started the car then slowly headed down the long driveway deep in thought and buried by memories.

"What do you think?" Felicia said, eventually breaking the silence.

"About Greedy?" I said, snapping out of my funk.

"Yeah."

"I think having Willy shot and swatting a fly would be identical to him," I said.

"And neither one would even register," Felicia said. "But I'm not sure he had it done."

"Me either," I said. "He seemed genuinely surprised the kid had his card. Maybe Willy was a gardener."

"Easy enough to find out," Felicia said. "What's Black Pearl?"

"It's an incredibly expensive cognac," I said.

"How expensive?"

"Somewhere between fifteen and twenty thousand a bottle," I said, glancing over at her.

"Wow. Have you ever had it?"

"Yeah, I picked up a case last year," I said. "I still have some at the house."

"You bought a whole case?"

"Nah," I said, shaking my head. "I stole it."

"You are so weird," she said, laughing.

We fell silent for a long time, alone with our thoughts. Then she spoke softly without looking at me.

"She's wasn't right for you."

"Really?" I said, glancing over. "By all means, enlighten me."

"A woman knows."

"You sure you're not using your cop's intuition?"

"I don't need it with this one. But I understand the attraction. There's something about her that gets your attention." She stared out the window. "Still, St. Croix was a long way to travel for a bit of closure, Doc."

I nodded but didn't respond.

"Brewster certainly liked you," I said after another lengthy silence.

"I noticed," she said, staring out the window. "I imagine he reacts the same way with a lot of the women he meets."

CHAPTER 9

Dupree chewed on the end of his brush as he took a couple of steps back to study the painting. Then he set the brush down and wiped his hands as he headed for the small fridge. He returned with beers and handed one to Harry who was gnawing on the end of his pen while staring down at his notebook.

"Thanks," Harry said, cracking the can. "You finished?"

"Finally," Dupree said, sliding down into an overstuffed chair and extending his legs. "It took me forever."

Harry studied the painting and nodded.

"It looks good to me."

"Yeah, it works. Thanks," Dupree said.

"You missed your calling," Harry said.

"It just took a while for me to figure out how to make money as a painter," Dupree said. "It won't be long before I say goodbye to bartending. And not a minute too soon."

"You really need me tomorrow night?"

"Yeah, I do," Dupree said. "Suzy backed out at the last minute."

"I'm not sure, Dupree," Harry said, shaking his head. "I've never done it before."

"How hard can it be? You hold the tray out in front of you, laugh at their jokes and do your best not to stare at the women."

"Still, I'm not comfortable being around all those people," Harry said, reaching for his beer.

"You've been on stage a million times," Dupree said.

"Yeah, in front of people. Not *among* them," Harry said. "There's a big difference."

Dupree laughed then took a long swallow of beer. His phone chirped and he answered on the second ring.

"Dupree…oh, hi…okay, yeah. I can do that…yup, all set…I'll see you then," Dupree slid his phone back into his pocket and glanced at Harry. "That was you know who. We need to be there at four."

"Four?" Harry said. "The party doesn't start until seven."

"You need to help set up," Dupree said.

"Me? What are you going to be doing?" Harry said.

"I need to run an errand before the party," Dupree said with a grin.

"Got it," Harry said, nodding. "Greedy is going to be out of the house?"

"Yeah. Boat trip," Greedy said. "And keep your schedule open."

"Where are we going?" Harry said, lighting a cigarette.

"That depends on what happens at the party," Dupree said.

"How much longer before we can head back to the mainland?" Harry said.

"It shouldn't be long," Dupree said, then nodded at the notebook in Harry's lap. "You finish the lyrics?"

"Nah, I'm still working on them," Harry said.

"Clear, cheer, fear, steer," Dupree recited. "Buck, luck, chuck, duck." He grinned at Harry and raised his beer in salute. "I expect a co-writing credit."

"Go screw yourself," Harry said. "I'm gonna head out and grab a beer. You in?"

"Nah, I gotta get started on a new painting," Dupree said.

"Already?"

"Hey, when the muse reveals itself, one follows the muse," Dupree said.

"Don't abuse the muse, just light the fuse," Harry said in a singsong voice. "Ignore the news, slip into your shoes…and just dance the blues."

"Stop it," Dupree said through a grimace.

"Sorry. What's the new painting?" Harry said.

"It's an abstract. I just need to splash a bunch of paint around and let it dry. It won't take long."

"Should I wait?" Harry said.

"Harry, not long is a relative term," Dupree said, shaking his head. "I'm an artist, not a miracle worker."

"Yeah, I get it," Harry said. "Still easier than coming up with something original."

"Exactly. And that's why I'm still schlepping drinks to rich people."

"But not for long," Harry said.

"Yeah, eventually life gives you a clear view of the road ahead. You just need to know which way to turn, right?"

"Hey, that's not bad," Harry said, picking up his pen. "I can use that."

"Yeah. You can call it the view from my truck."

***

I handed a snifter of Black Pearl to Felicia then took a sip of mine. I savored it then waited for her reaction.

"What do you think?" I said.

"I guess it's good," she said with a shrug. "But I can think of better ways to spend twenty grand."

"Can't argue with that," I said, taking another sip. I grabbed my phone and made the call. When it failed to connect, I shook my head and sat down in front of my laptop.

"What's the matter?" Felicia said over the top of her glass.

"He's changed his number again," I said, firing off a quick email.

"Who did?"

"Merlin."

"Who's he?" she said.

"An associate," I said. "He's always changing the number."

"Because?"

"Because he's Merlin," I said. "He'll get back to me soon."

"What does he do?" Felicia said.

"Anything he wants to," I said, then spotted the new email. "Here we go." I entered the new number into my phone and made the call.

"What's up, Doc?"

"Still not funny, Merlin," I said, putting my phone on speaker. "Are you still in D.C.?"

"No, I'm in Berlin."

"Nice. Make sure you go to Dots. They have the best coffee in the city. Are you busy at the moment? I need a favor."

"I'm working on something for our friend from Budapest, but I can make time."

"What are you doing for him?"

"You remember how he never shut up about his collection of artwork?"

"Sure," I said. "It was his pride and joy."

"Well, he was getting short on cash a few months ago and decided to sell off one of his paintings," Merlin said.

"He must have been broke. They're like children to him."

"Knowing the guy for the scumbag he is, I'm sure he would have preferred to unload one of his kids. But he was getting desperate," Merlin said. "So, he decided to sell a Van Gogh."

"He had a Van Gogh?" I said, surprised.

"He's got three," Merlin said. "But they're not top shelf. The one he was looking to unload is worth around five million. Or so he thought."

"It's not worth five?" I said, reaching for my cognac.

"No, it's not," Merlin said with a laugh. "He went to have it appraised and discovered it was a fake."

"Ouch," I said.

"Indeed. As you can imagine, he wasn't pleased to hear that."

"He bought a forged Van Gogh?"

"No, he stole it," Merlin said.

"And that's why he called you instead of the cops," I said, glancing over at Felicia who was frowning at me.

"Yeah. He's got me looking into the seedy underbelly of art forgers," Merlin said.

"And?"

"Nothing yet," Merlin said. "But I'll figure it out. What do you need?"

"I was wondering if you could do some digging into Brewster Greedy," I said.

"Greedy? Geez, Doc. Isn't it enough that she's divorcing him? Now you want to bury the guy?"

"His name turned up on a case I'm working," I said. "I met with him earlier today, and something seems off."

"Was Elle there?" Merlin said.

"She was."

"And how did that go?"

"Not well."

"Got it," Merlin said. "What do you need?"

"For now, financials," I said. "Poke around in Greedy's companies and see if anything jumps out at you."

"You want me to take a look at his personal accounts as well?" Merlin said.

"If you get a chance," I said. "But I have a feeling whatever he's doing is being washed through his companies."

"Yeah, unless he's a total idiot."

"He's not," I said.

"Okay," Merlin said. "When do you need it?"

"The sooner, the better."

"I should have something in a couple of days," Merlin said. "You flying solo down there?"

"No, I just brought on a new partner," I said, glancing at Felicia.

"Good. You're always better when you're not alone," Merlin said. "What's his background?"

"Hers," I said. "She's an ex-cop."

"Interesting. What's she like?"

"Beautiful and brilliant," I said, grinning at Felicia.

"She's there with you, isn't she?" Merlin said, laughing.

"She is," I said, laughing along.

"Okay," Merlin said. "Well, whoever you are, be gentle with my friend. And don't believe a word he tells you about me."

"I'll try to remember that," Felicia said. "It's nice to meet you, Merlin."

"I don't hear that very often," Merlin said. "Okay, I need to run. I'll call you soon."

"Thanks, Merlin," I said, then ended the call.

"I've never been to Berlin," Felicia said.

"I don't think Merlin has either," I said, then took a sip of coffee.

"You don't think he's there?"

"For all we know, he could be next door chatting with Sebastian," I said with a shrug.

"How is he going to get a look at Greedy's financials?"

"To tell you the truth, I'm not really sure how he does it," I said, taking another sip of cognac. "And it's probably better if I don't."

"Okay," Felicia said, confused. "He sounds like an interesting character."

"Merlin's...unique," I said. "But rule number one, never piss him off."

"Because?" Felicia said, raising an eyebrow.

"You don't want to know," I said, shaking my head.

"Let me guess, he's a spy."

"Ex-spy."

"Like you, huh?"

"It's a very long story," I said.

"I have time," Felicia said, flashing me a grin before sitting back in her chair and staring out at the harbor. "I thought ex-spies never talked about what they used to do."

"They don't," I said with a grin. "And that's why I couldn't have been one, right?"

"You are so weird," Felicia said, shaking her head. "But this guy Merlin doesn't mind talking about his past?"

"Merlin's situation is different," I said.

"He doesn't worry about getting shot or ending up at the bottom of the ocean?"

"No," I said. "Merlin knows way too much about too many people who matter."

"All the more reason to get rid of him, right?" Felicia said.

"Not until those people can figure out what Merlin's done with all his information," I said.

"And if anything did happen to him, all the dirt would come out?"

"I'm sure that's what all those people are worried about," I said, nodding.

"Does he have dirt on you, Doc?"

"At least six feet of it."

"But you're not worried about it coming out?"

"No, Merlin would never do that to me," I said.

"Okay. How did he end up working as a spy?"

"I recruited him," I said with a shrug. "And since I did, it was my job to babysit him. Nobody could stand working with him."

"Because?"

"Because he is one scary dude. And he's afraid of everything," I said without emotion.

"What?"

"He's a total germophobe," I said. "But apart from that, he can be very spooky to be around."

"So, he's a big guy?" Felicia said.

"Maybe five-one. In dress shoes," I said.

"That's tiny," she said, frowning.

"Yeah, all Merlin's growth was above the shoulders," I said. "If they wanted to get the real number about how smart he is, Merlin would have to be the one to invent the machine that could measure it."

"Nobody is that smart," Felicia said, shaking her head.

"Never say that to his face," I said, making solid eye contact with her.

"Why not?"

"Because it just pisses him off."

CHAPTER 10

I parked on the street and headed for the front door. I knocked softly and glanced around the neighborhood as I waited. Eventually, Felicia's grandmother opened the door partway then pulled it wide open when she saw me.

"Good evening, Mr. White," she said, waving me in. "Come in. Felicia's almost ready."

"Good evening, Mrs. Smith. And please call me Doc."

I followed her into the tiny living room and sat down. I glanced around the small, immaculately kept house and smiled at the old woman who'd sat down across from me.

"How is your new enterprise working out?" the woman said.

"Well, we have one client," I said. "It's a start."

"I need to thank you," she said. "I haven't seen her this happy in a long time."

"She's very special," I said softly.

"She is," Mrs. Smith said, pausing until she was sure she had my full attention. "But she's not as tough as she would lead you to believe. Please be gentle with her. Felicia's is still quite fragile."

Her comment about being gentle caught my attention, but before I had a chance to respond, Felicia entered the room attaching an earring. She beamed at me then frowned when she spotted the look on my face.

"What's the matter?" she said, glancing down at herself. "Did I miss a button?"

"Your hair," I said. "It's down."

"I thought it was time," she said. "Do you like it?"

It works for me.

I nodded to the voice as I stared at the long trail of thick hair that extended the length of her back.

"Yeah," I said with a grin. "I like it."

"You ready to go?"

"All set," I said, getting to my feet.

"Have a good evening, Grams," Felicia said, hugging her grandmother. "You need anything before we go?"

"No, I'm fine, dear," Mrs. Smith said, stroking Felicia's back. "You have a good time. I'll make up the couch before I turn in."

"Thanks, Grams," Felicia said, waving me toward the door.

"You look beautiful," I said as we crossed the small lawn.

"Thank you, Doc," she said, opening her own door and climbing into the passenger seat.

"How long has your grandmother lived here?"

"Forever," Felicia said, giving the old woman a final wave as I accelerated.

"What was her comment about the couch?" I said.

"I sleep on the couch," she said, staring out the window. "It's a one-bedroom."

"And you moved in after you left the force?" I said, treading lightly.

"I did," she said, finally making eye contact. "I've been having some financial troubles."

"Not anymore," I said to myself more than her.

"No," she said softly. "And I need to thank you again."

"No, you don't. You'll earn every penny."

"How do you want to handle tonight?" she said.

"I thought you might have a chat with Greedy," I said. "You'll get a lot more out of him than I will."

"While you work on his wife?" she said, flashing me a coy smile.

"Work is definitely the word for it," I said.

"What do you think Greedy is up to?" she said.

"I'm not sure," I said, turning up the music. "Maybe nothing. But a dead Moku Jumbie walking around with his business card in his wallet has got my attention."

"A get out of jail free card?" Felicia said.

"Maybe. What sort of stuff do the local gangs get up to down here?" I said.

"The usual," Felicia said. "If Willy was working for Greedy, why do you think he had him killed?"

"I imagine either Greedy was worried about Willy running his mouth or he was freelancing," I said. "You know, Willy wasn't happy with his cut and decided to try an end run."

"Makes sense," Felicia said. "Maybe Willy figured there was so much money floating around, Greedy wouldn't miss some of it."

"Big mistake," I said.

"Yeah, they always miss it," she said.

"That's been my experience."

"You learned that from stealing your own, right?" she said, grinning as she glanced over at me.

"I suppose," I said with a shrug. "Those guys probably missed it. If they managed to survive. But I'm sure they never knew where it went."

"Because you're that good of a thief?"

"No, but Merlin is," I said, returning her stare.

"I gotta meet this guy," she said.

"Be careful what you wish for," I said, laughing.

I pulled into the circular driveway fronting the Greedy property and came to a stop. A uniformed valet wearing a sleepy stare approached and handed me a ticket. Then he drove off to park the car as we headed for the front door.

"I think he just burned one," Felicia said with a chuckle.

We didn't even get a chance to knock before the door opened and another uniformed man greeted us.

"Good evening," he said, bowing slightly.

"Good evening," I said, then followed Felicia down the hall. "Nice touch with the bow, huh?"

"Yeah," Felicia deadpanned. "Colonialism dies hard."

I laughed as the sound of the party amped up. We came to a stop outside a massive room dominated by glass and tile. A bar was located on the other side, and I scanned the room and spotted Elle chatting with a small group.

"What would you like to drink?" I said.

"White wine is fine," Felicia said. "I'm going to take a look around outside and see who's here."

"I'm sure you know most of them," I said.

"This bunch? Doubtful," she said, then squeezed my hand. "I'll see you in a few minutes."

I watched Felicia stroll off then headed for the bar. As I waited to get the bartender's attention, I leaned my back against the long stretch of mahogany that would have been right at home in any pub. Elle spotted me and gave me a slight nod then resumed her conversation. I turned around and made eye contact with the bartender. We flinched simultaneously.

"Hey," he said with a puzzled look. "I think I know you."

"Yeah," I said, frowning. "But I can't remember where we met."

The bartender, a tall, thin black man, extended his hand across the bar.

"I'm Dupree."

"Dupree, of course," I said with a grin as I returned the handshake. "I know you from Blues Alley in D.C.."

"That's right, man," he said, grinning back. "I used to tend bar there. You'd come in from time to time to listen to the music."

"And drink," I said. "I love that club. Best jazz in the city."

"You got that right," Dupree said, concentrating hard. "You're...Doc."

"Very good," I said. "What the heck are you doing on St. Croix?"

"I couldn't handle the winters," Dupree said, wiping down the bar. "So, I decided to try the Caribbean."

"And ended up working for Brewster Greedy?"

"Nah, I don't work for the guy," he said. "I run a catering company and do high-end parties. I do some bartending occasionally just to keep my skills sharp. What can I get you?"

"A couple glasses of white wine, thanks," I said.

"I've got a nice pinot grigio and a chardonnay from Napa that ain't too oaky," Dupree said.

"Two of the pinot, please."

I watched him pour then took a sip and glanced around for Felicia. Deciding she was still outside, I sipped again as I studied the bartender who continued to give me the once-over.

"How long have you been on the island?" I said.

"About a year," he said, opening a fresh bottle and shoving it into a tub of ice. "Man, what a surprise seeing you."

111

I felt the presence of someone standing next to me and glanced over at Elle who was focused on the bartender.

"Dupree, be a dear and make me another Mimosa," Elle said, then leaned against the bar.

"You got it, Mrs. Greedy," Dupree said, then headed to the other end of the bar.

"Be a dear?" I said, raising an eyebrow at her. "What the hell happened to you, Elle?"

"What are you talking about?" she said, fixing a tight-lipped smile on me I'd seen a thousand times.

"It's an observation," I said. "An observation on change."

"I haven't changed a bit, Doc," she said, examining her nails. "I'm the same person I always was. You just chose not to see it."

"It must be the romantic in me."

"That must be it," she said with a soft laugh. "So, you decided to come tonight to see how the other half lives?"

"Don't you mean how the one-percenters live?"

"Fair enough," Elle said, blowing a strand of hair away from her mouth.

"Actually, I joined the one percent club several years ago," I said.

"Really?" she said, surprised. "Well, I know you didn't do it on a spy's salary. How did you make your money?"

"I stole it," I said, taking a sip of wine.

"Good for you," she said, nodding. "I hear it's a growth industry. And now you're a private investigator."

"It keeps my skills sharp," I said.

"I'll try to remember that," she said. "You know, in case I'm ever in need of your services."

"Like doing surveillance on a wayward husband?"

"Cheap shot, Doc," she said without emotion. "But no, I have all I need on Brewster."

"I'd be shocked if you didn't, Elle."

"Yes," she said through a sly grin. "I'm surprised you came."

"You know me, Elle. I'm a man of surprises."

"Actually, Doc, I always found you to be quite predictable. It's one of your better qualities."

"But from a short list, right?"

"Not at all," she said, nodding at the bartender when he handed her the drink. She took a small sip then set the glass down. "Dupree, dear, did you get a chance to take care of that thing we discussed earlier?"

"I did, Mrs. Greedy," he said. "You're all set."

"Wonderful," she said, then dismissed the bartender with a wave of the back of her hand. "That will be all for now."

"You've got him well trained," I said, unable to miss the dark stare Dupree gave her before heading off. "Most people just get a dog."

"Don't start, Doc," she said through another tight-lipped smile. "How's Merlin?"

"He's good," I said. "But I rarely see him."

"What's he doing these days?"

"Still making other people's lives miserable," I said.

"Playing to his strengths," she said, nodding. "Good for him. Tell him I said hi. Do you miss being a spy, Doc?"

"No."

"Because after trying to make the world a better place, you discovered, despite your best efforts, it just kept getting worse?"

"Pretty much," I said, nodding. "Decline of empire and all that."

"You really believe we're in decline?"

"Let's say we've peaked and leave it at that. But it's not my problem anymore."

"No, I imagine your time these days is relegated to more pedestrian concerns," she said, reaching for her glass.

"Like whether or not my husband had anything to do with that boy's death."

"What do you think?" I said, returning her stare.

She laughed loudly then drained half of her mimosa.

"I'm afraid my days of helping you solve problems are over, Doc. You'll have to ask my husband." She exhaled and glanced around the room before refocusing on me. "It was odd seeing you yesterday. It brought back a ton of memories."

"Some of them good, I hope."

"Some," she said. "Are you still dealing with the voice?"

"No, I'm fine," I said softly.

Hah!

"I was thinking earlier about the project we worked on in Vegas," she said, shaking her head. "So many memories."

"And?"

"It was…an interesting project to say the least. Actually, it turned out to be my last one."

"Yes, I know," I said, swirling the wine in my glass. "But you couldn't be expected to keep working after you married Greedy, right?"

"Don't kid yourself, Doc," she said, downing what was left of her drink. "Being married to that man is a full-time job."

"Well, I'm sure you're well compensated for the effort," I said.

Easy, big guy.

"But there must be something about married life that agrees with you," I said, ignoring the dirty look she was giving me. "You look fantastic."

"Thank you."

"But I don't remember you being a swimmer," I said. "How many laps are you doing?"

"A hundred a day," she said. "I started right after Brewster bought the sailboat. I decided that if we were going to be spending a lot of time out on the water, being a good swimmer might come in handy."

"Because you never know when you might go overboard?"

"Stranger things have happened," she said with a shrug.

"Well, the swimming is definitely working for you. And your breasts look great." I raised my glass to take a sip but paused and grinned at her over the rim. "They're new, right?"

"I almost forgot what a total dick you can be," she snapped.

"What can I say, Elle? You always bring it out in me."

We both sighed audibly then stared off into different corners of the room. I took a sip of wine and silently chastised myself. Elle smoothed some imaginary wrinkles from her silk blouse then shrugged again.

"Well, that didn't take us long," she said.

"No. We're just playing to our strengths, right?"

"Do me a favor, Doc."

"Sure. What is it?"

"We share some nice memories. Let's not sully them with reality, okay?"

"You got a deal."

"Why did you need to talk to my husband?"

"His business card was in the victim's wallet," I said, studying her reaction.

"I see," she said, pursing her lips. "Interesting. Do you really think my husband had something to do with that boy's death?"

"Do you?"

"Nice try, Doc. I have no idea," she said. "I stopped worrying about my husband's...proclivities a long time ago."

"If that's the case, why get divorced now?"

"It's time," she said as a simple statement of fact. "Like you always used to say, life is too short to be encumbered by dead weight.

"Cutting away the fat," I said, nodding.

"Exactly," she said, glancing around the room. "And Brewster is carrying around a lot of weight these days."

"Well, all that money must get heavy," I said, polishing off the last of my wine.

"Don't worry," she said, her voice cold and pointed. "He'll be shedding a lot of it soon."

CHAPTER 11

I watched Felicia meticulously tear a
paper napkin into tiny pieces as she studied the partygoers.
She gathered the scraps and wadded them into a ball before
tossing it into a nearby trash bin. She caught me watching
and gave me a small shrug.

"Sorry. Force of habit."

"You're bored," I said. "You about ready to go?"

"I am," she said, nodding at Brewster Greedy who was
regaling a group of people with a raucous story. "Do you
mind handling the goodbyes?"

"Not at all," I said, studying Greedy who was getting
louder and more animated. "He upset you, didn't he?"

"I'm a big girl, Doc," she said, fixing a stare on me.
"I'm fine."

"Okay, just checking. What was his pitch?"

"Well, let's see," Felicia said, flipping her hair behind
her shoulders as the breeze kicked up. "He started with how
the only way to make the ocean more beautiful would be to
have me out on the water."

"Geez," I grunted.

"Yeah, that's what I thought," she said, managing a small laugh. "Then he had to tell me all about his boat."

"Including the spacious master quarters, right?"

"Of course," Felicia said. "Then he made a reference about how I possessed some of the qualities he admired most in women."

"Such as?"

"A pulse and a vagina, I imagine," she said with a shrug. "I didn't stick around long enough for him to elaborate."

"How did he take it when you turned him down?"

"It barely fazed him," she said. "I imagine he's working from a long list of candidates."

I nodded and glanced around, spotting Elle chatting with a different group of guests. I got up from my chair.

"I'll meet you at the car."

I headed for Elle, shared a pleasant but perfunctory farewell, then approached Greedy. He gave me a quick once-over then accepted my outstretched hand.

"Heading off so soon?" he said.

"I need to get an early start in the morning," I said.

"Ah, the curse of the working class," he said with a cocky grin.

"Yeah, it's a problem. Thanks for the invitation, Brewster. It was a great party."

"Anytime, old man," he said, glancing around, I assumed, for signs of Felicia. "Maybe we'll catch up again soon."

"You can count on it," I said, then headed off with an over the shoulder wave.

I climbed into the car where Felicia was already in the passenger seat. She noticed the look on my face.

"What's the matter?" she said.

"I'm just wondering why so many nouveau riche Yanks feel the need to try to sound British," I said, frowning.

"What?"

"See you soon, old man. Be a dear and get me another drink," I said in a mocking tone as I started the engine.

"Did anyone ever tell you that you think too much, Doc?" Felicia said, laughing.

"Occupational hazard," I said, accelerating away from the house.

After we reached the highway, Felicia finally broke the silence.

"What do you think?" she said.

"About Greedy?" I said. "Oh, he's definitely involved. I just don't know how or why."

"Yeah, that's my take," she said. "What about her?"

"No, Elle's focus is on higher aspirations at the moment," I said, shaking my head.

"Like getting her hands on as much of her husband's money as she can?" Felicia said.

"While inflicting maximum pain," I said, remembering the tone of Elle's voice from our earlier conversation.

"And that's why neither one of them is willing to leave the house?" she said.

"That is strange, isn't it?"

"Yeah, they're definitely dug in," Felicia said, glancing at the mirror on the outside of her door. "Do you see it?"

"Yeah, they've been following us since we left the party," I said, checking the rearview mirror.

"I wonder whose cage we rattled," Felicia said.

"A black SUV," I said, taking another look in the mirror. "I saw a bunch of them at the party."

"The government has a whole fleet of them," Felicia said. "They wouldn't be that stupid, would they?"

"No, probably not," I said, keeping a close eye on the vehicle. "But the person who stole it might be."

122

"What do you want to do?" she said, studying the outside mirror.

"Let's see if we can have some fun with them," I said, accelerating.

**

"He's trying to get away," Emo said, staring out through the windshield from the passenger seat.

"He's on an island," Barry said, gripping the steering wheel tight. "Where the hell is he gonna go?"

"Yeah, you're right. And you saw the woman he's with. He's probably just in a hurry to get home. I know I'd be," Emo said. "But don't lose him."

"Relax, man. I know these roads like the back of my hand."

"Why are we following this guy?" Emo said.

"Harry said to find out where the guy lives," Barry said, turning off the headlights. "And try to get some idea if he's sleeping with her."

"Yeah, I imagine she's high on Greedy's list," Emo said. "You sure you can see without lights?"

"I don't need lights. What I need is a top-up," Barry said, removing a joint from his pocket.

"You're gonna stink up the car," Emo said, frowning.

"What do I care? It ain't mine," Barry said, taking a long drag before passing it to Emo.

"Whose car is it?" Emo said, then inhaled and held his breath.

"The commissioner of something or other," Barry said. "Don't worry. We'll have it back long before he's ready to leave."

**

I continued along the highway, noticed the SUV had turned off its lights then made a quick left onto the road that led up the hill to my house. I checked the mirror and spotted the SUV follow us without signaling.

"Interesting," I said, easing my foot off the accelerator. The trailing vehicle also slowed and maintained its position a couple hundred feet back. "If he planned on running us off the road, he missed his chance."

"Okay," Felicia said, annoyed. "Then what the hell are they trying to do?"

"Figuring out where I live is my first guess," I said.

"There's only about a dozen easier ways to find that out."

"I don't think we're dealing with a brain surgeon," I said, making another left that led to my street. "Hang on."

**

Emo took a final hit on the joint then tossed the roach out the window. He studied the car in front of them and pointed.

"Looks like he's slowing down," Emo said through a mouthful of smoke.

"Yeah, he must live around here," Barry said. "I wish the moon was out. It's dark up here."

"Turn the lights back on," Emo said.

"Yeah, probably a good idea," Barry said, flipping the headlights on then waving his hand to clear away the smoke. "You're wasting it, man. You're supposed to inhale and hold it."

"Don't tell me how to smoke a blunt," Emo snapped. "You're always doing that crap."

"Doing what?" Barry said, glancing over.

"Acting all superior," Emo said, pouting.

"Learn how to smoke properly and I'll stop," Barry said.

**

"Here we go," I said, taking another look through the mirror.

"What are you going to do, Doc?" Felicia said.

"I thought we'd introduce him to the neighborhood," I said, then hammered the accelerator. The SUV responded and quickly hit fifty. I took another look in the mirror and grinned when I saw the vehicle behind us respond in kind. "This is gonna be great."

"You need a hobby," Felicia said, without taking her eyes from the passenger side mirror.

As I sped toward my driveway, I veered right and gave the pothole a wide berth.

**

"Damn, I think he made us," Barry said, checking the speedometer that read fifty-two. "Man, I'm buzzed. I don't think we should have smoked that last joint."

"Uh-oh."

"What?" Barry said, glancing over at his wide-eyed friend.

**

I cringed and stifled a laugh when I saw the SUV hit the massive hole hard and almost come to a stop. The front end of the vehicle dipped down at a sharp angle, lost a headlight in the process before the back end landed. The SUV made it through the pothole, and I slowed down and shook my head at the car now slowly shimmying along the road.

**

"Hot damn," Emo said, grimacing as he clutched his back. "Now I know why they don't need traffic lights down here."

"That was a big hole," Barry said, massaging his neck while doing his best to control the wobbly SUV determined to head left. "I never saw it."

"No kidding," Emo said, shaking his head. "Did you blow a tire?"

"Probably a couple," Barry said, slowing down and eventually coming to a stop. "But that's the least of our problems. Did you hear that sound?"

"You mean the sound of the front end getting ripped off?" Emo said, unbuckling his seat belt and climbing out of the car. "Oh, man. What the hell have you done, Barry? The man is gonna kill us."

"Not if we get it back to the party before anybody knows it's missing," Barry said, studying the damage. "C'mon, it looks like we only lost the front tire. Go grab the spare."

"There goes my buzz," Emo said, heading for the back.

**

I kept driving until I was sure we were out of sight. I turned into a driveway, did a three-point turn then came to a stop at the edge of the street. I left the engine running but turned the headlights off.

"We're just going to sit here?" Felicia said.

"Yeah," I said, watching the road for signs of the SUV.

"You mind telling me why you don't want to hunt them down?"

"We're not armed," I said. "But they might be. I'd rather not end our evening by getting shot."

"I guess I can't argue with your logic," Felicia said, then settled back into her seat. "You made that look very easy, Doc."

"I've been doing this stuff a long time," I said, still watching for signs of the SUV. "And I told you this was an easy one."

Her laughter filled the car as I lowered my window and lit a cigarette. She frowned but said nothing. We waited in silence for about fifteen minutes, and I nudged her when I spotted the damaged, but drivable, SUV slowly wobble past us. I waited another minute until I was sure the car was gone then turned right and headed back toward my house. I parked next to the pothole, and we both climbed out. I spotted several shards of glass and plastic around the immediate area.

"He hit it hard," I said, laughing.

"What is that?" Felicia said, sniffing the air. "It smells like dead fish."

"Brake fluid," I said.

"A bent front end and no brakes," she said, laughing. "Good luck with that."

"Yeah, they should have quite an adventure. C'mon, let's get you home."

CHAPTER 12

Dupree came to a stop at the end of the long, inclined driveway then hopped out of the van and scanned the horizon. He arched his back and stretched then looked over at Harry.

"You remember our cover story?" Dupree said.

"If anybody shows up, we're plumbers."

"Electricians."

"Right, electricians," Harry said, nodding.

"Man, I gotta get me a place like this," Dupree said. "Look at that view."

"It won't be long," Harry said, opening the side panel and rummaging around.

"Yeah," Dupree said. "But not down here. We're gonna need to make ourselves scarce at some point. But I do like island life."

"I hear Ibiza is nice," Harry said.

"Nah, too much of a party place," Dupree said, heading for the van. "I'm getting too old for that scene."

"Probably lots of art collectors there," Harry said.

"They're everywhere, man," Dupree said, tucking a long tube under his arm.

"You sure nobody's home?" Harry said.

"They're going to be out on Greedy's boat all day," Dupree said, pointing out at the ocean where the enormous sailboat was becoming a distant speck. "You ready to do this?"

Dupree led the way then came to a stop at the bottom of the steps. He watched Harry study the exterior of the house. Then Harry spotted what he was looking for and shook his head in disgust.

"What's the matter?" Dupree said.

"They'll spend millions on paintings, but keep using ancient technology on their security system," Harry said, reaching for his phone. "They deserve to get ripped off. I'm not even going to break a sweat on this one."

"Good," Dupree said. "They won't know anybody has been in and out?"

"Not unless you break something inside," Harry said as he fiddled with his phone then nodded. "Okay, the front door is open."

"Just like that?"

"Yup," Harry said, draping the bag over his shoulder.

"You're the man," Dupree said, laughing as he headed up the steps and slowly opened the door. He paused to listen for the alarm then shrugged when he heard nothing but the wind and strolled in. Harry followed close behind and Dupree shut the door.

"We need to worry about any neighbors?" Harry said.

"Nah, they bought way up here for the privacy," Dupree said with a chuckle.

"Be careful what you wish for, right?" Harry said, glancing around the foyer. "Where is this thing?"

"It's supposed to be in the living room," Dupree said, wandering down the hall. Then he spotted what he was looking for and entered the room. "Man, this is one ugly piece of canvas."

"You got that right," Harry said, sitting down in an overstuffed chair.

"Hey, you wearing a clean uniform?" Dupree said with a scowl.

"Spotless," Harry said. "Relax, Dupree. Just do your thing so we can get out of here. It's two-dollar taco day at Maria's."

"Hey, that's right. Cool," Dupree said, opening the long tube he was carrying. He carefully removed a tightly rolled canvas and spread it out on the tile floor. "Give me a hand and hold this down while I grab the original."

Dupree lifted the painting off the wall and sat down on the floor with it in his lap. He carefully loosened the clasps on the back of the frame then removed the painting. He placed it on the floor next to the other and compared them.

"What do you think?" Dupree said, eventually glancing up at Harry.

"Man, you do good work, Dupree. They're identical."

"Thanks," Dupree said with a grin then frowned when Harry started pawing at them. "Hey, don't touch. You're going get 'em mixed up."

"Don't yell at me," Harry said. "I was just taking a closer look."

"Well, don't," Dupree said, rolling up the original and sliding it into the tube.

"Oh, I forgot to tell you," Harry said. "The man called this morning before he took the boat out."

"And?" Dupree said, raising an eyebrow.

"He wants to see us this afternoon after he gets back."

"Damn. How did he sound?"

"Madder than a rattlesnake with a hangover," Harry said.

"Don't start, Harry," Dupree said, scowling at his friend.

"What?"

"With the bad country metaphors. Just say the man ain't happy and leave it at that, okay?"

133

"Sorry to offend your refined sensibilities," Harry said. "But he's really pissed."

"I'm sure he is. You saw the car," Dupree said. "What the hell happened to it?"

"They hit a pothole doing fifty," Harry said. "Fortunately, the commissioner got hammered at the party and was sleeping it off."

"What did the guy say when he saw the car?" Dupree said.

"He freaked out at first. But Greedy played dumb then offered to buy him a new one," Harry said. "No harm, no foul."

"You got lucky. It was your job to babysit those two morons," Dupree said, as he began putting the new painting into the frame. "Why does he need to see me?"

"I don't know," Harry said. "He just told me he wanted to see us at the house tonight. And I sure wasn't going to argue with him."

"Damn. That can't be good," Dupree said, sliding the back of the frame into place and securing it. "Okay, let's hang this baby up and see how she looks."

They both studied the painting on the wall then Dupree nodded with a big grin. "I'm so good, sometimes I scare myself."

"How much is that thing worth?" Harry said, nodding at the tube that held the original.

"Maybe a million," Dupree said. "But that's black-market prices. I imagine it would go for more at auction."

"Geez," Harry said, shaking his head. "A million bucks for a bunch of lines and circles. Unbelievable."

"Too bad you wasted all that time in music school, huh?" Dupree said.

"No kidding. What's our take on this job?"

"A hundred."

"Each?" Harry said.

"No, we'll have to split it," Dupree said. "Still not bad for a day's work."

"Yeah," Harry said. "Hey, should I grab a couple beers for the road?"

"Only if there's more than a dozen in the fridge," Dupree said, glancing around to make sure they weren't leaving anything behind.

"I like our chances," Harry said, heading out of the room.

"And don't leave any prints on the fridge."

Dupree stood in front of the picture window that offered a one-eighty view of the ocean then glanced around the room and nodded.

"Yeah, I definitely need to get my hands on one of these."

CHAPTER 13

Dupree reached for the doorknob then paused and glanced at Harry.

"You ready for this?"

"As ready as I'm gonna get," Harry said with a shrug.

"This is your first come to Jesus with the man, right?"

"It is."

"Word of advice," Dupree said, opening the door. "Just keep your mouth shut and take whatever he gives you."

They entered the office and spotted Brewster Greedy sitting behind his desk talking on the phone. He nodded at the two chairs in front of the desk then snapped his fingers and pointed for them to take a seat. Dupree sat quietly and glanced around at the artwork on display. Then he heard Harry humming.

"Are you singing?"

"Yeah, it's the melody line to my new song," Harry said with a grin.

"Well, stop it," Dupree snapped under his breath, then beamed at Greedy who had finished his call and was glaring at them with both elbows propped on his desk. He rested his hands under his chin.

"Mr. Perkins. Mr. Wilder," Greedy said as he glanced back and forth at them through a narrow-eyed stare. Then his phone rang again, and he answered it on the first ring.

"We're on a last name basis," Harry whispered. "That can't be good, huh?"

"No," Dupree said softly. "So, shut up."

Greedy snapped at the person on the other end of the line then hung up and resumed his dark stare.

"Do I need to explain why you're here?" Greedy said.

"I've got some idea, Mr. Greedy," Harry said. "But feel free to expound."

Dupree rolled his eyes at his friend and slowly shook his head.

"What did I ask you to do last night, Mr. Wilder?" Greedy said softly.

"You asked me to follow the guy and find out where he lived," Harry said.

"And what's the operative word in that sentence, Mr. Wilder?"

"I beg your pardon," Harry said, frowning.

"You. That's the operative word, Mr. Wilder."

"Oh, got it," Harry said, nodding.

"But for some reason, you chose to delegate the task to a couple of stoners," Greedy said, leaning back and rocking in his chair. "Please. Enlighten me."

"Well, I'd been on appetizer duty all night," Harry said. "And I was due for my break."

Dupree lowered his head and massaged his temples.

"I see," Greedy said, rocking slowly. "So, you were tired. Is that what you're telling me?"

"Yeah," Harry said, nodding. "And hungry."

Greedy stared in disbelief at Harry then turned to Dupree.

"Would you care to comment, Mr. Perkins?"

"The man made a mistake, Mr. Greedy," Dupree said. "But I'm sure it won't happen again."

"That's two in the last week," Greedy said. "First, a case of pills goes missing and ends up on the streets of Christiansted."

"That wasn't my fault, Mr. Greedy," Harry said. "Not my job. I had nothing to do with that. The kid was freelancing."

"And I was forced to intervene to clean up the mess," he said, ignoring Harry's defense. "Then, wonder of wonders, the vehicle of a senior government official ends up on a joyride and gets trashed while he's a guest in my home."

"Yeah," Harry whispered. "That about sums it up."

"I have a question for you, Mr. Wilder," Greedy said, his chair coming to a sudden stop.

"Okay."

"Is that your best work?" Greedy said, again propping his elbows on the desk.

"Uh," Harry said, glancing at Dupree. "No, sir."

"Good answer, Mr. Wilder," Greedy said. "Because if it was, you and I really need to take a trip out on my boat."

"Cool," Harry said. "It's one hell of a boat."

Dupree sighed and focused on a painting hanging behind the desk.

"Are you actually that obtuse, or just screwing with me, Mr. Wilder?"

"I'm just nervous, Mr. Greedy," Harry mumbled. "And I'm really sorry. It won't happen again."

"I understand you have aspirations of becoming a country music songwriter," Greedy said, resuming his rocking.

"Yes, sir. I do," Harry said, brightening a bit.

"Good for you," Greedy said. "But try to remember one thing, Mr. Wilder."

"What's that, sir?"

"While you are in my employ, you aren't being paid for the power of your dreams. Do we understand each other?"

"Yes, sir."

"Excellent," Greedy said, then turned to Dupree. "I suppose you're wondering why you're here."

"I'm not paid to worry about stuff like that, Mr. Greedy," Dupree said with a shrug.

"Good answer," Greedy said, nodding before refocusing on Harry. "That's what I'm talking about, Mr. Wilder. It's really not that hard."

"No, sir."

"I invited you here to discuss a change I'm making," Greedy said.

"Okay," Dupree said, giving Greedy his undivided attention.

"Since you're the only one who appears to have half a brain around here, I've decided to promote you," Greedy said.

"You have?" Dupree said, raising an eyebrow.

"Yes. You are now officially in charge of local operations," Greedy said.

"Huh," Dupree grunted. "What exactly does that entail, sir?"

"It entails making sure everything I ask you to do goes off without a hitch," Greedy said.

"Makes sense. Yeah, I can do that," Dupree said. "Am I gettin' a raise?"

"At the moment, no. But I'll be happy to revisit that question after you've proven yourself."

"Okay," Dupree said with a frown. "Then how about a title?"

"A title?" Greedy said.

"Yeah, you know," Dupree said, leaning forward. "What should people call me?"

"How about Supervisor of Screwups?" Greedy said, glaring at Harry.

"What will I be doing, Mr. Greedy?" Harry said.

"If you know what's good for you, I imagine you'll be doing everything your new boss asks you to do," Greedy said.

"I'll be working for him?" Harry said with a frown.

"Unless you'd rather report directly to me," Greedy said through a crocodile smile.

"Uh, no, sir," Harry said, deflated.

"What do you need done, Mr. Greedy?" Dupree said.

"There's another shipment coming in on Friday," Greedy said. "I need you to coordinate everything and make sure that local gang doesn't do any more freelancing. How's that for starters?"

"You got it," Dupree said.

"I expect daily updates."

"Yes, sir," Dupree said, then pointed at one of the paintings. "Is that a Koons?"

"You have a good eye, Dupree," Greedy said with a smile as he glanced at the painting. "Yes, I just picked that one up. I think it works well in here."

"Yeah, it's sweet," Dupree said, then shrugged. "Actually, bold is probably a better word for it."

"Yes, bold," Greedy said, nodding as he stared at the painting. "I like that. Okay, gentlemen. That will be all."

Dupree and Harry got to their feet and headed for the door. Dupree hung back with a grin and waited for Harry to open it. After they left the office, Harry glared at Dupree.

"Don't be starting that crap, Dupree."

"What are you talking about?" Dupree said, turning coy.

"Crap like opening the door for you."

"You heard the man. You're working for me now."

"Dupree," Harry said, his voice rising in warning.

143

"Relax, man. I'm just having some fun with you."

As they headed for the front door, they spotted a leaf bouncing across the tile being carried along by the breeze. They watched it make its way toward them then Dupree nudged Harry with his elbow.

"Pick that up."

CHAPTER 14

I strolled down the Boardwalk then stopped in front of Brew. I looked down into the water at about a dozen Tarpon slowly circling, on the prowl for food scraps diners might toss their way. I sat down at an empty table just off the dock and stared out at the collection of boats anchored offshore. I smiled up at the waitress when she approached.

"Good afternoon, Suzy."

"Good afternoon, Doc. Haven't seen you in a while," she said, clutching a handful of menus.

"I've been a bit busy."

"Just you?" she said.

"No, they'll be two of us," I said.

"Okay," she said, setting two menus on the table. "You want a drink while you wait?"

"Is it too early for a beer?" I said with a grin.

"Not around here," she said, laughing. "Presidente?"

"Yes, please."

I leaned back in my chair and stretched my legs as I looked around. Moments later, a large uniformed cop came into view, and I studied him as he headed in my direction. When he got close, I stood and gave him a small wave.

"Mr. White?" he said, coming to a stop.

"Good afternoon, Chief Andrews," I said, extending my hand. "It's nice to meet you. Please, have a seat."

We sat down across from each other, and he looked around, waved to someone he recognized then gave me his undivided attention.

"How are you enjoying St. Croix, Mr. White?"

"Very much," I said, then sat back in my chair when the waitress returned with my beer.

They exchanged pleasantries then we ordered. After she departed, we sat quietly sizing each other up.

"I understand you're a private investigator," Chief Andrews said.

"I am. But I just got started."

"What did you do before that, Mr. White?" he said.

"I was a small-town cop," I said, taking a sip of my beer. "I thought I was ready for retirement, but I was wrong."

"I see. And you're working on Willy Johnson's murder," the chief said.

"Yes. His mother hired me to find his killer," I said.

"Have you had any luck yet?" he said, raising an eyebrow at me.

"I was about to ask you the same question, Chief."

"No, we haven't," he said, fiddling with his utensils. "I'm afraid we've hit a dead end on that one."

"It happens," I said, deciding not to push too hard early on. "Do you like being top cop, Chief?"

"I do," he said, nodding as he waved to a passerby. "But it comes with its challenges."

"I'm sure it does," I said. "And I can't imagine having a Moku Jumbie shot on the street makes your job any easier."

"Indeed," he said, his eyes narrowing. "So, where are you with your investigation?"

"Nowhere, really," I said. "I was hoping the video might help."

"Video?" he said, frowning at me.

"The video Willy's mom shot on her phone," I said.

"I'm not aware of any video."

I sat back and studied his expression. He appeared to be telling me the truth, and I filed that nugget away for later.

"Mrs. Johnson said the police looked at the video then returned it to her. They didn't find anything useful on it."

"But you did?" Chief Andrews said.

"Willy was shot by one of the stilt walkers," I said, then glanced up at our waitress who'd arrived with our food. She set our plates down in front of us, asked if we needed anything else then left. I took a bite of my sandwich and stared out at the water. "Your folks didn't share that bit of information with you?"

"No, they didn't," he said, toying with his salad. "I imagine you're wondering about the level of corruption that exists down here, Mr. White."

"I've heard the rumors," I said with a shrug then took another bite.

"Oh, they're more than rumors," he said, then speared a tomato wedge. "And while I must confess that I have a few officers who…bend the rules from time to time, I assure you, Mr. White, I am not one of them."

"Good to know, Chief," I said, starting to work my way through my fries. "And the local gangs don't make it any easier, right?"

"The gangs have become a real problem," he said, sitting back to wipe his mouth. "Have you come across them yet?"

"No," I said, shaking my head. "At least, not that I'm aware of. But I was followed home recently."

"I see," he said. "You need to be careful, Mr. White. Retribution is quite high on their list of priorities."

"I'll keep that in mind, Chief," I said, grabbing the other half of my sandwich. "Some of your people feel the need to go easy at times because they're afraid of what might happen to them or their families?"

"I have some, yes," he said.

"Do you worry about it?"

"I wouldn't be much of a husband or father if I didn't, Mr. White," he said softly.

"Okay," I said. "I get that."

"You have experience with groups like that?" he said.

"Unfortunately, I do," I said.

"Do you have any suggestions for me?" he said, returning to his salad.

"Well, it's not for me to say," I said. "But if you're unable to dig deep into gang activity, you might consider reaching out to the FBI. They might be willing to put some undercover agents down here."

"I'm sure they're around," Chief Andrews said, taking a sip of iced tea.

"But you can't be sure?" I said, pausing mid-bite.

"The FBI doesn't share much with me," he said.

"Because they think you might be part of the problem?"

"One would assume," he said with a shrug. "How's Felicia?"

"She seems to be doing well," I said, then drained the rest of my beer. "She's smart."

"She is," Chief Andrews said. "And an excellent cop."

"Not anymore," I said.

"Sadly, no," he said, staring out at the water. "Not one of my finer moments."

"Because?"

"Because I didn't take her initial complaints seriously," the chief said. "And by the time I did, too much damage had been done."

"So, you paid her to go away."

"My superiors felt it was the best option," he said. "You know, to avoid some rather bad publicity for the government."

"What would we do without money, right?"

"Yes. Most governments would be lost without it," Chief Andrews said.

"I've never seen one that wasn't," I said. "Did anything happen to the cops who harassed her?"

"Two of them got a week's suspension," he said. "I've tightened up on those behaviors since she left. Not that it makes any difference to Felicia's situation." Then he shrugged and shifted topics. "You mentioned you have a video of the murder?"

I reached for my phone, located the clip then handed him the phone. I watched his reaction as he studied the video. He ran it a second time, then handed me the phone back.

"The Moku Jumbie in yellow," he said.

"Felicia and I spoke with the people who run the training school and make all the costumes," I said. "They swear he wasn't one of theirs."

"No, I'm sure he wasn't," Chief Andrews said, pushing his plate away. "And I imagine he's long gone."

"What are the local gangs involved with, Chief?"

"The usual," he said with a shrug. "Drugs, theft, you name it."

"But why would they kill the kid?"

"What makes you think it was gang related?" he said.

"Let's call it a hunch," I said. "Did you know Willy?"

"Sure," he said, nodding. "He'd been in and out of trouble since he was a kid. I thought he'd cleaned up his act, but I must have been wrong."

"You can't keep an eye on all of them, Chief," I said.

"Indeed," he said, nodding as he glanced at his watch. "I need to run. I have a task force meeting at two."

"Task force? What are you dealing with?"

"It's our first meeting," he said. "I'm afraid we're facing a sudden influx of Fentanyl on the island."

"Fentanyl?" I said, grimacing. "That's nasty stuff."

"Yes, it's the worst thing I've ever seen," he said. "Whatever happened to the good old days when everyone just smoked weed?"

"Good luck with that one, Chief," I said. "I don't envy you."

"It's part of the job, Mr. White," he said, getting to his feet. "Thank you for lunch."

"You're welcome. It was nice meeting you."

"You will keep me informed if you find anything out about Willy's murder?"

"I will," I said, studying him closely. "As long as you're willing to extend the same courtesy."

He gave it some thought then nodded.

"I can do that," he said, then waved and headed down the Boardwalk.

CHAPTER 15

Felicia looked up when I entered the office. She was organizing items on her new desk that must have been delivered while I was at lunch. She put the finishing touches on her desktop then wadded up a bundle of bubble wrap and headed outside to toss it in the trash. When Felicia returned, I was already sitting at my desk studying my computer screen.

"How was lunch?" she said, stretching out on the couch.

"It was okay," I said. "The chief asked how you were doing."

"And?"

"I told him letting you get away was the biggest mistake he'll ever make," I deadpanned.

"Good," she said, laughing. "What did he have to say about Willy's murder?"

"Nothing," I said. "But he promised to keep us in the loop if he learns anything."

"Don't hold your breath," she said, staring up at the ceiling.

"But he did say they just formed a new task force to deal with an emerging Fentanyl problem," I said.

"I've heard about that stuff, but never had to deal with it," Felicia said.

"Imagine something fifty times stronger than heroin," I said.

"They give it to cancer patients, right?"

"They do," I said, scrolling through the page of search results. "But there's a huge black market for it. The stuff makes Oxy look like a candy bar." I studied the screen then opened my calculator and keyed in some numbers. I sat back in my chair and scowled. "That can't be right."

"What?" she said, getting off the couch and dragging her chair next to mine.

"I'm trying to do some basic math," I said, rekeying the numbers and examining the total. "No way."

"What are you trying to do?" she said, inching closer to get a better look at the screen.

"Get some idea of how much money somebody can make trafficking in Fentanyl," I said. "Let's try this again. There are about two milligrams of Fentanyl in a normal dose." I glanced over at her. "In pill form."

"Okay," she said, still staring at my screen.

"And a kilo of Fentanyl powder goes for around five grand. I'm sure it's even cheaper if you buy in bulk," I said, keying in another round of numbers. "There's a million milligrams in a kilo."

"You sure? That sounds like a lot."

"That's what I thought. But a thousand milligrams are in a gram. A thousand grams in a kilo. A thousand times a thousand is a million, right?"

"Whoever said Americans can't handle the metric system?" she said, laughing.

"And with a dosage of two milligrams per pill, that means you can produce a half million pills per kilo," I said, still stunned by the number.

"What does Fentanyl retail for on the street?" Felicia said.

"Between ten and twenty bucks a pill," I said, glancing over at her. "Geez, that's somewhere between a five and ten million return on a five-thousand-dollar investment."

"We're in the wrong business," she said, shaking her head.

"No kidding," I said, then shook my head again. "That can't be right."

"I think your math is fine, Doc. Andrews said a bunch of it just hit the street down here?"

"Yeah."

"You think it's related to Willy's death?" Felicia said.

"At those profit margins? It's certainly worth a look." Then my phone rang and I checked the number. "Hey, Merlin."

"What's up, Doc?"

"I'm putting you on speaker. I'm dealing with a math problem at the moment," I said.

"I thought I smelled smoke," Merlin said. "Who's listening in?"

"Felicia."

"Okay. How are you doing, Felicia?"

"I'm good, Merlin."

"So, what's the math problem?" Merlin said.

"I'm trying to calculate the profitability of Fentanyl," I said.

"It's between five and ten million per kilo," Merlin said. "At street prices."

"So, my math is right," I said, glancing over at Felicia.

"Why are you looking into that?" he said.

"Apparently, it just hit the streets down here," I said.

"Then get ready for Armageddon. That crap is incredibly profitable and lethal," Merlin said. "Always a lovely combination."

"Yeah," I said. "How's your hunt for the art forger going?"

"I thought it was going great," he said. "I found her."

"Her?"

"Esmeralda Winston," Merlin said.

"Esmeralda," I said, letting the name run through my memory bank. "Why does that name sound familiar?"

"She used to be the girlfriend of our old friend from Budapest," Merlin said.

"That's right," I said, nodding. "He was dating an artist. And she was stealing his paintings and replacing them with forgeries?"

"She was," Merlin said, then chuckled. "Not bad, huh?"

"Yeah, I like it. Very clever," I said. "How did our friend take the news?"

"About like you'd expect," Merlin said. "She had a studio in Paris, and our friend paid her a visit last night."

"How did that go?"

"She caught two in the back of the head," Merlin said.

"He shot her?"

"No, she was already dead when he got there."

"You believe him?"

"I do."

157

"Huh," I grunted. "Did Esmeralda have any idea you were looking for her?"

"What am I, an amateur?" Merlin snapped.

"Sorry," I said, then grinned at Felicia. "So, I take it our friend got his painting back."

"He did. Along with some others and a suitcase of Euros," Merlin said.

"I guess his cash flow problems are over, huh?"

"They are," Merlin said. "I got some stuff for you on Greedy."

"Cool," I said, reaching for a pen and pad.

"He made his early money in real estate," Merlin said. "Then he branched out."

"To what?"

"Currency manipulation to start with," Merlin said.

"Let me guess," I said, shaking my head. "He had help."

"He did."

"From us?"

"Yeah, that's the way it looks," Merlin said. "Greedy was getting tipped off from inside about emerging hot spots and unrest around the planet and started shorting various currencies. I'm sure he was kicking back to whoever was tipping him off."

"I'm so glad I'm out of there," I said.

"Me too. After that, Greedy started setting up different companies in several countries."

"What sort of companies?"

"I'm still digging into that," Merlin said. "Everything's registered offshore, including most of his money. It's a typical spiderweb. It's gonna take me some time to decipher all of it. If you need it."

"Yeah, I think I might. If you don't mind," I said. "Where are his companies located?"

"Let's see," he said over the sound of rustling paperwork. "He's got one in Brazil. A couple in Europe. And he moved into China a few years ago."

"What's he doing in China?" I said, perking up.

"Making knickknacks and toys for kids," he said with a laugh. "At least that's what the articles of incorporation say."

"I guarantee he's not making knickknacks," I said. "And the only toys he's interested in are the ones he buys for himself."

"I'll take your word for it," Merlin said.

"Hey, guess who I ran into the other night?" I said.

"Who?"

"Do you remember the bartender from Blues Alley?" I said.

"The tall black guy?"

"Yeah. Dupree."

"Huh? Cool guy. I always liked him. What's he doing down there?" Merlin said.

"He was tending bar at a party Elle and Greedy were throwing at their house," I said. "He told me he was running a catering company, but I have a feeling he's working for Greedy."

"You want to see what I can find out about him?" Merlin said.

"Yeah, it probably couldn't hurt," I said, then looked at Felicia. "You remember his last name?"

"Perkins," Felicia said.

"Dupree Perkins," I said into the phone. "And while you're at it, do some checking on a guy named Harry Wilder. He and Dupree seem to be thick as thieves."

"Got it," Merlin said. "Okay, I've gotta run. I've got a meeting with an art appraiser."

"Let me guess, our friend gave you a painting as a thank you," I said, laughing.

"Hey, you think I do this crap for free?"

160

CHAPTER 16

Dupree pulled into the parking lot outside
Club Horizontal then turned the engine off and reached for
his phone. Harry opened his door halfway then paused and
glanced over at Dupree.

"What are you doing?" Harry said.

"I'm making a phone call. What does it look like?"
Dupree said.

"He said he was going to be inside."

"I'm aware of that, Harry," Dupree said, holding the
phone to his ear.

"So, let's go inside. I want to get a lap dance."

"Knock yourself out," Dupree said. "C'mon, man. Pick
up the damn phone."

"You're not coming?" Harry said.

"In there? Not a chance," Dupree said, then spoke into
the phone. "Hey. We're outside." Dupree slid his phone
into his pocket. "He'll be right out."

"Why don't you want to go in?" Harry said, settling
back into his seat.

"Where do I even begin?" Dupree said, keeping a close eye on the entrance to the club. "Let's say I don't want fifty witnesses watching me talk to the guy and leave it at that."

"I don't want to go in there by myself," Harry said, scratching his sunburnt arms.

"Good call, Harry," Dupree said. "Besides, you wouldn't like it."

"Why not?"

"They don't play banjo music," Dupree said with a grin. "And in the last couple months, two guys have gotten stabbed in there. Not to mention another who got shot last week. But you go right ahead. They're gonna love you."

"Maybe another time," Harry said.

"There he is," Dupree said, nodding at the front door. He flashed his headlights once to get the guy's attention then got out of the car and called out. "There's the man. You been making it rain in there, TeeMac?"

They exchanged an elaborate handshake, and the young man stumbled backward a few steps before regaining his balance.

"Who are you again?" the man slurred as he shivered in the night air.

"I'm Dupree. And this is Harry."

"Yeah," TeeMac said, doing his best to focus as he glanced back and forth at them. "How you doing?"

"Better than you, it appears," Dupree said. "How much of that stuff you been eating?"

TeeMac merely shrugged before shivering again.

"It's cold out here," he said.

"Yeah, it must be all the way down to seventy-five," Dupree deadpanned. "And me without my muff."

"Where's Emo?" TeeMac said, glancing around the parking lot as he swayed on his feet.

"Emo and Barry went for a boat ride this afternoon," Dupree said. "They ain't back yet."

"I've always dealt with Emo," TeeMac said.

"Well, you're dealing with me now, TeeMac," Dupree said, studying the man's face. "Man, where the hell did your pupils go?"

"What?"

"Look at that, Harry. The man's got no pupils."

"Yeah, I noticed," Harry said.

"Are we all set for Friday?" Dupree said.

"Huh?" TeeMac said, then flinched and jumped back. He recovered and forced a small smile. "Sorry. I've been seeing iguanas all night."

"You're hallucinating, man," Dupree said. "Keep eating that crap and you ain't gonna make it to your next birthday."

"Is that some sort of threat?" TeeMac said, attempting to look tough but failing miserably.

"It's just an observation, my man," Dupree said. "Look at you. You're a mess. I expect you to clean yourself up a bit before Friday or we're gonna have a problem."

"Friday? Oh, right. Friday," TeeMac said, nodding. "Yeah, we're cool."

"What's the plan?" Dupree said.

"I'm gonna meet him at midnight," TeeMac said through a round of tremors.

"Where?"

"A half-mile offshore. On the north side near Salt Bay Preserve."

"Okay," Dupree said. "If it was good enough for Columbus, it's good enough for us, right?"

"Who?" TeeMac said.

"I take it you're not much of a history buff," Dupree said, glancing over at Harry and shaking his head. "Just head for the beach after you make the pickup and flash your lights when you get close to shore. We'll find you."

"Yeah," TeeMac said. "Got it. Anything else? My beer's getting warm."

"Just one more thing," Dupree said.

"What's that?"

"It's a hundred cases, TeeMac," Dupree said, placing a hand on the man's arm to emphasize his point. "Not ninety-nine. Or ninety-eight. A hundred. Are we clear?"

"Yeah, I got it," TeeMac said through a vacant stare.

"Repeat it."

"A hundred cases."

"Good man," Dupree said. "And in case you're thinking about doing something foolish, just remember what happened to your associate."

"Who?"

"Willy."

"Willy," TeeMac whispered through another round of shivers. "Yeah, Willy."

"Another tragic outcome of the life you lead," Dupree said. "But there's no reason for history to repeat itself, right?"

"What?"

"Never mind, TeeMac," Dupree said, shaking his head. "Let's keep it simple. A hundred cases. Friday. Midnight. Salt Bay Preserve."

TeeMac nodded, his shivering almost out of control.

"You better get back inside out of the cold," Dupree said.

"Yeah," TeeMac said, nodding.

They watched him stagger his way back inside the club then climbed into the car.

"What a waste of oxygen," Harry said.

"Don't be like that, Harry," Dupree said, starting the car. "The man's got a problem."

"At the rate he's going, he's not going to last the week," Harry said.

"Yeah, that sounds about right," Dupree said, after giving it some thought.

"All that Fentanyl is going kill him," Harry said.

"Yeah. I'm sure that's the way Greedy is going to make it look."

CHAPTER 17

Samson led me down the driveway,
apparently determined to separate my arm from the
shoulder socket then growled at the work crew.

"Easy," I said, then bent down to pet the dog's back.
"They're just here to fix the road."

A man strolled over and slowly lowered a hand in front
of the dog's head. Samson sniffed it then wagged his tail.

"Good morning," the man said. "He's a good-looking
dog. Is he yours?"

"Good morning. No, he belongs to my neighbor." I
said. "But I walk him every day."

"What's his name?" the man said, kneeling down to
rub the dog's head.

"Samson."

"Sounds about right," he said. "Are you Doc?"

"I am. Nice to meet you."

"Same here. I'm Harold," he said, extending his hand.
"Sorry, I didn't get a crew out here earlier to fix this thing."

"Don't worry about it," I said. "Actually, your timing
worked perfectly."

"One hell of a hole," Harold said, shaking his head as he stared down into the pothole. "We'll be out of here in a couple hours max."

"Take your time," I said. "I'm not going anywhere until later on."

"Felicia said she's working for you," Harold said.

"She is," I said.

"You're a lucky man. Tell her I said hi."

"I'll do that," I said, giving him a wave as I headed off with Samson leading the way.

We walked for about a half hour before heading back up the driveway. The road crew had filled the hole, and a couple of guys were tamping the dirt and rock down before a layer of asphalt was applied. I let Samson off his lead, and he raced for Sebastian's house and sat waiting for me on the porch. I knocked then let myself in.

"You're back," Sebastian said, lowering the newspaper. "How was your walk, Samson?"

The dog gently placed his front paws on Sebastian's lap. After receiving enough attention, the dog stretched out on the floor and glanced back and forth at us.

"He's a great dog," I said, sitting down in a chair across from him.

"He is," Sebastian said softly. "I'm going to miss him."

A wave of emotion surged through me as I studied his wistful expression.

"You've got a long time to go, Sebastian," I said eventually.

"No, I don't, Doc," he said. "And we both know that. You think I'm losing all this weight because I'm on a diet?"

Despite the gravity of the conversation, I laughed.

"Fair enough, Sebastian."

"Good. So, let's not dance around that subject, okay?"

"Okay," I whispered.

"I've been putting my affairs in order," Sebastian said, then grinned when Samson rested his head on his feet. "And I've only got a couple things left I need to take care of."

I sat quietly and waited for him to continue.

"The first is Samson," he said, then laughed when the dog cocked his head at the mention of his name. "I was talking about you, not to you."

"What would you like to do with him?" I said.

"I thought you might be interested in taking him," Sebastian said.

"I'd love that," I said, nodding. "No sense putting him through more change than necessary."

"He'll be very happy with you," Sebastian said.

"Don't worry. I'll take good care of him."

"I know you will," he said. "The other remaining question is what to do with the house."

"Don't you have someone you can leave it to?"

"Actually, no," Sebastian said. "So, I thought I'd sell it."

"Makes sense," I said. "Would you like some help finding a real estate agent?"

"I'd like to avoid that if possible."

"I guess you could just put an ad in the paper and see how that works," I said, shrugging.

"I'd rather not," he said, shaking his head.

"Why do I think you have something on your mind, Sebastian?"

"Very good, Doc," he said. "You don't miss a thing. I thought you might be interested in buying it."

"Me? Why would you think that? I'm not even sure I'm going to stay on the island."

"Oh, you're not going anywhere," Sebastian said.

"Why do you say that?" I said, leaning forward in my chair.

"Because I've seen the way you look at her," he said softly.

I leaned back and draped a leg over my knee.

"Is it that obvious?" I said after an extended silence.

"Doc," he said, laughing. "At this point, everything in my body has pretty much stopped working. Except for my eyes. My eyesight remains quite good."

"What would I do with the place? If I do decide to stay, I'll just buy the place I'm in. I love that house."

"Rent it out," Sebastian said with a shrug. "Rent it to her. She can't sleep on her grandmother's couch forever."

I sat quietly trying to process the idea. Then I leaned forward again.

"But if you don't have anyone to leave the house to, who would you give the sales proceeds to?"

"To the Preservation Society," Sebastian said. "For the turtles."

"You have been busy," I said, again smiling at him.

"At my age, all I have left is time to think, Doc."

"Okay," I said, nodding. "Let me give it some thought."

"That's fine," he said, his eyes twinkling. "Just don't take too long."

"I'll do my best. You are something else, Sebastian."

"Yes, a rare breed, wouldn't you say? Could you do me one more favor?"

"Of course. What do you need?"

"Are you going to the grocery store later?"

"Actually, I am. I'm out of milk," I said. "What do you need?"

"A bottle of Jameson."

"But you quit drinking a decade ago," I said.

"I did. But this seems like a good time to start again."

"Do you really think that's a good idea, Sebastian?"

"I think it's the best idea I've had in years."

I flashed a sad smile in his direction then got up and petted Samson who was still stretched out across the old man's feet.

"I'll stop by as soon as I get back from the store."

"Thank you, Doc. Oh, there's just one more thing."

"A case of beer to chase it down?" I said, pausing at the door.

"No," he said through a phlegmy chuckle that turned into an extended round of hacking coughs.

I waited until he finished and had wiped his mouth with a handkerchief.

"What is it, Sebastian?"

"Don't let me die in the hospital, Doc."

CHAPTER 18

I leaned back in the lounge chair and took a long look out at the harbor then began reviewing my notes. The wind whipped across the gallery, and I couldn't miss a black patch of clouds making its way across the water. Felicia stepped outside carrying a tray of food.

"You bought a lot at the store," she said, setting the tray down before sitting down on the lounger next to mine.

"Yeah, I figured since I was there, I'd stock up," I said, sitting up and eyeing the selection. I built a small nosh plate then got settled back in. "Did you get a chance to swing by and give Mrs. Johnson an update?"

"I did," Felicia said, sampling a Dolmades.

"How is she doing?"

"Not well," she said, studying the clouds. "I hated having to tell her we haven't made much progress."

"It won't be long," I said, scanning my notes.

"What are you working on?" she said, stretching out.

"The history of stilt-walking," I said, reaching for a wedge of Edam. "You can still find them in a lot of places."

"They're all over the Caribbean," Felicia said.

"Yeah," I said. "And Asia."

"Asia?" she said, glancing over at me.

"To be more specific, China. Maybe Russia."

"You think Greedy flew a shooter in?"

"Not necessarily," I said, going in for some more cheese. "But if we assume he's behind the Fentanyl."

"And we do," she said, nodding.

"Yeah. Then it makes sense he'd use someone he's familiar with. You know, to keep the circle as tight as possible. And if we also assume his factory in China is producing that crap, maybe someone from there was either the shooter or organized the hit."

"It's a good theory," she said with a shrug. "I'm not sure it helps us, though."

"No, it doesn't," I said.

"What I don't understand is why he dropped some of it here. He could make some money on it, but nothing like he could on the mainland. It sounds like a lot of risk for not much reward. You know, in the grand scheme of things."

"But to somebody like Willy, it would have been a fortune," I said.

"You think he decided to do some freelancing?" Felicia said.

"I do," I said. "And when Greedy found out about it, he put a stop to it."

175

"And send a message to anyone else who might be thinking about doing the same thing," she said, nibbling on a slice of apple. "Sure, that works."

"This lunch is way too healthy," I said, surveying the tray.

"Well, excuse me," she said with a laugh.

"Did Greedy elaborate when he was hitting on you at the party?" I said, turning to face her.

"I told you I didn't stick around long enough to hear the details," she said, frowning.

"Not about that," I said, shaking my head. "His boat. When he was talking about his boat, did he go into any specifics about some of the trips he takes?"

"Let me think," she said, setting her plate down. "He talked about some of the day trips he likes to take. And he mentioned sailing the islands off of St. Thomas and the BVI." She stared out at the water, deep in thought, then turned back to me. "Florida. He mentioned he was putting a crew together for a trip to Miami."

"Did he say when?" I said.

"No, I don't think so," she said. "You think he just sails the stuff to the mainland on his own boat?"

"Yeah, I think he might," I said. "If I had that much money at stake, I'd be keeping a close eye on it."

"But how is he getting the product here?" Felicia said.

"By boat, I imagine," I said. "Where's the closest Caribbean port that can handle oceangoing cargo ships?"

"Probably the Dominican Republic," Felicia said.

"How far away is that?"

Felicia grabbed her phone and did a search. A few minutes later, she looked up.

"The ports on the northern side of the island are about three hundred fifty nautical miles from here," she said.

"Do ports still put arrivals and departures on their websites?" I said, now convinced I was on the right track.

"I'm sure they do," she said, refocusing on her phone.

"See if you can find any Chinese ships in port," I said as the rain began to pound the corrugated gallery roof.

"Bingo," she said eventually. "There aren't any in port at the moment, but one is scheduled to arrive tomorrow. And you'll never guess where it's registered."

"Shanghai," I said.

"Well done," she said, laughing. "That's where Greedy's factory is located, right?"

"It is," I said, deep in thought. "You're the nautical expert around here. If you were going to do a three-hundred-fifty mile run across open water, and wanted to do

177

it safely but as quickly as possible, what sort of boat would you use?"

Felicia gave it some thought.

"I'd probably go with a powercat," she said.

"What's that?"

"You know what a catamaran looks like, right?"

"Sure. I'm not a total idiot," I said.

"A powercat is like a catamaran without the sails," she said.

"How big are they?" I said.

"Fifty, sixty feet. Maybe a bit bigger," Felicia said. "Certainly big enough to handle rough seas."

"How fast are they?"

"I think the high-end ones have a cruising speed around twenty-five knots. A tricked out one could even be a little faster."

"English, please."

"It's about thirty miles an hour," Felicia said.

"That's a twelve-hour trip," I said. "Assuming non-stop."

"And good weather. But you could definitely do it in a day. As long as you got an early start."

"What about range? Can they go that far without having to stop for gas?"

"There aren't a lot of gas stations out there, Doc," she said, laughing. "But sure, all you'd need to do is add an extra fuel tank. People do it all the time."

"Tomorrow is Thursday," I said, staring out at the rain. "There's no way they could unload, pay off whoever they're working with at Customs, then head out, right?"

"I wouldn't want to do that run at night," Felicia said.

"They'll be leaving Friday morning," I said, nodding.

"You're sure? Just like that?"

"Greedy is going to want to get his hands on it as soon as possible," I said. "It's Friday. Saturday at the latest."

"How big a shipment do you think it is?" she said.

"Good question," I said, getting up off the lounge chair.

"Where are you going?" she said.

"To get my bottle of vitamins."

I returned a few minutes later carrying a small plastic bottle.

"Good idea," she deadpanned. "You know, given your age."

"Funny," I said opening the bottle and removing one of the pills. "It's pretty big."

"I suppose," she said with a shrug. "But I'm sure you can get it down."

"The average dose of Fentanyl is two milligrams. That's tiny," I said. "And there's a hundred pills in this bottle. You could easily fit five hundred Fentanyl pills in a bottle this size."

"Yeah, you could," she said, examining one of the vitamins.

"And you can produce a half-million pills from a kilo of powder," I said, reaching for my phone and launching the calculator.

"More math?" she said with a grin.

"Yeah, worst part of the job," I said, grinning back. "If we assume five hundred pills per bottle, you need a thousand bottles per kilo." I grabbed my pen and paper and began sketching. "Say you had a box a couple of feet long and maybe a foot and a half wide."

"Okay," she said, studying the drawing.

"If you were using bottles a little smaller than the vitamin one, you could probably fit a couple hundred across the bottom of the box, right?"

"Maybe even more," she said, nodding. "And you could stack them."

"Yeah," I said. "I think you could get a thousand in a box that size. And the boxes would be easy to carry."

"Sure, the heaviest thing would be the bottles," she said. "So, each box would be worth somewhere between five and ten million?"

"Yeah, if my math is right."

"It is," she said, stunned by the number. "How much do you think Greedy's bringing in?"

"Who knows?" I said with a shrug. "But if he's going to all that trouble, it's gotta be at least fifty, maybe a hundred kilos. It could even be more."

"He's bringing the product over in stages," Felicia said.

"Yeah, and that's smart," I said. "If one of the deliveries went south, Greedy wouldn't lose the whole thing. I don't know. But we do know it's at least the second delivery. Maybe this is the last one before he heads to Florida. Storage on a powercat wouldn't be a problem, would it?"

"On a sixty-footer? Nah, there'd be tons of room," she said. "We're talking hundreds of millions of dollars, Doc."

"We are," I said, stretching out on one of the lounge chairs. "And that's why Greedy is going to want to get his hands on it as soon as possible."

"Friday?"

"That's my best guess at the moment," I said, closing my eyes to enjoy the sound of the rain.

"They'll probably use another boat to do the pickup," Felicia said.

"Yeah, that's what I was thinking. No sense docking in town and running the risk of somebody seeing you."

"Like us?" she said.

"Are you free Friday night?" I said, opening my eyes and glancing over at her.

"Well, I'd prefer dinner and a movie, but I suppose I can make an exception," she said. "How do you want to handle it?"

"The easiest way is to just follow the guy driving the van to the pickup spot," I said, closing my eyes.

"Makes sense," she said, stretching out on her lounger.

"Do you know who Willy used to hang out with? You know, during his younger years before he tried to go straight?"

I waited out a lengthy silence until she responded.

"TeeMac," she whispered. "Son of a gun."

"Who's TeeMac?" I said, sitting up.

"He's a player in one of the gangs down here," she said, sitting up. "And he and Willy were really tight."

"He doesn't happen to have a boat, does he?"

"As a matter of fact, he does," Felicia said. "It can't be that easy, Doc."

"Don't overthink it," I said. "A lot of times it is."

"We need to figure out who'll be driving the van," she said.

"Dupree and his buddy, Harry," I said. "I'm sure Greedy is worried about somebody else trying to freelance. And those two seem to be the most likely candidates to make sure the deal doesn't head south."

"Because?"

"Because they're mainlanders he brought down here," I said. "And while Greedy needs some help from the locals, he doesn't trust them."

"Makes sense," she said. "And you think he trusts those two more?"

"Nah," I said, shaking my head. "But he's got proximity to them."

"And has managed to put the fear of God in them?"

"I'm sure Greedy considers himself a deity," I said, closing my eyes as the rain intensified. "I'm gonna take a nap."

"I think I'll join you," she said, then laughed. "But from over here."

"It's a start."

CHAPTER 19

After Felicia had left for the day, I took Samson for his evening walk, then showered and changed. I was sitting on the gallery sipping a beer when my phone rang.

"What's up, Doc?"

"Hey, Merlin. I'm just sitting here enjoying the sunset. What are you up to?"

"I'm about ready to go to bed. It's been a long day."

"Did you sell your painting?"

"I did," Merlin said. "I still can't believe what people pay for those things. That's kind of why I'm calling."

"Okay," I said, frowning as I reached for my beer.

"I got some information on those two guys," Merlin said. "You'll never guess where Dupree went to college."

"Bartending school," I said with a grin.

"Yeah, funny," he said. "Dupree got his MFA from the Maryland Institute. The college of art."

"That's in Baltimore, right?"

"It is," Merlin said. "That might explain why he was tending bar in Georgetown."

"Yeah, probably making some extra money while he was in school. He's a painter?"

"That's what he got his degree in," Merlin said. "But I couldn't find any of his stuff online. It's like he finished school, then either stopped painting or couldn't sell anything."

"That's interesting," I said, taking a sip.

"Yeah, who goes through an intense program like that and just quits?" Merlin said. "And that got me thinking."

"I'd be shocked if it didn't," I said, getting up and pacing the gallery. "You think we might have stumbled onto some sort of forgery ring?"

"You said Greedy was a big-time collector, right?" Merlin said.

"Yeah, his place down here is full of paintings. I wouldn't know a valuable piece of art if I fell over it, but Felicia says a lot of them were done by famous artists."

"You're such a philistine," Merlin said, laughing.

"Guilty."

"But why would Greedy even bother?" Merlin said. "He can obviously afford to just buy them."

"Maybe he does it because he can," I said with a shrug. "Or Dupree is freelancing."

"That's possible," Merlin said. "But if this is an organized ring, it has to lead back to Greedy."

"Let me guess," I said, coming to a stop. "Our friend in Budapest has crossed paths with Greedy."

"Nice to see you haven't lost all your skills," Merlin said. "They met several years ago at an art auction in Paris."

"Did you get that from our friend?"

"I did," Merlin said. "Greedy and Elle have been at a couple of dinner parties he threw at his place in France."

"And they talked art, right?"

"According to our friend, that's all they talked about," Merlin said. "Their shared love of the art world."

"Was he dating Esmeralda at the time?" I said.

"He was," Merlin said. "And our friend thinks that she and Greedy had a little thing going on between them."

"Wow," I said, sitting down and lighting a cigarette. "I gotta give Greedy credit for this one. That's a brilliant scam."

"Yeah, I like it too," Merlin said. "The beautiful part of it is there's never any crime reported. People have no idea the thing hanging on their wall they paid millions for is a fake."

"And if they do try to sell it at some point, they wouldn't have a clue about how or when it happened. It could have been swapped out years ago."

"Yeah, and you'd only need a few people to pull it off," Merlin said. "Somebody who knows their way around security systems and, of course, the forger."

"And you just wait until the people are out of the house. In and out before you know it," I said, then exhaled smoke, deep in thought. "Hang on."

"What?" Merlin said.

"Greedy loves to take people out on his boat for the day," I said.

"Rich people who collect art?"

"Yeah, that would be my first guess," I said, shaking my head. "Man, this guy might be smarter than I've been giving him credit for."

"Well, if he's running Fentanyl out of China, I'm sure he can handle stealing some paintings," Merlin said. "Be careful with this guy, Doc."

"Yeah, I will," I said, then crushed my cigarette out. "What about Dupree's buddy, Harry?"

"Another interesting story," Merlin said. "Harry's a Juilliard grad."

"Juilliard?" I said, surprised by the news. "Well, there's no way that guy's a dancer. Musician?"

"Bingo," Merlin said. "I made a few calls."

"To who?"

"Does it matter?" Merlin snapped.

"No," I said, laughing at his ongoing unwillingness to share his sources. "What does he play?"

"Apparently, any instrument he picks up," Merlin said. "But he's trying to break into the business as a country songwriter."

"Really? Huh," I grunted as I picked at the label on my beer bottle. "So, he's never made any money with his music?"

"It doesn't look like it," he said, then waited out a lengthy silence. "Is there something on your mind, Doc?"

"You mind doing a little more digging into him?" I said.

"I'm sure I can fit it in. What do you need?"

"Get Harry's work history and see if he's spent any time working around electronics, surveillance, security systems, stuff like that."

"That's a good thought," Merlin said. "You think those two are smart enough to pull something like that off?"

"I think they might be," I said. "And if the only thing they're doing is following Greedy's instructions, I'm sure they can handle it."

"Okay," Merlin said. "I'm beat, so I'm gonna sign off."

"Thanks, Merlin. Great job, as always," I said.

"No problem," he said. "It's still early there. You got plans for the night?"

"Yeah, Felicia and I are heading out to hear some music," I said, glancing at my watch. "Actually, I need to get going." I was about to hang up then paused. "Hey, can I ask you a question?"

"You can ask, sure."

"How much did you get for the painting?"

"Somewhere north of a hundred bucks," Merlin deadpanned.

"Got it," I said, laughing. "Later."

CHAPTER 20

I picked Felicia up and we headed for the Nauti
Bar. I eventually found a spot to park in the crowded lot,
and we strolled across the gravel to the outside area where
the band was in full swing. We stopped to listen, and
Felicia waved to several people.

"They're good," I said.

"Yeah, they are," she said above the noise, swaying in
place to the music. "They're the house band on
Wednesdays. It's open mic night."

"Cool," I said, glancing around and spotting Dupree
standing off to one side. I nudged Felicia and nodded at
Dupree then realized she had her eyes on someone else.
"Who's that?"

"That's the infamous, TeeMac," she said, studying the
young man.

"He looks twitchy," I said.

"Yeah. He's on something," Felicia said. "I think I
might go have a chat with him."

"Okay. I'm gonna say hi to Dupree. You want a
drink?"

"Maybe in a few minutes," she said, giving me a small wave as she headed off.

I wandered over to Dupree who remained focused on the music until he realized I was there.

"Hey. Good evening, Doc."

"Good evening, Dupree," I said, bumping fists with him. "What brings you here?"

"Just catching some tunes," he said, through a sleepy-eyed stare. "And my buddy is gonna play in a bit. Giving the man some moral support and all that, you know?"

"Got it," I said. "How's the catering business?"

"Huh? Oh, yeah. It's good."

"I loved those crab puffs you served at Greedy's party," I said.

"What?" he said, glancing over. "Oh, yeah. They're always a big hit. Old family recipe."

"From Maryland?"

"Why do you say that?" Dupree said with a frown.

"Well, anything that good dealing with crab has to be from Maryland. They've got the best crab cakes in the country."

"You got that right," Dupree said, nodding.

The band finished the song, and we were finally able to talk without shouting. I spotted Harry making his way to the bandstand carrying a guitar case.

"Isn't that your buddy, Harry?" I said.

"That's him," Dupree said. "He's got a new song he just wrote he's dying to hear live. And he needs to run through the chord changes with the band."

"What kind of music does he write?" I said.

"Country," Dupree said. "I'm afraid Harry's got a terminal case of rhyming disease."

"Rhyming disease," I said, laughing. "That's funny."

"Yeah," he said, grinning at me. 'I try to talk to the man about writing some different stuff, but he don't listen. But he's good at it. I gotta give him that."

I focused on Felicia who was doing her best to talk with the obviously impaired TeeMac. Dupree had spotted the conversation as well and was watching it closely.

"She really work for you?" Dupree said.

"She does. But works with me is a better description."

"She's a beautiful woman," Dupree said as a statement of fact. "You having any luck figuring out who killed that kid?"

"No," I said, shaking my head. "Not yet."

"But you're still looking, right?"

192

"We are," I said. "But it's been hard to catch a break."

"Tough job," Dupree said, staring out at the harbor. "And not without its dangers, I imagine."

"When one searches for honey, one must occasionally expect to get stung."

"Not bad, Doc," Dupree said, grinning at me. "That would look good on a tee shirt."

"Words to live by."

We both focused on the stage when we heard the thrum of an amplified acoustic guitar.

"Here we go," Dupree said, taking a long swig of his beer.

Harry approached the microphone.

"This is a new one," he said to the crowd then counted the band in and launched into an up-tempo and very catchy pop-country song with surprisingly intricate chord changes.

"You're right," I said to Dupree. "He is good."

"Yeah," Dupree said, tapping his foot.

I listened to the first two verses, dripping with references to some of life's basic challenges, then laughed out loud when I heard the words to the chorus.

"I thought you'd like that," Dupree said.

"It sucks getting old," I said. "Can't argue with the man."

"Yeah, I think Harry's onto something with this one. Kind of a timeless theme, huh?"

I spent the next few minutes glancing back and forth between Harry and Felicia's conversation with TeeMac then the song finished to loud applause. Harry thanked the crowd then put his guitar back in its case. He motioned to Dupree who nodded yes as he waved his empty bottle in the air.

"Always leave them wanting more," Dupree said, then flinched when he spotted TeeMac clamoring up onto one of the picnic benches and looking around with a wild stare. "What the hell is he doing?"

"It looks he saw a mouse," I said.

"I better go see if the man needs any help," Dupree said. "Good seeing you, Doc."

"You too, Dupree. Hey, I almost forgot. I'm having a barbecue at my place and was wondering if you and Harry want to come."

"That sounds great," Dupree said. "When's the party?"

"Friday night," I deadpanned. "We'll probably get the grill going around eight. So, anytime you're ready, just swing by."

"Friday?" Dupree said. "Nah, no can do. Sorry, Doc, I'm already booked."

"That's too bad. Maybe next time."

"You can count on it," Dupree said, giving me another fist bump before heading off. "TeeMac. What are you doing? C'mon, man. Get the hell off that table."

Felicia started to make her way back and pointed at the front door. I followed her inside and ordered drinks then joined her at a table where she was watching hockey on one of the screens.

"You're a hockey fan?" I said, setting her wine glass in front of her.

"No, but it's better than golf," she said pointing at another screen.

"What's the deal with TeeMac?"

"He thought he saw an iguana. He said one has been following him around the last couple of days," she said, shaking her head. "He's whacked out of his mind. Are hallucinations a side effect of Fentanyl?"

"I think they can be. Especially after large doses," I said, taking a sip.

"Well, he's definitely been eating something," Felicia said. "And I'd be very surprised if they were pot cookies. What did Dupree have to say for himself?"

"He can't make it to the party," I said.

"What party?"

"The barbecue at my place on Friday," I said with a grin.

"Got it," she said, laughing. "Let me guess. He's already booked."

"He is."

"Well done, Doc."

"Thanks. But let's not get ahead of ourselves. Before we leave, make sure you invite TeeMac."

"Given how high he is, he might accept," Felicia said.

"No, I'm sure he'll remember Friday night," I said. "And Dupree will definitely be reminding him."

"If nothing else, it should be an entertaining evening," she said, taking a sip.

"Better than dinner and a movie?"

"I'll let you know next Friday," she said.

"You're asking me out?" I said, pausing mid-sip.

"I am," she said, grinning as she placed a hand over mine. "But you're paying."

"I knew there had to be a catch."

CHAPTER 21

Dupree stepped back from the canvas
and studied the painting as he cleaned his brush. He
finished the last of his beer then glanced at the photograph
taped to an easel next to the half-finished painting. Dupree
touched up a small section of the canvas then turned around
when he heard the music.

"What's that you're playing?" he said to Harry who
was on the couch fingerpicking his way through a
complicated set of chord changes.

"It's a new one," Harry said, not looking up from the
fretboard. "I'm gonna call it Life Imitates Art."

"Art who?" Dupree said with a grin, sitting down
across from Harry and closely watching how his hands
worked together.

"Funny," Harry said, finishing with a flourish. He set
his guitar down then focused on the painting. "It looks
good."

"Thanks," Dupree said. "I was up most of the night
working on it."

"When's the last time you painted one of your own?"
Harry said. "You know, an original."

"It's been years, man," Dupree said, shaking his head. "I just can't do it."

"You never have any original ideas?" Harry said, heading to the fridge for fresh beers.

"Oh, I got a ton of ideas. I've just never been able to bring 'em to fruition."

"Well, you're a great copycat. I'll give you that," Harry said. "You must have always colored inside the lines when you were a kid."

Dupree laughed and took a long swig of his beer. He sighed contentedly then set the bottle down.

"Who's the guy who painted that one?" Harry said, nodding at the half-finished canvas.

"Koons," Dupree said. "That's one of his early ones. He does a lot of different stuff now using various mediums."

"Is he popular?" Harry said, reaching for his guitar.

"Yeah," Dupree said with a laugh. "You could say that. One of his pieces sold a while back for over fifty million."

"Fifty? Geez," Harry grunted. "What do you think Greedy paid for that one?"

"I have no idea. And remember to keep your mouth shut about it. The man doesn't need to know anything. Got it?"

"Relax, Dupree. But it's a tricky one. You sure about this?"

"We'll be fine," Dupree said. "But I thought we might use a different split on this one."

"Like what?" Harry said, raising an eyebrow at him.

"Eighty-twenty. You know, since you aren't going to have to disable the alarm."

"Not fair."

"Don't pout," Dupree said. "And no veiled references in those new lyrics. I know how you like to get cute with those."

"Relax," Harry said, resuming his fingerpicking.

"Okay, new topic," Dupree said. "Friday night."

"What about it?"

"You're gonna be on the boat with TeeMac," Dupree said.

"On the water at night?" he said, removing his hands from the guitar. "Not gonna happen, Dupree."

"Oh, it's gonna happen, Harry. You saw TeeMac last night. The man's liable to fall overboard."

"I don't like being out on the water at night."

"Neither do I," Dupree said with a big grin. "And that's why you're going."

"Give a man a little power, and it always goes to his head," Harry said, strumming a power chord.

"You want this to work or not?"

"Yeah," Harry grunted. "Why doesn't the man just take his sailboat out there and meet the guy bringing the stuff over?"

"Too conspicuous. You know how the guy works. He tells everyone he's stocking supplies for his trip to Florida, and nobody bats an eye when they see a bunch of people carrying stuff down the dock."

"You ever tried it?" Harry said.

"Fentanyl?"

"Yeah."

"Are you out of your mind?" Dupree said. "You might as well eat rat poison. That crap will kill you right on the spot if you ain't careful."

"You think I'll be safe out there with TeeMac?"

"Just keep him focused on what needs to be done, and you'll be fine," Dupree said, then focused on Harry. "But the man has been seeing lizards, so keep your eyes open, just in case."

**

"I've been thinking about Friday night," Felicia said, glancing up from her planting.

"What about it?" I said, turning the hose off and looking around at the progress we'd made. Looking to spruce up the front of the house, I'd asked her to help me select some local plants and flowers that were easy to maintain. "It looks good. Adds a lot of color."

"Yeah, it does," she said, getting to her feet and brushing the dirt off her hands. "I thought instead of both of us being on shore keeping an eye on Dupree, I'd take my boat out."

"To get a feel for who's bringing the stuff over?"

"Yeah. If we're trying to put an end to Greedy's operation, identifying who he's working with out of the DR wouldn't hurt. And I'm still wondering if he might have some of the local cops in his pocket."

I sat down on the front steps and spotted Samson tearing across the lawn heading straight for us. I gave her idea some serious thought then nodded at her.

"I like it. Do you have night-vision glasses?"

"No, but I figured you might," she said, sitting down next to me and rubbing the dog's head. "Hey, Samson." The dog dropped the tennis ball, and Felicia leaned forward to pick the sodden object up. "That's disgusting." She fired it across the lawn and watched the dog tear after it.

"Actually, I do have a couple sets," I said, trying to remember where I'd put them.

"What about walkie-talkies?"

"Yeah," I deadpanned. "It's called an iPhone."

"Duh," she said, laughing.

"Just don't try to get too close to them."

"Not my first rodeo, Doc," she snapped.

"Sorry. Just be careful. That's all I'm saying."

Samson returned with the ball and dropped it at my feet. I threw it then wiped my hand on my shorts.

"I need to ask you something," Felicia said, then nodded for me to follow her onto the gallery.

We sat down on separate lounge chairs, and I threw the ball again before giving her my undivided attention.

"What's up?"

"You remember telling me about how you stole most of your money?" she said softly.

"I do. What about it?"

"Tell me more."

"Why?"

"Humor me," she said, loosening her ponytail.

"Okay. Most of my money came from two jobs."

"Jobs you did with your gang of ex-spies?"

"Actually, we preferred the name posse," I said. "And they weren't all ex-spies."

"But Merlin was involved, right?"

"Of course," I said. "We couldn't have done it without him."

"What about the others?" she said, turning toward me and folding her legs underneath her.

"There were two. One of them isn't around much. The other is dead."

"What happened to him?"

"He got shot in Italy," I said, exhaling as the memory washed over me.

That was a bad night.

"The worst," I whispered.

"What?"

"Nothing."

"Were you there?" she said softly.

"He died in my arms."

"I'm so sorry, Doc."

"Yeah. He was a good guy," I said, choking back the emotions. "But to answer your question, we stole the money from some despicable people."

"What were they up to?" she said.

"You don't want to know," I said, shaking my head. "It'll just ruin your day."

"Try me."

"One of them was an arms dealer running surface-to-air missiles to some folks who had no business getting their hands on them," I said. "We stole thirty million from him."

"Thirty million?" Felicia said, stunned.

"Well, we did have to split it," I said with a soft chuckle.

"So, you decided to steal it, just like that?" she said, leaning forward.

"No, Merlin and I talked about it for a long time," I said. "But in the end, that's what we decided to do."

"Just because you could get away with it?"

"I'd be lying if I told you that wasn't part of it," I said with a shrug. "But the main reason was that we didn't want the thirty million used for other things."

"Like what?"

"Sowing additional seeds of discontent around the world," I said.

"The thirty million would have gone back to the government if you hadn't taken it?"

"Let's just say it would have been added to a very unusual account."

"I don't know anything about how that world works," she said.

"Consider yourself lucky."

"Being a spy always sounded so romantic," she said. "You know, working anonymously in the shadows while trying to make the world a better place."

"It had its moments," I said, lighting a cigarette.

Few and far between.

"You never feel guilty about taking all that money?" she said.

"Actually, I don't. I like to think I'm putting it to better use than others would have. At least that's the way I justify it."

"Justification would be the word for it," she said, scowling. "You don't seem to spend much of it."

"I give a lot of it away," I said.

"To who?"

"To people who need it."

"You are so weird," she said, laughing.

"Guilty," I said. "But despite what you might think, I do have some semblance of a moral code. And an underlying philosophy about life."

"This I gotta hear," she said, stretching out on the lounger.

"It's all about trying to manage the good versus evil that lurks within all of us," I said.

"You truly believe we all have the capacity for evil?"

"There's no doubt about it," I said. "I used to have grand designs about what needed to be done. Lofty goals, if you will. Now, I pick my spots."

"To do what?"

"To try and leave the place better than I found it," I said softly.

"Have you?"

"I don't know," I said, staring directly into her eyes. "I'm not done yet."

"Okay," she whispered. "What about Merlin?"

"What about him?"

"Does he share your philosophy?"

"Merlin is…complicated," I said. "But compared to me, he has the chance to leave the world in much better shape. Or a whole lot worse."

"Why is that?"

"Because of his technology skills. I've seen him bring small countries to a standstill."

"I gotta meet this guy," she said.

"I think he'd like you."

"You think?" she said, striking a playful pose.

"You never know with Merlin," I said, laughing. "And the world will be fine as long as he doesn't get too pissed off." I studied her closely and turned serious. "You're asking about my money because you're wondering if I plan on stealing Greedy's, right?"

"It did cross my mind," Felicia said.

"No, that's not going to happen," I said.

"I want to believe you, Doc."

"For that money to be stolen, he would have already unloaded the Fentanyl. And there's no way I'm going to let that crap hit the streets."

"Good answer," she said, nodding. "What's your plan for Greedy?"

"I'm trying to figure out a way to sink his boat with him and the Fentanyl on it," I said with a shrug. "They both deserve to be on the bottom of the ocean."

"That shouldn't be hard to do."

"He's gonna have other people on the boat," I said. "That's the problem."

"Let me guess," she said. "You can't justify taking out the crew, right?"

"No, I can't. I'm sure they're just trying to make a living. Illegal as it is."

"You do have a strange moral code," she said, staring at me.

"I like to think of it as layered," I deadpanned.

"Okay, Doc," she said, laughing. "Whatever floats your boat. What about Dupree? Do you plan to take him down?"

"I'd like to cut Dupree a break if we can," I said.

"You don't think he had anything to do with Willy's murder?" Felicia said.

"No, Dupree's not a killer," I said. "And whatever forgery ring he's involved in has to be respected."

"What?" she said, frowning.

"I've always been a big fan of clever white-collar crime. That forgery ring has got panache. A real sense of style and wit. You gotta respect that. As long as nobody gets hurt in the process."

"That woman Esmeralda just got shot. Did you forget about that?"

"That's a different element," I said, raising a finger to emphasize my point. "And definitely something that needs to be followed up on. But Dupree wasn't involved in that. In fact, if he isn't careful, he might end up being the next one catching a couple in the back of the head."

"You think Greedy is starting to tie up some loose ends?"

"Maybe," I said, frowning. "The situation with Esmeralda could have just been the result of an affair gone bad. Greedy might have been worried she was going to start running her mouth."

"It's possible," she said.

"The trick to dealing with people like Greedy is to always assume the worst. I've found you're rarely disappointed."

"You think Dupree is pretty much just following orders?"

"When he needs to, yes. But that's not all of it. Dupree's up to something."

"Like what?"

"I'm not sure," I said, shaking my head.

"We're still a long way from figuring out who shot Willy."

"Actually, we're a lot closer than you might think."

CHAPTER 22

Dupree draped a leg over his knee, doing his best to listen and smile for the man who seemed to have an endless supply of stories about himself and loved to tell them. The current topic was squash, the sport not the vegetable as Dupree had learned after asking an embarrassing question about the man's favorite way to cook it. His eyes drifted to the painting behind the desk until he realized Greedy was staring at him, waiting for a response. Dupree frowned, unsure if Greedy was looking for an answer or merely validation. He went with the latter.

"That's most impressive, sir."

"Yes, well, I've spent a long time perfecting my game," Greedy said, reaching for a box of cigars. He held it out to Dupree.

"Oh, no, but thank you, sir."

"You sure? They're Cuban," Greedy said, lighting the cigar and quickly creating a cloud of smoke that hovered over the desk. "Talk to me about Friday."

"Yes, sir," Dupree said, nodding. "We're all set."

"What time are you meeting them?"

"Around midnight."

"Excuse me?" Greedy said, raising an eyebrow.

"Sorry, sir. Midnight."

"There you go. So, what's the plan?"

"Harry is going to be on the boat with the local kid. I'll have the van on shore. As soon as I see their signal, I'll confirm it and they'll head for the beach."

"Have you checked the measurements of the van?" Greedy said.

"Yes, sir. If the boxes are the size you say they are, we'll be able to load them all in one trip."

"Excellent," Greedy said, then glanced at the door when he heard the soft knock. "Come in."

Elle, wearing a long tee shirt over her bathing suit, entered the office but remained near the door. She nodded at Dupree then focused on her husband.

"You wanted to see me?"

"Not exactly," Greedy said. "But it was unavoidable."

"Go screw yourself, Brewster."

"There's my girl," Greedy said with a grin. "I just wanted to let you know that I'll be leaving on Monday."

"My prayers have been answered," Elle said. "Where are you going?"

"I'm taking the boat to Miami."

211

"You and your latest batch of chippies?" she said, leaning against the door.

"It's called a crew," Greedy said.

"How long are you going to be gone?"

"Probably a couple of weeks. But don't worry, I'll be back," he said through an evil grin. "I have some business to take care of once I get there. Then I'll just fly back."

"Okay," Elle said.

"Will you still be here?"

"Oh, you can count on it," Elle said.

"I still don't understand why you don't head to our place in France," Greedy said. "Or California."

"The weather here agrees with me," Elle said through a cold stare. "Is that all you wanted?"

"That's it."

"I'll be in the kitchen for the next hour," she said, exiting. "So, make yourself scarce.'

Greedy shook his head at the door then focused on Dupree.

"Well, that was pleasant. Nice of her to stop by."

"Yes, sir," Dupree said.

"Do me a favor while I'm gone," Greedy said.

"Sure. What do you need?"

"Just keep an eye on her. Let me know what she gets up to. And make sure nothing disappears from the house." Greedy noticed the frown on his face. "What's the matter?"

"It's really none of my business," Dupree said, shaking his head.

"No, something's on your mind. Go ahead."

"I can't help but think it would be easier for you to just give her this place. It sure ain't about the money. And who needs the hassle?"

"There's a principle involved here, Dupree," Greedy said, fixing a cold stare on him. "Behavior has consequences."

"Sure, I get that," Dupree said. "And again, it's none of my business. But it seems like things between the two of you have run their course."

"They have. But the battle isn't over."

"And what happens if it takes forever to end?"

"I'll just shoot all the survivors," Greedy said with a laugh.

"Sounds like a workable strategy," Dupree said, again glancing at the painting behind the desk. "I do like that Koons. You mind if I get a closer look?"

"Knock yourself out. That's what it's there for."

Dupree got up and approached the canvas. He leaned in close then took a few steps back to take the entire painting in.

"Are you an art lover, Dupree?" Greedy said.

"Not much. But I do find parts of it interesting," Dupree said, sitting back down.

"Like what?"

"The money, mainly. It seems strange that people are willing to part with so much of their hard-earned cash to get their hands on it. Especially some of the stuff I see," Dupree said.

"It's an acquired taste," Greedy said. "But you should give it a shot. I think you'd come to appreciate it. You seem to have an eye for it."

"Yeah, maybe when I've got a couple million laying around I don't know what to do with."

"You recognized that one as a Koons right away the other day," Greedy said.

"It's kind of hard not to, sir. His stuff is everywhere. You consider your collection an investment?"

"No, they're like my children," Greedy said, glancing over his shoulder to give the painting a loving stare. "I'd never sell them."

"Good to know," Dupree said, nodding.

"But speaking of economics," Greedy said, leaning forward. "There's no reason for the Dragon Lady to know anything about our current project. Do you understand what I'm saying?"

"Yes, sir."

"There's no reason why she should get her hands on half of that money."

"No, sir. And she wouldn't be able to carry it around anyway, right?"

"Exactly," Greedy said, slapping the desk with both hands. "That will be all for now. Keep me posted."

"Yes, sir," Dupree said, heading for the door.

"Oh, Dupree."

"Yes, sir?"

"If you don't screw this up, I'll make it worth your effort."

"I'd appreciate that, sir," Dupree said as he left the office.

Outside, Harry was waiting by the car, and Dupree hopped in and started the engine.

"How did it go?" Harry said.

"I thought the man would never shut up," Dupree said, turning right at the bottom of the driveway. "Fortunately, the missus showed up and got him off the stories about himself."

"He didn't mention when he was setting sail, did he?"

"He did," Dupree said, glancing over at Harry. "Monday."

"That means we can head out Tuesday, Wednesday at the latest."

"Yeah," Dupree said, glancing out at the passing scenery. "I'm gonna miss the place."

"You want me to book the flight?"

"Let's wait," Dupree said. "I thought we'd take the ferry over to St. Thomas and spend a few days there."

"Okay," Harry said, settling back into his seat. "I've been thinking."

"Don't overdo it," Dupree said with a chuckle. "It always seems to get you in trouble."

"Yeah," Harry said, laughing along.

"So, what's on your mind?"

"I think I should move to Nashville," Harry said. "You know, if I'm gonna get serious about songwriting."

"Sure, I get that," Dupree said. "That's where all the deals get done, right?"

"Yeah," Harry said. "But I'm worried about loose ends. What are we going to do about the kid?"

"I'm still thinking about that," Dupree said. "The way he's going, he ain't gonna last long. I suppose we could just let nature run its course."

"But if it doesn't, and the kid starts talking, he's gonna be a problem."

"Yeah," Dupree said, nodding as he stared out at the road. "I was hoping Greedy might mention something about getting rid of him, but he didn't say a word."

"Do you think TeeMac even knows who he's working for?" Harry said.

"The thought probably hasn't even crossed his mind," Dupree said, heading straight through the green light at the bottom of the bypass. "But he knows us."

"And that's the problem," Harry said. "Why do you think Greedy isn't worried about the kid?"

"Because he's got the one thing you need during times like this," Dupree said, slowing down to maneuver the car through a rough patch of road.

"What's that?"

"Plausible deniability."

CHAPTER 23

Harry stood on the dock next to the St. Thomas ferry that was buttoned up for the night and studied the lights heading his way. As the boat neared the dock, Harry got a good look at TeeMac who was behind the wheel and appeared to have the craft under control. Whether or not that control extended to the driver was still up for debate. Harry used his foot to stop the boat from bumping the dock then hopped onboard.

"Good evening, TeeMac," Harry said, sitting down on the bench seat that ringed the front half of the boat.

"Good evening. What's your name again?"

"George," Harry said.

"That's right. George," TeeMac said through a sleepy stare.

"You been behaving yourself today, TeeMac?"

"What? Oh, yeah. I'm good. But I'm gonna need a top-up at some point."

"How about we hold off on that until we take care of business?" Harry said, pointing out at the water.

TeeMac nodded in agreement then opened the throttle. Harry was thrown back onto the seat and spent the next few moments struggling to regain his balance. The boat sped over the calm water through the darkness while Harry did his best to keep breathing and not obsess over the multitude of possible calamities lurking dead ahead.

**

Dupree turned the music up then glanced through the rearview mirror. Seeing no sign he was being followed, he lowered the window and let the night air fill the van. He barely heard his phone buzz above the music.

"This is Dupree."

"Hey, Dupree. It's Doc."

"Doc?" Dupree said, frowning as he turned the music down. "How's the party?"

"It's still raging," Doc said.

"We must have a different definition," Dupree said, laughing. "I don't hear a peep."

"I came inside to make the call. But everyone seems to be having a good time."

"Sorry I couldn't make it."

"No problem. Duty calls, right?"

"What? Oh, yeah. Duty does indeed. What can I do for you?"

"I thought we should get together for a drink," Doc said.

"A drink?" Dupree said, taking a quick look through the rearview mirror.

"Yeah, you know. A beverage of the alcoholic variety."

"Got it," Dupree said, laughing again before turning serious. "Does this have anything to do with that kid's murder?"

"Maybe. But only indirectly as far as you're concerned."

"Doc, I told you, man. I had nothing to do with that," Dupree said, slowing down and listening hard.

"And like I told you, I know that," Doc said.

"Why do I get the feeling you're messing with me, Doc?"

"Can't help you with that, Dupree. Maybe it's a guilty conscience. And I've heard that smoking too much weed can make you paranoid."

"Nah, I ain't smoking tonight."

"Probably a good idea," Doc said. "Do you want to drink some free booze or not?"

Dupree slowed down to thirty as he gave the question some thought.

"I suppose it couldn't hurt," he said eventually.

"Glad to hear it," Doc said. "Nauti Bar tomorrow. Around two?"

"Yeah, I can make it. See you then, Doc."

Dupree slid his phone back into his pocket, replayed the conversation in his head then shook it off as probably nothing. He hit the gas pedal hard and turned the music back up.

**

"What's up, Doc?" Felicia said with a laugh into her phone.

"Not you too. Where are you?"

"I'm drifting off the north shore. I'm all set. It's a beautiful night out here."

"I'll take your word for it."

"You don't like being out on the water?"

"Never been much of a fan," Doc said. "Especially at night."

"And yet, you live on an island. You are so strange," Felicia said.

"Guilty. Dupree's on his way. He just drove by where I'm parked."

"What direction is he headed?"

"North shore," I said. "Just like you predicted."

"It made the most sense," she said. "Did you talk to him?"

"I did. We're meeting for drinks tomorrow. Have you tried the night vision goggles yet?"

"I have. They're amazing," Felicia said.

"Okay. Just keep your eyes open and your head down," he said, then ended the call.

Felicia raised the night vision glasses and scanned the surface of the water.

"It's so good to be back," she whispered to herself.

**

Harry gripped the side of the boat as it continued to speed across the water. TeeMac maintained his dead-eyed stare with both hands on the wheel then slowly pulled the throttle back. The bow rose then the boat planed, and TeeMac turned the engine off. The boat gently bobbed in the water amid the darkness of a new moon.

"This is the spot?" Harry said, getting to his feet.

"Yeah," TeeMac said, lighting a cigarette.

"What are you doing?" Harry said when he picked up the familiar scent.

"What does it look like?"

"It looks like you're doing something stupid," Harry said, waving off TeeMac's offer of the joint.

"I gotta take the edge off," TeeMac said through a cloud of smoke.

"Just not too much, okay? We're working here." Harry looked out at the surface of the water and shook his head. "This is nuts. How is the guy going to find us?"

"He knows his way around," TeeMac said with a shrug.

"But he's Dominican," Harry said. "Does he spend a lot of time over here?"

"He lives here," TeeMac said. "But he ain't Dominican."

**

Dupree parked the van in a cul-de-sac and turned the engine off. He hopped out, removed his sandals and felt soft sand envelop his ankles. He strolled toward the water, about thirty feet from the van, and glanced up and down the beach. With not much to see through the darkness, he sat down on a large piece of driftwood and made a call.

"Hey," Dupree said. "Where are you?"

"According to TeeMac, we're here," Harry said.

"Good. How's the kid holding up?"

"So far, so good. He just smoked a joint."

"What?" Dupree said way too loud. He glanced around then whispered into the phone. "Have you lost your mind,

Harry? What the hell are you doing letting the kid smoke weed?"

"Hey, I'm not his mother," Harry snapped. "Relax, Dupree. Strange as it sounds, I think it helped. Took the edge off, you know."

"Just keep him under control," Dupree said, digging his toes deep into the sand. "And call me as soon as you're done."

Dupree hung up without waiting for a response.

**

I parked between two large palms, grabbed my backpack then hopped out and began the quarter-mile jog to where Dupree's van was located. A couple hundred yards into my trek, I fought off the stitch in my side and silently vowed to start getting to the gym. A few minutes later, I spotted the van and came to a stop. I grabbed my night vision glasses from my backpack and surveyed the area while trying to catch my breath.

**

TeeMac pointed at the approaching light then switched on the white light attached to the stern. Harry felt a surge of adrenaline as he watched the boat get closer.

**

Felicia grabbed her phone and placed the call with one hand while keeping the binoculars fixed on the approaching craft.

"Here we go," she said, then hung up.

**

The boat slowed and turned off its lights. TeeMac nodded to the man behind the wheel as he tied the boats together. Both were soon gently bobbing in tandem.

"Good evening, TeeMac," the man said with a small nod then fixed a cold stare on Harry.

"Good evening, Walt," TeeMac said.

"Who's this?" Walt said.

"That's George," TeeMac said.

"How you doing?" Harry said.

Walt nodded at him then focused on TeeMac.

"Let's get this done."

**

Felicia lowered the glasses, stunned by what she was seeing. She placed the call and whispered when he answered.

"Hey."

"Hey," Doc said. "What's going on?"

"The other boat just got here. And you'll never guess who it is."

"Let's say you're right about that and move on," Doc said. "Who is it?"

"You remember the night Willy was killed?" Felicia said.

"Not an easy one to forget, Felicia."

"The first two cops that showed up. And I pointed out that one of them was a despicable human being?"

"Yeah, I remember. Him?" Doc said, obviously surprised by the news.

"Walt Samuelson," Felicia said. "I can't believe it. Well, I can, but…well, you know. Son of a gun."

"He drove over here from the DR?" Doc said. "I wonder if he's supposed to be on vacation."

"Easy enough to check," she said. "Okay, they're starting to load."

She ended the call and resumed her surveillance.

**

"Just start stacking them in the stern," TeeMac said, handing one of the boxes to Harry.

Harry, surprised by how light the box was, did as instructed and they soon had an efficient process working.

"Leave a space down the middle and don't go over four boxes in a stack," TeeMac said.

Ten minutes later, Harry glanced around, wiped his hands on his shorts then headed for the bow where TeeMac was on the verge of a heated conversation with the guy in the other boat.

"What's the matter?" Harry said.

"Stay out of this, George," the man named Walt said without taking his eyes off TeeMac.

"C'mon, let's get out of here," Harry said, tugging TeeMac's elbow. "Whatever you guys are arguing about, you can do it on shore."

TeeMac jerked his arm away and gave Walt a defiant stare.

"Hand it over," TeeMac said.

"I just told you, TeeMac," Walt said. "I'm keeping a case for my trouble."

"Hey, that's not gonna happen," Harry snapped, then flinched when he caught a glimpse of the gun in the guy's hand. "Easy. Hang on. I'm sure we can figure something out."

"It's already figured out, George," Walt said, still focused on TeeMac. "My man here thought he was going to get away with something. Didn't you, TeeMac?"

TeeMac shrugged and stuffed both hands into the front pouch of his hoodie.

"What's going on?" Harry said, glancing back and forth at both men.

"Much to my surprise, TeeMac decided to keep a case for himself from the last shipment," Walt said. "But he also decided not to tell his business partner about it. Isn't that right, TeeMac?"

TeeMac remained silent but did manage a small shrug.

"Now, he tells me the Fentanyl is gone along with all the cash he made selling it," Walt said. "Which I know is a lie. So, instead of beating it out of him, I'll just keep this last case for myself, and we'll call it even."

"I can't let you do that, man," Harry said.

"They'll never miss one box," Walt said.

"I wouldn't be too sure about that," Harry said. "Did you hear what happened to the last kid who tried it."

"Hear about it?" Walt said, laughing. "Man, I was there when it happened."

"Sure, I get it," Harry said, nodding. "You were at Jump Up watching the Moku Jumbies."

"He's a cop," TeeMac whispered.

Harry cocked his head, stunned by the news. He stared at Walt who continued to point the gun at TeeMac.

"Perfect," Harry said. "Man, I really need to start doing something else with my life."

"You're too late, George," Walt said to Harry then stared at TeeMac. "Rule number one, don't screw your business partner."

"They'll kill me," TeeMac said, rocking on his heels as the boat bopped in the water.

"No need to worry about that, TeeMac," Walt said, laughing as he raised his pistol. "They're not gonna get the chance."

TeeMac pulled a handgun from the front pouch of his hoodie and fired once. Harry hit the deck as a second shot rang out almost simultaneously.

**

Doc frantically pulled his phone from his pocket and made the call. A wave of relief washed over him when Felicia answered on the first ring.

"Are you okay?" he said.

"I'm fine."

"What the heck was that?" Doc said.

"TeeMac and Walt just shot each other," she said.

"Dead?"

"Too soon to tell," Felicia said. "But from five feet, my guess would be yes."

**

Harry got to his knees and surveyed the mayhem in front of him. TeeMac was on his back, his hoodie rapidly turning several shades darker. Walt was bent over facedown, the upper half of his body draped over the side of TeeMac's boat. He checked both men for signs of a pulse then looked out at the water with a bewildered stare. He heard his phone buzz and held it up to his ear, his hands shaking so badly he almost dropped it in the water.

"Hey," Harry said.

"Who's the idiot firing a gun?" Dupree said.

"They just shot each other," Harry whispered, glancing back and forth at both bodies.

"What the hell did they do that for?"

"The cop was trying to keep a case of pills for himself," Harry said.

"Cop?"

"Yeah, it caught me by surprise, too."

"Damn," Dupree whispered.

"What do you want to do?" Harry said.

"Well, for starters, I want to get the pills loaded in the van and get the hell out of here."

"What about these two?" Harry said.

"Let me think for a sec," Dupree said.

Harry focused on trying to get his breathing back to normal as he waited out the silence.

"You got all the boxes loaded?" Dupree said.

"Apart from the one the cop was going to keep," Harry said.

"Well, get that one loaded, then put TeeMac on the other boat."

"You want me to carry a dead body?" Harry said.

"You got a better idea?"

"Every idea I have is better than that one."

"Suck it up, man," Dupree snapped. "Just toss him on the other boat, then head for shore. I'll shine the flashlight from the beach."

"What are we going to do with the boat?" Harry said.

"One thing at a time. Okay, Harry?" Dupree said, then hung up.

**

Felicia placed the call as she continued surveying the scene playing out about a hundred yards away.

"Hey," Doc said. "What's going on?"

"It looks like Harry is putting TeeMac's body on the other boat," she said.

"Yeah, that makes sense. Take care of the Fentanyl first, then figure out what's next."

"They'll probably just let the powercat drift and wait for somebody to find it," Felicia said.

"Too bad that's not gonna happen," Doc said.

"You want me to tow it back, don't you?" Felicia said.

"Yeah," he said. "And we'll need to call the police chief."

"What are we going to tell him?"

"Good question," Doc said, then fell silent. Eventually, he continued. "You want to call him?"

"No."

"Okay, I'll take care of it," Doc said. "How long will it take you to get back to Christiansted?"

"Probably about an hour," Felicia said.

"I'll have him meet us at the dock next to the ferry."

"What are you going to be doing?"

"I'm gonna follow Dupree and see where he puts the stuff," he said. "I'm betting he'll end up at Greedy's place, but I want to be sure. Oh, do you have a tarp or a blanket on your boat?"

"Way ahead of you, Doc," she said, managing a small laugh. "The last thing I want is two dead guys staring up at me."

"Okay, stay safe."

**

Dupree slammed the back door of the van and glanced around the immediate area. He spotted Harry smoking a cigarette standing a few feet away.

"How are you holding up?"

"Not bad for a guy who just saw his life flash in front of his eyes, I guess," Harry said, crushing the cigarette out with his foot.

"Pick that up," Dupree said, nodding at the cigarette butt.

"Now, you're an environmentalist?"

"It's called potential evidence. Pick it up."

Dupree put his hands on his hips as he stared out at the water. Then he nodded and turned to Harry.

"Okay, we'll just let the other boat drift," he said. "Let other people worry about what a crooked cop and a local gang thug were doing out on the water at night."

"Makes sense," Harry said, giving himself the once-over. "Man, I'm soaked."

"Well, you ain't done getting wet," Dupree said, pointing. "Drive TeeMac's boat about a mile down. There's more beach access down there. When you get a couple hundred feet from shore, point the boat out to deep water and put it in gear at slow speed."

"And?" Harry said.

"And then jump in and swim to shore," Dupree said. "I'll flash my headlights."

"This sucks."

"Don't pout, Harry," Dupree said, laughing. "We're in the home stretch."

"This is my last job, Dupree. What are we gonna tell Greedy?"

"When in doubt, go with the truth," Dupree said, climbing in behind the wheel. "Or a well-crafted facsimile."

CHAPTER 24

I was already waiting when I spotted Felicia's boat slowly making its way toward me. She expertly guided her boat next to the dock along with the powercat she was towing. She shut the engine down and tossed me a line. I tied her boat off then removed the tow line and used it to secure the catamaran.

"Nice boat," I said, glancing around before spotting the tarp on the deck. "Did you take a look at them?"

"Just a quick one," she said, extending an arm. I helped her up onto the dock, and she tugged her baseball hat further down over her forehead. "TeeMac took one in the chest. Walt got shot in the throat."

"You okay?"

"I'm fine," she said. "It's just been a while since I've dealt with something like this. There's so much blood."

"Yeah. You want to stick around and talk to the chief or take off?"

"No, I need to stay," she said, then nodded at the man strolling along the dock.

I couldn't miss her flinch and stiffen at the sight of the police chief but said nothing.

"Good evening, Chief," I said, extending my hand.

"Good morning is probably more appropriate," he said, returning the handshake. "Good evening, Felicia."

"Good evening, Chief," she said softly through an intense stare.

"How have you been?" he said, rocking back and forth on his heels.

"I'm good," she said.

"I'm glad to hear it," he said, then focused on me. "You said you had something to show me."

I climbed onto the catamaran and tiptoed my way to the tarp being careful not to step in blood. I pulled it halfway back and looked up at the chief. He stared down then shook his head and motioned he'd seen enough. I put the tarp back and climbed onto the dock.

"TeeMac and Walt," the chief said, shaking his head. "That's quite a pair. Walt was supposed to be on vacation in Florida. I guess he changed his mind."

"Maybe he liked the beaches better in the DR," I said.

"DR?" the chief said, frowning. "Maybe you better catch me up, Doc."

I spent the next few minutes outlining most of what we knew. When I finished, he whistled softly and stared out at the harbor.

"What a mess," he said. "How much Fentanyl did they bring over?"

"It looked like a hundred cases," I said.

"That's enough to kill everyone living on this island," he said.

"It's enough to kill everyone in the Caribbean," I said.

"None of it was supposed to land here," Felicia said. "Willy was freelancing. But he got caught with his hands in the cookie jar."

"By who?" the chief said.

"Brewster Greedy," I said.

"Greedy? Huh," the chief said, deep in thought. "I've never liked him."

"Join the club," I said.

"Where's the Fentanyl at the moment?" the chief said.

"At his house," I said.

"Then I suppose I should head over there and arrest him," the chief said, then noticed my reaction. "What's the matter?"

"It's not my call, Chief, but I'd wait."

"For what?"

"Until he arrives in Miami," I said. "Why get only one side of the players when you can get both?"

He gave it some thought then frowned.

"I have no jurisdiction over there," he said.

"No, but the FBI does," I said. "I'm sure they'd be very appreciative of the tip. And…they'd owe you."

"You're suggesting I barter with them for some help with our gang problem," he said.

"Not just help, coordinated help," I said. "Working directly with you. Keeping you in the loop."

"Interesting," he said, again staring out at the water. "You sure Greedy is going to Miami?"

"Positive," Felicia said.

"Okay," he said eventually then reached for his phone. He made a short call. "One of my guys is on his way."

"Tony, right?" Felicia said.

"Yes. He's still my go-to guy when I need discretion," the chief said. "I could use more like him."

"You had your chance," Felicia snapped as she glared at him.

"Yes, I suppose I did," he said softly.

We shared a lengthy, awkward silence. Fortunately, a man wearing shorts and a tee shirt soon approached at a brisk pace. He came to a stop in front of us, and we exchanged greetings.

"How are you doing, Felicia?" he said with a warm smile.

"I'm good, Tony. How are Mary and the kids?"

"Just great. You should swing by the house. It's been too long."

"I'll do my best," she said. "Tell Mary I said hi."

"Will do," Tony said, then focused on the chief. "Okay, what do you need, Chief?"

"TeeMac and Walt Samuelson are under that tarp," the chief said, nodding at the catamaran.

"I take it they're not catching forty winks," Tony said.

"No, I'm afraid they're not," the chief said.

"Geez," he said, pursing his lips. "Well, not that it matters, but Walt lasted a lot longer than I thought he would."

"I'll fill you in on the details later," the chief said. "But for now, I need you to get the boat out of here."

"Nice boat," Tony said, glancing around the craft. "Where do you want me to take it?"

"Park it at the dock at my house," the chief said. "Call Xavier and tell him to start doing his thing with the bodies. Then head up to the house and have a quiet word with my wife about keeping the kids away from the dock until I can get home."

"Got it," Tony said, nodding. "Anything else?"

"Just that if this leaks, it will be your last official act as a member of the force," the chief said.

"Okay, that's pretty clear," he said, giving us a small wave as he climbed down onto the boat and carefully made his way to the driver seat.

We untied the lines and watched as he drove off with another wave.

"Who were the two guys making the pickup?" the chief said.

Felicia and I glanced at each other then I shrugged.

"We didn't get a good look at them," I said.

"No, it was really dark," Felicia said. "New moon and all that."

"Okay," he said, obviously not believing a word we were saying. "But let me ask you this."

"Go ahead," I said.

"Why on earth were you out there in the first place?"

"That's a good question, Chief," I said with a grin.

"Thanks. Sometimes they just come to me," he said, maintaining his stare.

"We were following up on a lead about Willy's murder," I said.

"I see. And?"

"And we're not sure yet," I said. "Hopefully, it won't be long."

He continued to stare at me for a long time then eventually gave me a small nod.

"Okay. Somehow you two managed to take down my most crooked cop and a local gang leader in one night. I guess I shouldn't look a gift horse in the mouth. Is that how that saying goes?"

"That's it," I said, extending my hand. "We'll be in touch as soon as we know more, Chief."

"All right. We're done here," he said, shaking hands with me. "It was good seeing you, Felicia. Nice work. Both of you."

We watched him head down the dock then I studied Felicia's face as she stared after her ex-boss.

"He's okay," I said. "He just did a crappy job handling your situation."

"It doesn't matter," she said. "I'm happy now. That's what's important."

"Oh, you're happy," I said, laughing. "Good to know."

"Don't get cocky, Doc," she said, laughing along. "I'm gonna take the boat back then get some sleep."

"Good idea," I said, squeezing her hand. "I think I'll do the same. I need to be fresh for cocktail hour with Dupree."

"You need any help with him?"

"No, I think it should be handled one on one," I said.

"Okay. I wish we could be in Miami to see the look on Greedy's face when a couple dozen FBI agents swarm his boat.

"Oh, Greedy's never gonna make it to Miami."

CHAPTER 25

I was sitting by myself nursing a beer and enjoying the view of the harbor when I spotted Dupree pull into the parking lot. He got out, stretched, then saw me and confidently strolled in my direction with a fixed grin. I got up to share a fist bump then sat back down across from him at one of the picnic tables.

"Well, you don't look too hungover," Dupree said with a laugh then waved at the waitress who approached. "Good afternoon, Marissa."

"Good afternoon, Dupree. What can I get you?"

"What are you drinking there, Doc? Presidente. Sounds good."

"You ready for another, Doc?" she said.

"Yes, please," I said, draining the last of my beer and handing her the empty bottle.

Dupree watched her stroll off then pressed his sunglasses tight and focused on me.

"Okay, Doc. I'm here. How can I help you?"

"I'm thinking about using your catering services for my next party," I deadpanned.

Dupree flinched briefly then studied me with a big grin.

"Yeah, the crab puffs, right?" Then he shrugged. "Okay, you caught me. So, I'm not a caterer." He sat back and beamed at the waitress arriving with our drinks. She left and Dupree continued. "No harm in telling a little white lie from time to time."

"No, there's not," I said. "I do it all the time."

"There you go," Dupree said, then took a long swig and burped. "Perfect. Nice and cold. But for the record, I do make one hell of a crab cake."

"I guess you can't spend all that time in Maryland and not learn how to make them, huh?"

"Yeah, I did spend a lot of time there," Dupree said, taking a smaller sip. "So what? You already know that."

"You're a man of many talents, Dupree," I said, lighting a cigarette.

"Bad habit."

"Dreadful," I said, holding out the pack to him.

"Maybe just one," he said, grabbing a cigarette and leaning forward for me to light it. He took a puff, exhaled a cloud of smoke then resumed his stare. "What talents are you referring to, Doc?"

"I didn't know you were a painter."

He sat quietly, stared off then took another drag and a sip of beer.

"Yeah, I went to art school. Ancient history."

"You're good," I said, tapping ash.

"You seen some of my stuff?" he said, surprised.

"I'm sure I have," I said, grinning at him. "I just don't know which ones they were."

Dupree gave his two-day stubble a vigorous scratch.

"What are you looking for, Doc? A self-portrait? I'm a little rusty, but I'm sure I could knock something out that would look good on your wall."

"Thanks for the offer, but no. I have a hard enough time just looking in the mirror," I said. "I only want to clear a few things up before I go any further."

"Sure, I get that. Get your facts straight before heading too far down the wrong road. What's on your mind?"

"Art forgery," I said softly.

"Don't know him," Dupree said, laughing it off. "Let me guess. You've seen him *hanging* around."

I sat quietly waiting for his laughter to subside. Eventually, he realized I wasn't going to let the topic go.

"You got something specific to talk about Doc, or are you on a fishing trip?"

"I do have something on my mind," I said, nodding.

"Then lay it on me, man. I got nothing to hide."

"It's too bad about what happened to Esmeralda," I said with a shrug.

"What?" he said, even his sunglasses unable to hide the shock.

"That's odd, Dupree. I mention a name, and you say what. Most people would have said who."

"You're not making a lot of sense, Doc," he said, going for casual. "If I didn't know better, I'd swear you'd just burned one."

"Okay, Dupree. I just wanted to give you a chance, that's all."

"A chance to do what?"

"To save your own ass."

He sat back and folded his arms, staring off into the distance.

"Esmeralda's dead?"

"She is," I said, nodding.

"What happened to her?"

"She caught two in the back of the head."

"Damn," he whispered. "What a waste."

"So, you did know her."

"Barely."

"Dupree, we're going to get along a lot better if we stop lying to each other," I said, crushing out my cigarette.

"But how do I know you're telling me the truth?"

I laughed and leaned forward with my elbows on the table.

"You're a funny guy, Dupree. When was the last time you saw Esmeralda?"

"Don't be starting with that crap, Doc. We both know I haven't been off island in months."

"How would I know that?"

"I thought we were going to stop lying to each other," he said with a glare then drained his beer. "First, you start insinuating I had something to do with that stilt walker's death, now you're trying to pin what happened to Esmeralda on me. I'm a lot of things, Doc. But I ain't a killer."

"I know that, Dupree."

"Then what the hell are we talking about here?" he said, his temper flaring. He raised two fingers to the waitress before taking a few deep breaths.

I slid a large envelope across the table.

"They're a little grainy," I said. "But the lighting last night wasn't great."

Dupree stared at the envelope like it was going to bite him, but eventually opened it and removed a small stack of photographs. He flipped through them slowly, studied each one then slipped them back into the envelope and slid it across the table.

"Who the hell are you, Doc?" he said, studying me hard.

"Just a PI who's trying to figure a few things out."

"Yeah, and I'm Pablo Picasso," he said, then glanced up when the waitress arrived with fresh beers. He waited until she departed then resumed his cold stare. "You FBI?"

"No, you can relax, Dupree," I said. "As long as you're willing to play."

"Do I have a choice?"

"Of course," I said with a shrug. "People always have choices. But if I were in your shoes at the moment, I'd choose mindfulness."

"What the hell are you talking about?"

"I'm talking about the process of focusing your full attention on whatever is happening in the present."

"What is that? Some sort of pop psychology crap?" Dupree said.

"It's a Buddhist tenet."

"Buddhist, huh?" he said, giving it some serious thought. "I always liked those guys. It's like they've somehow managed to learn everything by thinking about nothing."

"I can see why you'd think that," I said. "But at the moment, we're talking about staying in the present."

"Mindfulness, huh?"

"Yeah. You're in one hell of a mess, Dupree."

"No shit," he whispered. "What do you need to know?"

"Talk to me about Brewster Greedy."

"Okay," he said, leaning forward.

"When's he leaving for Miami with the Fentanyl?"

"Monday."

"How many deliveries are on board?"

"At the moment?" Dupree said, managing a grin.

"Funny," I said, laughing. "Yeah, at the moment."

"Two. He'll be loading last night's shipment sometime today."

"Are you involved in that?"

"Nope," he said, shaking his head. "If I were, I wouldn't be sitting here with you drinking beer."

"Fair enough. How big a crew will be on board?"

"Six," Dupree said.

"A captain?"

"Sure."

"Bodyguards?"

"A couple."

"And the others?"

"Use your imagination," he said.

"Got it."

We both fell silent. I watched Dupree pick at the label on his beer bottle.

"Tell me about the forgery ring," I said after a lengthy silence.

"I don't know a lot about it," he said, then caught my expression. "I'm serious, man. I just follow orders."

"When did Greedy come up with the idea?" I said.

"What?" he said, confused. Then he shrugged. "I'm not sure. But I've been doing my thing for about a year."

"And that's why he brought you to St. Croix?"

"Sure. Let's go with that."

I thought about the cryptic nature of his comment before continuing.

"The forgery ring is brilliant," I said.

"Yeah, it is," he said, grinning and nodding in agreement. "I wish I'd thought of it. You interested in busting it up?"

"Only if I have to. I imagine it will morph into something else after Greedy goes down," I said, giving him a hard look to let him know I'd been thinking. "Unless it already has."

"Morphed? You lost me, Doc," he said. "But I gotta say, you're talking like you're a fan of white-collar crime."

"I do like clever scams with some style and wit to them," I said. "But what I don't like is people getting killed in the process."

"Esmeralda," he whispered.

"Exactly. And I'd really hate to see you be next."

He flinched again but remained silent as he took a series of small sips.

"How many fake paintings have you done since you got here?" I said, grabbing another cigarette and sliding the pack across the table.

"About a dozen," he said, staring down at the cigarettes before finally taking one.

"Harry gets you into the houses, right?"

"Yeah," Dupree whispered. "The man's a genius when it comes to security systems."

"And you wait until Greedy takes the owners out on his boat for the day and you guys go in," I said.

"You are so close, Doc," he said, laughing. "You have no idea how close you are."

"What are you talking about?" I said.

"Never mind," he said, shaking his head. "But trust me, you're gonna like it."

I frowned but decided to file further questions away for the time being.

"Did you tell the cops about last night?" Dupree said.

"It was kind of hard not to, Dupree. Two dead bodies are a little tough to explain."

"I didn't have anything to do with that," he said.

"I know," I said. "But we had to bring the police chief in. Especially since one of the victims worked for him."

"Really?" Dupree said. "I did not know that."

"I think I believe you."

"So, I can expect a visit from the boys in blue soon?"

"I don't see why."

"You didn't tell them about me and Harry?" he said, raising an eyebrow.

"Not yet," I said with a grin.

"I suppose I should thank you for keeping your mouth shut."

"You're welcome."

"Okay, Doc. Let's cut to the car chase," he said, exhaling a cloud of smoke. "What do you need from me?"

"The name of the guy who shot Willy."

"We gonna go over that ground again? How many times do I have to repeat myself? I don't have a clue about how that went down. Or who the shooter was."

"Then you're going to need to find out, aren't you?"

"C'mon, Doc. How the hell am I supposed to do that?"

"Tell Greedy you need some help dealing with a situation. Tell him somebody is making your life miserable. But make sure Greedy knows it doesn't have anything to do with the Fentanyl. No sense getting him excited. Ask him for the name of the guy he used on Willy."

"So, I'm just supposed to walk into the man's office and ask him for the guy's name?"

"Yeah. And his address and phone number would be good, too."

"And who exactly would I want to put a contract hit on?"

"Oh, that's an easy one," I said, draining the last of my beer.

"Who?"

"Me."

He stared at me in disbelief then took a long drag on his smoke.

"You are one strange dude," he said.

"Guilty," I said with a shrug before turning casual. "What are you going to do next?"

"You mean after you take Greedy down?"

"Yeah."

"I imagine I'll be leaving the island," Dupree said.

"And go where?"

"Probably another island. I like the idea of being surrounded on all sides by water."

"Then why would you leave?"

"Self-preservation, mainly," he said, shrugging.

"Nobody's going to be looking for you, Dupree," I said.

"They're not?"

"I don't know why they would. You're just a bartender, right? And a part-time painter."

"Don't forget the catering," he said with a grin. "But I'm done with bartending."

"Then do something else down here."

"Like what?"

"Like working for me."

I didn't see that one coming.

"Think about it," I whispered to the voice.

"I will," Dupree said.

"What?"

"I said I'd think about," Dupree said, frowning at me.
"You were talking to me, right, Doc?"

"Who else would I be talking to?"

CHAPTER 26

I felt a moist, warm breath on my neck, and I glanced into the back seat where Samson was simultaneously looking for attention while keeping a close eye on the sights we drove past. I reached back with one hand to pet his head, and the dog responded by trying to climb into the front seat and help me steer.

"Stay," I said firmly, and the dog immediately turned his attention to Felicia sitting in the passenger seat. I laughed when the dog managed to get half of his body in her lap. "He's not used to being in the car."

"He'll get used to it," she said, stroking the dog's head. "I've always been scared of pit bulls. But this guy is a total sweetheart."

"He is," I said, glancing over at her. "And obviously drawn to great beauty."

"Don't start," she said, laughing. "You're going to adopt him, right? You know, if anything happens to Sebastian."

"I am. And the question is when, not if," I said, staring out at the road.

"Yeah," she whispered. "It's so sad."

"He's had one hell of a run," I said, accelerating when we hit the four-lane highway that led to Frederiksted.

"I can't believe Sebastian agreed to a live-in," Felicia said. "Is she a nurse?"

"She's more of a nursing assistant, housekeeper combination," I said. "It made sense to have someone around full-time keeping a close eye on him. You know, since he's started drinking again."

"Thanks to you," she said.

"I couldn't say no to him," I said softly as I passed a car filled with rubberneckers. "I sense judgment."

"Maybe a little," she said. "But I suppose, if it makes him happy, what's the harm, right?"

"That's how I read it," I said.

"Where did he find her?" Felicia said, her arm draped over the dog who was being lulled to sleep by the car ride.

"I found her."

"Let me guess," she said, laughing again. "You're paying for her, right?"

"It's not much," I said. "And it's cheap peace of mind."

"For you or Sebastian?"

"Both of us, I guess," I said, studying the road. "Do I go right at the end of the highway?"

"Yeah," she said, gently rubbing the dog's head.

"I'm buying Sebastian's house."

"Really?" she said, surprised. "I thought you loved the place you're in."

"I do."

"Then what on earth would you want with his?"

"I thought I'd give it to you," I said, glancing over.

Her expression turned dark, and she shook her head.

"Absolutely not."

"Why not?"

"I'm not a charity case, Doc," she said, glaring at me.

"Who said you were?" I said, making solid eye contact. "Actually, it was Sebastian's idea."

"Why on earth would he say that?"

I fell silent, my eyes now fixed on the road in front of us.

Be straight with her.

I nodded then exhaled and focused on her.

"Because he said he couldn't miss the way I looked at you," I whispered.

"Now you're taking matchmaking advice from a ninety-year-old?" she said, softening.

"He also pointed out that you can't sleep on your grandmother's couch forever."

"I'm very aware of that, Doc," she said, the dog now on full alert from the sharp tenor of our conversation. "It's okay, Samson." She stroked the dog's back until he drifted off again. "Just take the road up the hill and make a left."

"Okay," I said, slowing down to twenty. "So, what do you think?"

"Are you out of your mind, Doc? You can't give me a house."

"Why not?"

"Because people just don't do things like that."

"There are thousands of divorce lawyers who'd disagree with you."

She laughed and shook her head.

"This is different. And you know it."

"Maybe," I said. "I suppose we could work out some sort of monthly payment plan."

She scowled but seemed to be giving the idea some serious thought.

"But there is another option," I said, grinning at her.

"What's that?" she said, cocking her head.

"You could just move in with me."

She laughed long and hard before leaning in close and giving me a kiss on the cheek that caught me completely off guard.

"Nice try," she said, settling back into her seat. "But just for the sake of discussion, how much a month are we talking about?"

**

Dupree knocked softly then poked his head inside the office. Greedy waved him in and pointed at the chair in front of the desk. Dupree settled in and glanced around as he waited for Greedy to finish his phone call. His eyes settled on the Koons and he stifled a smile. Greedy ended his call then set his phone on the desk and began rocking in his chair as he gave Dupree the once-over.

"What have you got for me, Dupree?"

"Well, as far as I can tell, the cops don't have a clue about why those two shot each other," Dupree said.

"As far as you can tell?" Greedy said, fixing a hard stare on him.

"The word on the street is the police chalked it up to getting lucky. You know, a corrupt cop and a gang kid taking each other out. And since there wasn't any evidence on either boat, they've already closed both cases."

"Good," Greedy said, nodding. "That saves me a ton of work. Nice job, Dupree."

"Thank you, sir. You all set to get out of here?"

"I am," he said with a grin. "That phone call was from my most recent addition to the crew. She's packing today and wanted to know what she'll be wearing on the trip."

"Wardrobe. Sure, I get it," Dupree said, then grinned. "Did you tell her, not much?"

Greedy laughed and rocked a bit faster.

"Yes, clothes are going to be the least of her concerns," Greedy said. "Don't forget what I asked you to do while I'm gone."

"No, sir, I won't. Keep a close eye on your missus and report back."

"Good," he said, coming to a stop and grabbing a map sitting on the desk. "If there's nothing else, I need to finish mapping out our route. I like to change it up and visit some new islands."

"Smart," Dupree said, nodding. "Where are you going this trip?"

"Turks and Caicos," Greedy said, without looking up from the map. "I've sailed past several times, but never actually stopped. So, I thought we'd spend a couple of days exploring."

"Nice," Dupree said, nodding. "Sounds like a fun trip."

"You're still here, Dupree," Greedy said, glancing up. "Is there something else?"

"Actually, there is one thing I could use some help with," Dupree said.

"Okay," he said, sitting back in his chair and resuming his rocking. "What is it?"

"I need the name of a shooter."

"What?"

"Yeah," Dupree whispered.

"What on earth do you need with a shooter?"

"There's a guy who's making my life difficult," Dupree said.

"Difficult?" Greedy said, his voice rising as he leaned forward and placed both elbows on the desk. "Does this have anything to do with me?"

"Oh, no, sir," Dupree said, shaking his head. "It's nothing like that. This deals with something I was involved with years ago on the mainland. I figured the statute of limitations had run out, but this guy doesn't seem to be able to let it go."

"You been a bad boy, Dupree?" he said with a grin.

"It wasn't one of my finer moments, sir. And I'd really like to finally put it all behind me. If you know what I mean."

"I do," Greedy said, nodding. "Loose ends, right?"

"Exactly. I knew you'd understand, sir."

262

"Who's the guy?"

"The guy who supposedly set up shop down here as a PI," Dupree said. "Doc White."

"You're kidding," Greedy said, unable to control his smile.

"I wish I was. He's like a dog on a bone. According to my guys in D.C., that's why he's down here."

"Huh," Greedy grunted. "And here I thought he was down here to see if he could get the Dragon Lady back."

"No, he's here for me," Dupree said. "And he's definitely got me in his sights."

"That can't be fun," Greedy said, his hands steepled under his chin. "I always like a man bearing gifts, Dupree."

"What's that, sir?"

"You. Bearing gifts," Greedy said, then reached for his phone and began scrolling through it. "You're going to need the best."

"The guy who took out the stilt-walker?" Dupree said, leaning forward.

"Yes. Among others," Greedy said, scribbling a note and sliding it across the desk. "If he asks, feel free to tell him I recommended you get in touch with him. But apart from that, keep my name out of it."

"Will do," Dupree said, glancing at the phone number before folding the note and sliding it into his pocket. "Thank you, sir. I appreciate it."

"Don't mention it," Greedy said, refocusing on the map and dismissing Dupree with a wave of the back of his hand.

"Have a good trip, sir," Dupree said, heading for the door.

"Oh, you can count on it."

Dupree exited the office and waited until he reached his car before making the call.

**

I looked up and down the desolate stretch of sand then kept a close eye on Samson as he began exploring.

"It's so beautiful," I said, then pointed off into the distance. "What's that beach way over there?"

"Sandy Point," Felicia said. "It's where the last scene from The Shawshank Redemption was shot."

"Really? I thought that was in Mexico."

"Most people do," she said, her hair blowing in the stiff breeze. "But it was filmed down here."

"I'd like to see it," I said.

"We can't do that," she said, nodding for me to follow her as she walked to the water's edge. "It's closed at the moment."

"Why's that?" I said, surprised by the news.

"It's a major turtle nesting area. And during hatch season, it's closed to the public. And the rest of the year it's only open on weekends."

My phone buzzed and I checked the number before answering. Felicia frowned at me.

"It's supposed to be a day off, Doc," she said.

"Sorry. But I need to take this one. I'll keep it short. Hey, Dupree…Great. Good job." I listened carefully but couldn't miss Felicia keeping a close eye on my conversation. "That's perfect…No, just the phone number is good enough. Just text it to me…Thanks…What are we doing? Felicia's giving me a tour of the island…Yeah, I'll give it my best shot. Talk to you later."

I ended the call and stood at the edge of the water with the phone in my hand.

"Did he get it?" Felicia said.

"He did. It's a Miami area code."

"And he's the guy who killed Willy?" she said.

"He is," I said, making a call.

"Who are you calling?"

"Merlin," I said, holding the phone to my ear and turning around to block the wind the best I could. "Hey…Yeah, everything's good…I need your help…Do you remember the guy we used to use for diversion before we brought Gene onboard? Yeah, that's him. I can never remember his name…I'm about ready to move on Greedy. But he's going to be on his boat with a crew…Yeah, that's what we need…Yes, Merlin, I know it would be easier to just take them all out. But we're not going to do that…Greedy plans to stop in Turks and Caicos for at least a day. Let's do it there…Nice. That's perfect…Who knew that would come in handy? And I need you to run down what a guy named Nikolai Kilovich has been up to…Yeah, financials. Travel history. The usual. I'll text you his number…Great. Let me know."

I ended the call, my mind racing.

"Who's Gene?" Felicia said.

"He's the guy who died in my arms," I said softly.

"I'm sorry," she said softly.

"Don't worry about it," I said, whistling at Samson who stopped then began racing back down the beach toward us.

"And Nikolai Kilovich?" she said.

"He's our shooter," I said, bending down to greet the dog. "Good boy. What a good boy."

"Dupree delivered," she said, sitting down on the sand to play with Samson.

"He didn't have much choice," I said, sitting down next to her. "It's such a beautiful spot."

"It is," she said, staring out at the water. "You really want this guy working with us?"

"Yeah. Dupree has the potential to be a star," I said. "And do a lot of the crap we don't want to."

"I'll take your word for it," she said. "He is funny. I have to give him that."

"Yeah. And smart. That's a good combo," I said. "Where's our next stop?"

"I thought we'd have our picnic in the rainforest," she said, pushing herself up out of the sand and brushing her shorts.

"Works for me," I said, also getting to my feet. "Lead the way."

"That I can do," she said, grinning as she squeezed my hand. "Are you sure this is the way you want to spend the day?"

"Are you kidding?" I said, following her back to the car. "This is perfect. But I wouldn't mind boozing it up a bit and getting buzzed at some point."

"I can do that, too."

CHAPTER 27

I sat up to refill both glasses then settled back into the lounge chair. The wind was up, and a tiny sliver of moon seemed to be playing hide and seek as the clouds came and went. I stifled a yawn before taking a sip of wine then closed my eyes and listened to the night air.

"Thanks for a wonderful day," Felicia said, breaking a long silence.

"No, thank you," I said, my eyes still closed. "You're a great tour guide."

"What was your favorite part?"

"Is that a trick question?" I said, opening my eyes and glancing over at her.

She laughed then sat up and tied her hair into a single braid. She sipped her wine then shook her head.

"I've had too much to drink."

"You're not driving," I said, then took another sip.

"You sure you want to handle Greedy that way?" she said, sitting up and folding her legs underneath her on the lounger.

"I am," I said softly as I sat up. "Does it bother you?"

"Actually, it does."

"Greedy's a monster."

"Oh, it's not Greedy who's the issue. Well, he is…but that's not what I'm talking about."

I sat back, fully prepared for what I knew was coming.

"It's the taking the law into our own hands that bothers me," she whispered. She picked up her glass, swirled wine then tossed back a mouthful.

"Force of habit," I said. "Or, you might say, a learned behavior."

"I'm serious, Doc," she said, fixing a stare on me.

"So am I," I said with a shrug. "Trust me, it's the best way to deal with creatures like him."

"I still don't like it."

"Nobody likes it," I said, lighting a cigarette. "And if you did, I'd be worried about you."

"There has to be some kind of moral code," she said, topping off both our glasses. "If there isn't, we're all pretty much screwed."

"It's hard to apply a moral standard to people that don't have one," I said, exhaling a cloud of smoke.

"Isn't that what the justice system is for?" Felicia said.

"One would think," I said. "But you know how this would play out if Greedy simply got arrested. He'd have an army of lawyers spinning lies and tying things up for years."

"He's sitting on a boatload of Fentanyl," she said, protesting. "It's kinda hard to spin that."

"Greedy would blame somebody on his crew," I said. "Maybe the captain. Or Dupree. Maybe even Elle. You name it. Trust me, he and his lawyers would come up with something plausible. People like Greedy have enormous clout when it comes to getting out of trouble."

"Is this the part of the story where you start talking about the privilege of color?" she said.

"Yeah, him being white certainly wouldn't hurt," I said. "But in cases like this, the only color that really matters is green."

She gazed out over the gallery, deep in thought. Eventually, she spoke without looking at me.

"Do you remember the night Willy was killed?" she whispered.

"Of course. I'll never forget it."

"When we were leaving the restaurant, I made a crack about how strange you were," she said, strands of her ponytail fluttering in the breeze. "And you said the word I was looking for was damaged."

"I did," I said, nodding. "What about it?"

"You weren't joking, were you?" she said, finally making eye contact.

"I'm surprised you even have to ask," I said, laughing as I crushed my cigarette out.

"And that's what all those years in espionage did to you?"

"You know, I go back and forth on that question," I said, scratching the back of my head. "And I wonder if the people who recruited me knew something I didn't at the time. You know, like they had figured out what made me tick long before I did."

"I imagine they're good at that sort of thing," Felicia said.

"You have no idea," I said. "But I can definitely tell you doing that sort of work didn't help."

"Okay," she said, nodding.

I could tell she was heading somewhere with the conversation but tiptoeing her way through it as if treading on thin ice. I waited for her to continue at her own pace.

"I'm surprised you're so open about it," she said, facing me. "About what you used to do."

I leaned back and sipped wine.

Keep going.

272

"My inability to talk about it in the past with people I cared for cost me dearly," I said softly.

She gave my comment some thought then placed her elbows on her knees and leaned forward.

"You're talking about Elle, aren't you?"

"Among others," I said with a shrug. "But she's probably the best example."

"And the reason you came here," Felicia said, exhaling.

"Yeah," I said, nodding. "But she's not the reason I'm thinking about staying."

"Good answer, Doc," she said, laughing.

The tension on the gallery subsided, and I felt myself relax.

"When we split, there were so many unanswered, even unspoken, questions," I said. "And so much bad blood had built up."

"And you thought you could repair the damage?"

"I have to admit that, at first, I had some goofy romantic notions," I said. "But that quickly disappeared. Then it became a matter of answering some questions for myself."

"Closure," she said, nodding. "You're talking about closure."

"That's a big part of it," I said. "But there was also an element of trying to figure out if we could rebuild the friendship."

"I get it," she said. "I've tried to do that myself a few times." She drained the last of her wine. "Without much success."

"It's hard," I said, holding out my glass as she reached for the bottle.

"What were your first thoughts when you saw her?"

"Contempt, primarily," I said, then attempted to clarify my point. "Not for what she was, but for what she's become."

"What exactly is that?"

"A sellout," I said.

"That's harsh, Doc," she said, frowning.

"I know," I said, taking a sip. "It's what I do."

"Thanks for the warning," she said with a grin. "Don't beat yourself up too much, Doc. Life's too short."

We both settled back down on our loungers and stared out at the evening sky.

"You never told Elle you were a spy?" Felicia said after a long silence.

"I did…eventually," I said. "But it was too late by the time I was capable of doing it."

"She wondered what else you were keeping from her, right?"

"You're a smart woman," I said, glancing over at her.

"Thanks," she said, taking a sip before again focusing on me. "Is there?"

"Is there anything else I'm keeping from you?" I said, returning her stare.

"Yeah," she whispered.

I took a few deep breaths then exhaled loudly.

Be straight with her.

"There is one thing," I said.

"Is it good?" she said, raising an eyebrow.

"No. It sucks."

Hey. Don't start.

She turned toward me and tucked her legs underneath her. She sat quietly, waiting for me to continue.

"It's okay if you don't want to tell me," she said, apparently thinking the conversation was over.

"No, I need to do this," I said, staring down at my hands that were starting to shake. I clasped them tight then nodded to myself. "I hear voices."

Felicia flinched like I'd slapped her. I remained silent until she recovered.

"What?" she whispered.

"Actually, it's only one voice," I said, shrugging.

"I think I need to hear more, Doc," she said, putting her wine glass down.

"Yeah, I'm sure you do. I've got it pretty much under control these days. But it comes back during times of stress." I reached for my cigarettes. "Over the years, we've figured out a way to co-exist."

Co-dependent is probably a better term.

"Yeah," I said, nodding.

"What?"

"Oh, sorry. I was just responding to the voice."

"It's here? Now?" she said, for some reason looking around the gallery.

"You can't actually see him," I said, laughing.

"Just checking," she said, shaking her head. "So, it's a guy's voice?"

"It is."

"Do you know whose voice it is?" she said, still stunned by my revelation.

"I do," I said, fixing a stare on her. "It's my brother's voice."

"Your brother?" she said, cocking her head.

"My twin brother," I whispered. "My *dead* twin brother."

"Oh, my God," Felicia said. "What happened to him?"

"He got shot," I whispered again. "It was a case of mistaken identity."

Felicia flinched again and stared at me in disbelief.

"Somebody was trying to kill you, and they shot your brother by mistake?"

"Yeah, that's a good summary," I said, nodding.

"Where did it happen?"

"China."

"What were you doing in China?" she said, gently probing.

"Sowing and exploiting seeds of discontent. I can't go into the specifics. But I'm sure you can use your imagination. Anyway, he flew over to visit me. And the Chinese authorities gunned him down on the streets of Shanghai."

Don't go there. It wasn't your fault.

I ignored the voice and gulped wine.

"What happened next?"

"As soon as I saw him bleeding out on the street and figured out what had happened, I got out of China," I said.

"You and the people you worked for let the Chinese think they'd gotten the right guy?" she said.

"Yeah."

"That's sick," she said, obviously disgusted by the idea.

"You'll get no argument from me," I said, topping off our glasses.

"I thought I'd had enough," she said, reaching for her wine. "But after that little nugget, I'm gonna keep drinking."

"Good plan," I said, chuckling. "Anyway, the subterfuge worked well. And it came in handy."

"And that's when the voice started?" Felicia said.

"Yeah, he made his presence known occasionally," I said. "It freaked me out at first."

"I can imagine," she said, shaking her head. "And you just kept working?"

"I was on the sidelines for a while," I said. "Eventually, they put me back out there."

"You must have gone to counseling, right?"

"Oh, I was couched by several different people," I said, taking a sip.

"Couched?"

"You know, grilled by a whole bunch of shrinks."

"And they decided you could keep working?" she said, frowning.

"Actually, I finally managed to convince them I was okay," I said.

"Why on earth would you do that?"

"What else was I going to do?" I said softly.

"Geez, I don't know, Doc," she said, staring in disbelief at me. "Find a girlfriend, travel, walk in the woods, sit in a tree and learn how to play the flute."

I laughed but she maintained her deep frown.

"And the voice kept getting worse?" Felicia said.

"Not until later," I said.

"Something else happened?"

"Yeah. And it was right up there with what happened to my brother."

"Can you talk about it?"

"Some of it," I said, again staring out at the harbor. "I was in Mongolia looking for a way to get our hands on some of their natural resources."

"Why?"

"Because they have a lot of them and we wanted some," I said with a shrug. "In particular, molybdenum."

"I'm not even going to try pronouncing that," she said, laughing. "What is it?"

"It's used in missiles, aircraft, the oil industry, some nuclear stuff," I said. "Or as I like to call it, the Big Four."

"You were there covertly?" Felicia said, already halfway through her fresh glass.

"Of course," I said. "And there was a group of Chinese insurgencies in the area making trouble."

"For you?"

"No, the Mongolians, primarily," I said. "They and the Chinese don't play well in the same sandbox. Anyway, I was heading through a mountain pass and came under attack. Somebody was firing an automatic rifle in my direction. So, I had to do something about it."

"Makes sense," she said. "So, you took care of the problem?"

"I did. I took him out with a headshot," I said.

"I'm sure you didn't have a choice," Felicia said.

"No, I didn't," I said with an exhausted sigh.

"You must have been used to the job by then. Why was that one a problem?"

"He was nine."

"Sweet Jesus," she said, rubbing her forehead with both hands. "Nine?"

"Yes. And quite good with a Kalashnikov," I said, then lowered my voice to a whisper. "Just not good enough." I exhaled and reached for my cigarettes. "After that, the voice pretty much moved in full-time."

"No wonder it's still around. I doubt if you could dig it out with a melon baller," she said, staring at me. "That's an incredible story, Doc."

"You asked."

"I needed to know," she said, swirling the wine in her glass. "So, let me see if I've got this straight. You stole all your money, shot one of your ex-girlfriends, a nine-year-old, and who knows how many more. And you hear voices in your head."

"Yeah, I'm quite a catch, huh?"

Her laughter filled the gallery then she stretched out on her lounge chair with a goofy grin.

I love this woman.

"Me too," I whispered.

"What?"

"Nothing," I said, topping off our glasses to empty the bottle.

"What a day," Felicia said. "A great day."

"Apart from the last ten minutes, right?"

"No, Doc," she said, making solid eye contact. "Actually, that was the best part."

"I'll never understand women," I said, shaking my head.

"Don't worry. I'll help you." She stared out at the harbor. "I've been thinking about something the past few days."

"Only one? Count your blessings."

"Shhh," she said, raising a finger to her lips. "This is important."

"You're not quitting, are you?" I said.

"Not a chance," she said. "Now hush. This is good."

"Whatcha got?" I said, my temples beginning to pound from too much wine.

"I think it's time we started sleeping together."

"Okay," I said, bolting upright.

"Not tonight, you idiot," she said, laughing. "We've both had way too much to drink."

"Good call," I said, nodding as I stretched back out. "I'd hate to disappoint you right out of the gate." I glanced over. "Maybe in the morning."

"As long as we're not too hungover."

"I don't like our chances," I said, rubbing my temples.

"Me either," she said. "But it won't be long."

"You have no idea how happy that makes me," I said, closing my eyes. "I'm beat. You mind just sleeping out here on the gallery?"

"Not at all," she said, slurring her words. "I'm very comfortable."

"Yeah, it's good," I said. "I sleep out here a couple times a week."

"We're going to need to buy a double lounge chair."

"I'll get on it first thing in the morning," I said, yawning.

We both fell silent, and I immediately began dozing off.

"Doc?" Felicia whispered.

"Yeah."

"If you break my heart, I'll hunt you down like a dog."

"I think I believe you."

CHAPTER 28

I was woken from my dream by the sensation of my shorts being tugged and pulled down.

"I thought you wanted to wait," I said, my eyes still closed.

"What?" a groggy Felicia said from the adjacent lounger.

I opened my eyes, spotted her still sprawled out then glanced down. Samson had his teeth sunk into cotton, determined to get my attention.

"What the hell?" I said, forcing myself awake. "Knock it off, Samson. I'm trying to sleep."

The dog continued unabated, and I finally realized what he was doing.

"What's wrong?" I said, sitting up. "Is it Sebastian?"

At the sound of the old man's name, the dog emitted a low growl and maintained a solid grip on the bottom hem of my shorts.

"What's going on?" Felicia said, sitting up. She groaned then began massaging her temples. "Ugh, I feel like crap."

"I think something might be wrong with Sebastian," I said, working my way off the lounge chair.

Trailed by Felicia, I followed the dog as he raced across the lawn and waited on the top step, barking loudly. I opened the door just as I heard the sound of sirens and stepped inside. All the lights were on, and I strode through the empty living room to the kitchen then down the hall that led to Sebastian's bedroom. Inside, I found his live-in nurse bending over the old man using a stethoscope on his chest. She looked up from her work, calm but obviously concerned.

"He's having a hard time breathing," she said, grabbing Sebastian's wrist to check his pulse.

"I heard the ambulance," I said, approaching the bed just as Felicia entered the room. "You called them, right?"

"I did," she said, then gave Felicia a small wave before focusing on Sebastian. "I never would have known he was having trouble. The dog woke me up."

"Me too," I said, watching the dog who was sitting on his haunches staring up at the old man. I bent down to stroke the dog's head, but he remained fixated on Sebastian. Then I spotted the old man staring up at me with a distant stare. "Good evening, Sebastian. Just try to relax. We're going to get you to the hospital."

With some difficulty, he managed to wiggle a finger in my direction. I leaned over the bed.

"Don't forget your promise, Doc," he managed to get out.

"I won't," I said, gently squeezing his hand.

I heard the sound of people outside the room, and Felicia stepped back to let two paramedics enter. They went to work immediately, and Felicia and I left to give them room. The dog reluctantly followed us but kept pacing from the living room to the kitchen and back.

"How do you feel?" I said, looking at Felicia who continued to massage her temples.

"Like crap. You?"

"About the same. I'm going to follow the ambulance. You mind staying here and keeping an eye on Samson? He's pretty rattled."

"No problem."

We watched the paramedics roll the stretcher across the floor. Sebastian was strapped tight, and an oxygen mask covered his face. I got up, grabbed Samson's collar until they had left, then walked him over to Felicia. She held the dog and gently petted him.

"Give me a call as soon as you hear something," she said.

"Will do," I said, heading outside and being greeted by the early morning light.

At the hospital, I sipped bad coffee and checked my messages as I waited for an update on Sebastian's condition. I noticed I had missed a call from Merlin. I grimaced through another sip as I waited for him to answer.

"What's up, Doc?"

"Did I wake you up?"

"No, I've been up," Merlin said. "But I'm surprised you are."

"I'm at the hospital."

"Are you okay?"

"I'm fine. It's my neighbor."

"What's wrong with him?"

"He's ninety," I said, tossing the half-filled cup into the trash. "Sorry, I missed your call."

"No problem. I just wanted to let you know we're all set."

"Good," I said, nodding. "How much is he charging me?"

"Fifty," Merlin said. "It's a little high, but you seemed to be on a short timeframe. I figured you couldn't be bothered negotiating."

"Yeah, good call," I said. "You mind fronting it? I'll pay you back as soon as things settle down a bit here."

"Already done," Merlin said.

"Thanks. Any update on Kilovich?"

"He's definitely your guy," Merlin said. "You going to take him out?"

"That's one option," I said.

"Well, you'll be doing society a favor. Are you all set on your end?"

"I'm about to find out. I'll talk to you later."

I ended the call and scrolled through my phone for the number.

**

Dupree stood on the deck and glanced around. He pressed his sunglasses tight and shook his head.

"Look at this thing," he said, awed by the boat.

"It's incredible," Harry said, his feet spread to help deal with the gentle rocking of the sailboat, moored a few hundred feet offshore. "That's a lot of teak."

"The man knows how to live," Dupree said, nodding.

Dupree ignored the chirp of his phone when they spotted a small runabout slowing down as it approached the sailboat. They walked to the stern and helped three women onboard. They were dressed identically in tailored shorts and white golf shirts, and all three gaped as they looked around.

"Wow," one of the women said, then finally spotted Dupree and Harry. "Good morning."

"Good morning," Dupree said, then took a step back when Brewster Greedy's head came into view.

Greedy hopped onto the deck and beamed at the women.

"Why don't you ladies take a look around?" he said. "Feel free to go below deck and pick out your quarters. We'll meet as a group before we set sail and run through the trip."

The women grinned at each other then headed off. Greedy watched their departure then leaned over the stern to chat with the man driving the runabout. The small craft headed back toward shore, and Greedy turned his attention to Dupree and Harry.

"Good morning, gentlemen," he said. "Can I ask what you're doing here?"

"I was just taking a final look to make sure the shipment is all set," Dupree said.

"Okay," Greedy said, nodding. "Did you count them to make sure nothing's gone missing?"

"I did, sir," Dupree said. "Three hundred cases."

"Excellent," Greedy said, nodding. "And speaking of things going missing, make sure you keep a close eye on the Dragon Lady while I'm gone. If she manages to steal anything from the house, I'm going to hold you personally responsible. Do we understand each other?"

"Yes, sir," Dupree said.

"Okay. That will be all," Greedy said, pointing at the small boat tied to the stern.

"Have a good trip," Dupree said, stepping onto the ladder.

"I like my chances," Greedy said with a cackle.

**

I was about to try the call a second time when I spotted a grey-haired man wearing a white coat heading my way. I stood up and extended my hand.

"Mr. White?" he said, returning the handshake.

"Yes, sir. How is he?"

"He's stable," the doctor said. "But I'm afraid that's about the best news I'm going to have."

"Yeah," I whispered. "How long will he need to be here?"

"He's going to need round the clock care, Mr. White."

"He already has that," I said. "I only ask because Sebastian made me promise I wouldn't let him die in here."

The doctor gave it some thought then nodded and gave me a small smile.

"I'm sure he did. He's a tough old bird. Okay, Mr. White. He'll need to stay for at least another day. If his vitals return to somewhere near normal and stay there, I'll let him go home."

"Thanks," I said. "Can I see him?"

"I'd rather you wait until tomorrow. He's still in intensive care, and I gave him something for sleep."

"Okay," I said, extending my hand again. "I'll stop by in the morning."

"That will be fine," the doctor said then gave me a small wave and headed off down the hall.

I walked outside, leaned against the side of my SUV and lit a cigarette. Then my phone buzzed.

**

"Hey, sorry I couldn't pick up," Dupree said.

"No problem," Doc said. "Did you get it done?"

"I did. I tucked it way in the back in one of the stacks."

"The same kind of box?"

"Identical," Dupree said, stretching his legs out and leaning back against the side of the runabout. "But it's heavier than the others. If he grabs it, he's gonna know right away something's up."

"He won't," Doc said. "Thanks, Dupree."

"Happy to help," Dupree said. "I still don't see how you're gonna pull this off."

"That's good," Doc said, laughing. "When are you guys heading off island?"

"I'm taking my man Harry to the airport just as soon as we dock. But I've got a few things to take care of before I go."

"I imagine you've got a lot of packing to do," Doc said.

"Not as much as you think. Why do I still think you might be setting me up, Doc?"

"I don't know, Dupree. Maybe a lack of trust from prior relationships?"

"Yeah," Dupree said with a chuckle. "That must be it. When do you need me back on the island?"

"You're taking the job?"

"I am. At least until something better comes along," Dupree said.

"Something better that doesn't include the threat of jail time?"

"Let's just say I'm intrigued by the idea of working with you, Doc."

"As good a reason as any. Tell Harry goodbye for me and tell him I hope he makes millions."

"Will do," Dupree said. "I should be back in a couple of weeks."

"Okay," Doc said. "And remember Dupree, black market prices are never as high as retail. So, don't be getting greedy."

"Getting Greedy? I thought that was your job, Doc."

Dupree slid his phone into his pocket then stared out at the water.

"What did he have to say for himself?" Harry said, easing the throttle back as the runabout approached the dock.

"He said he hopes you make millions," Dupree said.

"You really taking the job?" Harry said.

"Yeah," Dupree said, getting up to grab the dock. "It sure beats the alternative."

"Could be fun," Harry said, hopping out of the boat and tying off the stern. "Hey, you busy on Friday?"

"Friday?" Dupree said, tying the bowline to a cleat. "Man, I'm lucky if I know what I'm doing the rest of the day. What's going on?"

"I'm doing a showcase in Nashville with some guys I know," Harry said. "It should be good."

"I don't know, Harry," Dupree said, strolling down the dock. "All those cowboy hats and rednecks in one place always makes me nervous."

"Your loss," Harry said, gently punching Dupree on the shoulder. "You gonna miss me?"

"Almost as much as I'd miss my horse," Dupree deadpanned through a slow drawl.

"Yeah. Funny," Harry snapped as he dug through his shorts for his car keys.

"Let's go. Time is short and we ain't getting any younger." Dupree grinned at Harry. "And we both know how much that sucks."

CHAPTER 29

I found Felicia and Samson on the gallery sound asleep sharing the same lounge chair. The dog heard me coming, hopped down and greeted me with a vigorous tail wag. Felicia stirred then sat up yawning.

"How's he doing?"

"The doctor said he's stable but will need to stay there at least another day," I said, sitting down on the adjacent lounger and immediately making room for Samson when he climbed up next to me. "How are you feeling?"

"Like crap," she said, reaching for a bottle of water and chugging. "You?"

"I'm okay," I said. "But I could use a nap."

"Did you talk to Dupree?" she said, then took another long swallow.

"I did. We're all set," I said, then caught the expression on her face. "You still don't like the idea, do you?"

"I'll learn to live with it," she said. "Has Greedy set sail yet?"

"Yeah, I spotted his boat on my way back," I said, reaching for my phone.

"Who are you calling?" she said, stretching both arms over her head.

"Our shooter." I got up and leaned against the railing to block the wind. I made the call and lit a cigarette while I waited.

"Hello?" said a man through a heavy Russian accent.

"Nikolai?"

"Who is this?"

"Someone who needs a job done," I said, glancing at Felicia who was paying close attention.

"I don't think I know you," he said.

"We haven't met," I said. "But our mutual friend in St. Croix gave me your number and highly recommended you."

"St. Croix?" the man said, obviously puzzled. "Okay, got it. Which one?"

I was so startled by his question that I almost dropped the phone. Felicia noticed my reaction and stared at me. I remained silent as my mind raced. I shook my head in disbelief then answered the Russian's question.

"Her," I whispered into the phone.

"Describe her to me," he snapped.

"Five-six, blond, blue eyes, and the kind of woman who can make you question every decision you've ever made in your life."

The Russian chuckled through the phone.

"Yes, I agree. So, you need a job done?"

"I do. But I don't want to discuss the particulars over the phone."

"Me neither," Nikolai said.

"But I'll be in Miami in a couple of days. Will you be around?"

"Call me when you get here," he said, then hung up.

Stunned, I slipped my phone into my pocket and rubbed my forehead.

"What's the matter, Doc?"

"Greedy's not behind the forgery ring," I said, sitting down at the table and crushing my cigarette out.

"He's not?" she said, puzzled. She looked out at the harbor, deep in thought then her eyes widened. "No way. Her?"

"Yeah," I said, nodding and reaching down to pet Samson who was nuzzling my leg. "I need to get out there."

"Where?"

"Greedy's house," I said, getting to my feet. "Merlin told me this morning that another painter died yesterday."

"The same way?"

"Merlin didn't know."

"Are you going to confront her?" Felicia said.

"At some point, I'm sure I will. But first, I've got to save Dupree's butt."

"You think she's tying up her loose ends?" she said.

"That's my first guess," I said. "Geez. That's diabolical. I never knew she had it in her."

"Maybe she doesn't," Felicia said.

"Maybe."

"You want me to come with you?"

"No, I need to do this one alone," I said.

"Okay, but be careful," Felicia said. "And try not to repeat yourself."

"What?" I said, cocking my head at her.

"Shooting your ex-girlfriend," she said, then patted the lounger and called Samson.

"I'll do my best," I said, heading for my bedroom to grab my gun.

**

Dupree gently placed the frame back on the wall and stepped back to admire his work. He rolled up the original

Koons, slid it into a long tube then draped it over his shoulder. He turned to leave but stopped short when he saw Elle leaning against the doorjamb giving him a quizzical stare. She was wearing her bathing suit and dripping water on the tile.

"What are you doing in here, Dupree?" she said, entering the office and glancing around.

"Just making sure I haven't left anything behind," he said, forcing himself to stay cool.

"What's in the tube?" Elle said, heading straight for him.

"Nothing."

She stood in front of the fake Koons and studied it before nodding.

"You are good," she said, sitting down behind the desk and putting her feet up. She rocked slowly, concentrated hard then grinned at him. "Let me guess. You decided the Koons would make a nice parting gift."

"Yeah," Dupree said with a playful shrug. "Let's call it part of my severance package."

"I see," she said, lowering her feet and reaching inside one of the desk drawers. Dupree took a nervous step back. "Relax, Dupree," she said, laughing as she placed a briefcase on the desk. "Since you decided to pop in unannounced, we might as well settle up, right?" She opened the briefcase and turned it toward him.

Dupree stared at the bundled stacks of hundreds filling the briefcase.

"How much is in there?" he said, grabbing one of the bundles and rifling through it.

"Half a million," she said, putting her feet back up. "Just like we discussed. But that was before I found out you were stealing from me."

"Actually, Elle," Dupree said, sitting down across from her. "If you think about it, I'm stealing from him."

"Perhaps," she said, staring at him as she continued rocking. "But stealing, Dupree? Such a despicable thing to do."

"Well, you would know," Dupree said, closing the briefcase to enable better eye contact.

She laughed and lowered her legs onto the tile.

"No, I'm sorry, Dupree. This won't stand. I just can't let this one go."

"C'mon, Elle. It's one painting. And trust me, he's never gonna miss it."

"Sorry, Dupree."

"Hey, I've done a dozen paintings for you," Dupree said in protest. "First, you wanted fakes of some of the paintings in the house. Then you just had to have some of the others you saw around the island."

"So? Haven't you been adequately compensated for your efforts?" Elle said with a shrug.

"I took a lot of risks for you," Dupree said. "And so did Harry."

"Harry, that's right. I almost forgot about him. Where is he?"

"He's off island."

"Where?"

"Bulgaria," Dupree said, keeping a close eye on her movements. "Tell you what, Elle. How about I take the Koons and this briefcase and head out. And if it ever happens, the next time we see each other, we'll just pretend we never met."

"You make it sound so easy, Dupree," she said, draping a leg over her knee.

"Well, it sure ain't hard," he said.

"I have a better idea," she said, reaching into the desk drawer directly in front of the chair.

**

From the door, I raised my gun and racked a shell into the chamber. Elle, startled by the loud click, looked up at

301

me and dropped the gun she was holding. She started to lean down to retrieve it.

"Leave it, Elle," I said, then walked across the office and bent down to pick it up. I ejected the clip then emptied the round in the chamber. I examined the gold-plated nine-millimeter then shook my head. "Nice gun. Nothing's too good for Greedy, right?" I tossed the gun on one of the couches.

"What the hell are you doing here?" Dupree said, his eyes wide.

"Apparently, saving your life," I said, sitting down next to him and keeping my gun pointed at Elle.

"You were gonna shoot me?" Dupree said, glaring at Elle. "After all I've done for you?" He shook his head then looked at me. "Man, I gotta tell you, Doc, you can't trust anybody these days."

"Words to live by," I said, then glanced around. "You got the original Koons?"

"Yeah," Dupree whispered.

"What's in the briefcase?" I said.

"Half a million," he said.

"Okay," I said, nodding. "Not bad for a day's work, huh?"

"Doc, I can explain all of this," Elle said through a tight smile.

"I can't wait to hear it," I said. "You know where she keeps the other paintings you forged?"

"Actually, I do," Dupree said. "They're in a footlocker at the end of her bed."

"How the hell do you know that?" Elle snapped.

"I'm nosy," Dupree said with a shrug.

"And it's not a footlocker, you moron," she said. "It's a cedar chest."

"Go grab the paintings and get out of here. Make yourself scarce," I said.

"Hey, now wait a minute," Elle said, glaring at me.

"Just like that?" Dupree said.

"Unless you'd rather stick around," I said.

"No, it seems like a good time to hit the road. Can I take that?" he said, nodding at the briefcase.

"I don't see why not," I said. "It's your money, isn't it? Oh, make sure to unload all the paintings as soon as you can."

"Why?" Dupree said, suspicious. "Are you trying to set me up, Doc?"

"Geez, Dupree," I said, scowling at him. "Do we have to go down that road again? For chrissakes, work with me here. But don't worry, nobody is going to come looking for them."

"Are you sure?" Dupree said, reaching for the briefcase.

"Almost positive," I said with a grin.

"All right," he said, snapping the briefcase latches shut. "Thanks, Doc. You're the man. I owe you. Big time owe you."

"Yeah, I guess you do," I said, then had a thought. "Hang on. Hand me the briefcase."

Dupree shoved it across the desk. I opened it and removed five of the bundles then closed the briefcase and slid it back.

"What are you doing?" Dupree said, raising an eyebrow at me.

"I'm taking fifty," I said, stacking the bundles in front of me.

"What for?"

"To cover an unexpected expense," I said.

"Geez, Doc," Dupree said, scowling at me.

"Really, Dupree?" I said, staring back in disbelief. "You're actually going to argue the point?"

"Yeah, you're right. Forget I even mentioned it," he said, grabbing the briefcase off the desk. He draped the tube over his shoulder then focused on Elle who was sitting quietly with her legs tucked underneath her. "I can't believe you were gonna shoot me." He headed for the door. "Man, I'm so done with people. I'm getting myself a dog."

"Hey, Dupree?" I said, calling after him.

"Yeah."

"Remember. Black market prices," I said.

He gave it some thought then beamed at me from the doorway.

"One of these days, you gotta explain how your brain works, Doc."

"I'll do that. Just as soon as I figure it out," I said. "But I'm serious. Be smart about how you handle the next few days."

"Don't worry, Doc. I won't get greedy."

His laughter echoed off the tile as he headed down the hall. I focused on Elle who was staring back at me. It was impossible to miss the anger and frustration in her face emerging, I was sure, from a combination of current events and a well-developed, yet poorly defined, sense of shared history.

"Okay, Elle," I said with a sigh as I placed my gun on the desk. "Let's chat."

CHAPTER 30

We stared at each other across the desk, a distance of four feet that might as well have been the Atlantic. Like so many times in the past, I knew she was waiting me out, silently challenging me to go first. I decided the standoff wasn't worth the energy and launched.

"The forgery ring was brilliant, Elle."

"Thanks, Doc," she said, unable to suppress her grin. "I knew if anyone would appreciate it, it would be you."

"At first, I couldn't figure out the pattern," I said.

"Pattern?"

"Yeah. I knew there had to be one. And then it sorted itself out."

"I'm not following you, Doc," she said, resuming a slow rock.

"Of course, you are," I said, spinning my gun on the desk and watching it rotate.

"Why don't you put that thing away?" she said, nodding at it. "We both know you're not going to shoot me."

"You're right," I said, then grabbed the gun and set it on the chair next to me. "I couldn't do that." I lit a cigarette then exhaled a cloud of smoke up at the ceiling. "Greedy won't mind if I smoke in here, will he?"

"I really don't care," she said, reaching for the pack. She leaned forward and waited for me to light it. "So, what's this pattern, Doc?"

"The paintings you were having forged came from your own houses," I said. "At least, initially."

"Very good, Doc," she said, grinning at me. "You haven't lost your touch."

"Thanks," I said, taking another drag as I studied her expression. "You were forging all of Greedy's favorite paintings. And probably the most valuable."

"They're worth a fortune," she said, shaking her head. "And now you've given them all away."

"I'm sure you'll be able to handle the financial hit."

"Don't be so sure about that, Doc," she whispered.

Her comment caught me by surprise. I sat quietly, working my way through the cigarette then sat back and draped a leg over my knee.

"What I didn't understand at first, was why you'd rip yourself off."

"And?"

"And I decided it must have something to do with the divorce settlement. What was it, Elle? Some sort of plan to inflict as much damage on Greedy as possible?"

"That was certainly part of it," she said, tapping ash onto the desk and not bothering to brush it off.

"And the beautiful part of it was Greedy didn't have a clue he was admiring a bunch of fake paintings," I said, laughing. "I bet you enjoyed listening to him when he'd start prattling on about them to your dinner guests."

"I loved it," she said, laughing loudly. "He's such a pompous ass."

"And yet you married him," I said.

"Don't start, Doc," she said, shaking her head. "And you're not as smart as you think you are."

"Why's that?"

"Inflicting damage on Brewster was only a small part of why I did it," she said softly.

I sat back in my chair, folded my arms across my chest then rubbed my chin.

"Money?" I said through a confused frown.

Elle didn't respond. She just kept rocking back and forth with a fixed stare, again challenging me to continue. I concentrated hard, then the questions rolling around my head coalesced, and the answer floated to the surface.

"Holy crap," I whispered. "You signed a prenup."

Elle could only manage a small nod.

"That seems out of character," I said, frowning. "Why on earth would you do that?"

"I didn't have a choice," she whispered. "Brewster was insistent."

"You should have worked a little harder," I said with a grin.

Her eyes flared wide as she muttered a string of expletives under her breath.

"I'm sorry, Elle. That was a cheap shot."

"Why do you have to be such a dick?"

"That's a really good question," I said. "So, the paintings were going to be your post-divorce nest egg?"

"Yeah," she said, crushing her cigarette out on the desk. "Now, that idea is shot to hell. Thanks to you."

"How's your cash supply these days?"

"Not great. But I'll get by until the divorce is finalized." She noticed my distant stare. "What's on your mind, Doc?"

"How much do you know about Greedy's businesses?"

"What?" she said, confused.

"Your husband's businesses. How much do you know about them?"

"Enough to know they're all incredibly boring," she said. "And I can't wait until I don't have to listen to any more of his stupid stories."

"Explain his businesses to me," I said.

"Why on earth do you want me to do that?" she said, genuinely confused.

"Because your answer is going to determine what I decide to do with you," I said with a shrug.

"Cryptic Man," she said, shaking her head. "Damn. I'm so glad I got away from you."

"I'm sure you are, Elle," I said, accepting the insult without a return volley.

"Brewster does finance, real estate, and has some manufacturing companies," she said, reciting from memory.

"Do you know what he's up to down here?"

"You mean apart from taking chippies out on his boat?"

"Yeah, apart from that," I said.

"I have no idea," she said, shaking her head. "But I have a feeling you're about to tell me."

"He's running Fentanyl out of China," I said, then watched her reaction closely.

"Fentanyl?" she said, frowning. "That sounds familiar. What is it?"

"It's the crap that killed Prince," I said. "It's like heroin on steroids."

"And my husband is smuggling it?"

"Right now, he's sailing to Miami with three hundred cases of it onboard."

"Three hundred cases?" she said, still confused. "What does that even mean?"

"Actually," I said, correcting myself. "It's three hundred and one. Millions and millions of tiny little pills selling for about ten bucks a pop on the street."

"My husband is involved in something that's going to net him hundreds of millions?" she said through a tight-lipped grimace. "That son of a bitch."

"And here I thought you might be concerned what that crap might do to thousands of kids," I said. "Silly me."

"Don't even go there, Doc," she snapped. "Of course, I worry about that. Or I would have if you'd given me a few seconds to think about it. That's really what he's doing?"

"That's his plan," I said. "But it's not going to happen."

"What is going to happen to him?" she said, leaning forward.

"I imagine he'll be arrested when he docks in Miami,"
I said, lying through my teeth. I studied the look on her face
as she focused on the far wall deep in thought. Then I
laughed. "I can see the hamsters turning the wheel. Don't
even think about it."

"Think about what?"

"Calling to warn him."

"Why not?" she said with a grin. "It sounds like
enough leverage to help me cut a much better deal."

"Because that would make you an accessory," I said as
a statement of fact.

"You'd really do that to me, Doc?"

"Just because I can't shoot you doesn't mean I won't
have you arrested."

"Okay," she said, nodding. Then she brightened. "Hey,
maybe Brewster will get shot, and I'll inherit everything."

"It wouldn't help," I said, shaking my head as I caved
and reached for another cigarette.

"Why not?"

"Think about it," I said, then sat back and waited for
her to connect the dots.

"Ah, crap. They're going to seize all of Brewster's
assets," she sighed. "That's it, isn't it?"

"Right down to that chair your cute little butt is sitting on."

"Oh, a compliment," she said, managing a small laugh. "It is cute, isn't it? I thought you hadn't noticed."

Not very likely.

"It's hard to miss," I said.

"Did Brewster have that stilt walker killed?" she said, resuming her rocking.

"He did," I said, then decided to push. "He used the same guy you used on Esmeralda."

She flinched as her eyes went wide. She had a hard time recovering.

"I knew it," she whispered.

"Knew what?"

"As soon as I heard you were working on the kid's murder, I knew you'd eventually put it together."

"Why do you say that?"

"Because it's what you do," she said with a shrug. "But I thought I had some time."

I remained silent as she tucked her knees under her chin and stared at me.

"Merlin," she whispered.

"Yeah," I said.

"That little phobic," she said, shaking her head. "How did he put it together?"

"We got lucky. He was helping our friend from Budapest out."

"Merlin was helping him?"

"For a price."

"Geez, I can't stand that Hungarian. He's a total pig and barely walking upright. But, of course, he and Brewster got along great." She sighed loudly. "As I soon as I saw it, I knew I had to have that painting. It's worth a fortune."

"Who was helping Esmeralda get past the security systems?"

"I have no idea," Elle said. "It wasn't my problem."

"And you had her taken out because you were worried she would start talking?"

"That was the major reason. And the fact she was sleeping with Brewster had something to do with it." She noticed the look I was giving her then continued. "But I found that out back in the day when I still cared if he was cheating on me."

"What about the forger you were using in California?"

"What about him?" she said, confused by the question.

"He's dead," I said. "Don't try to tell me you didn't know anything about that."

"Swear to God, Doc," she said, making solid eye contact. "I had no idea. Poor Julio."

"Who do you think killed him?"

"I don't know," she said. "I'm very sorry to hear that news. Julio was a gentle soul. But he ran with a really rough crowd. The tortured artist lifestyle and all that. Maybe he didn't pay his dealer. Or he slept with the wrong woman. Who knows?"

"You weren't worried about him talking?" I said, finishing my cigarette.

"No," she said, shaking her head. "And given all the drugs he was doing, he was gonna be dead within a year." She gave me a wide-eyed stare. "I panicked when I saw you, Doc. That's why I had Esmeralda taken out. She would have folded as soon as anybody starting asking her questions. Not to mention she hated my guts."

"And Dupree?" I said.

"Dupree could have been a big problem," Elle said. "He's way too smart."

"He is," I said.

"What are you going to do about him?"

"I just hired him," I said.

"To do what?" she said, stunned.

"I'm not exactly sure," I said, shaking my head. "But I like hanging out with him."

"You are so frigging weird."

"Guilty."

She studied my expression for several moments before continuing.

"And what about me, Doc?"

"That's a much harder decision," I said, staring back at her.

"Maybe we can rekindle things," she said with a grin.

"Us?" I said, laughing. "If Dupree were still here, he'd be asking if you'd just burned one."

"Yeah," she said, nodding. "Bad idea. But I suppose it was worth a shot." Then she turned serious. "Are you going to have me arrested, Doc?"

"You know, Elle, that question has been rolling around my head since I figured out you were behind this whole thing."

"And?"

"And I have to give you credit for the forgery ring," I said. "It is one of the coolest scams I have ever come across. And I've seen a lot."

"Thank you, Doc."

"But putting out a contract hit is something else altogether."

"If it makes a difference, Esmeralda wasn't a nice person."

"It doesn't," I said, shaking my head.

"Okay. So, what have you decided?"

"I've decided you don't look good in orange."

"You're right," she said. "I don't. You're letting me go?"

"For now," I said, nodding. "Long term, I'm still not sure."

"You're going to let it hang over my head, right?"

"I am."

"Okay," she said, nodding. "How long have I got?"

"You mean, how long do you have to head back to your places in California and France to grab the rest of the paintings?"

"Uh-huh," she said, leaning forward. "How long before Brewster's assets are frozen?"

"Probably three or four days," I said.

"That's long enough," she said. "I need those paintings, Doc. Or I'll have to start over from scratch."

"You could always go back to work," I said, grinning at her. "Or find another Greedy."

"If you don't mind, I think I'll keep my plans to myself," she said, getting to her feet.

"Just one thing, Elle," I said, accepting her offer of a handshake.

"What's that?"

"When you leave St. Croix, don't come back."

"That won't be a problem," she said, rocking on her heels. "Anything else?"

"No more contract hits," I said.

"Don't worry, Doc," she said, adjusting her two-piece. "That was merely temporary insanity."

"So, it was my fault?" I said, laughing.

"Yeah, that's the way I see it," she said. "You can let yourself out."

"Okay. Goodbye, Elle."

"Goodbye, Doc," she said, extending a hand. "I'd give you a hug, but I'm still wet."

"As good an excuse as any," I said, returning the handshake.

"It was good seeing you, Doc. It was nice catching up."

"It was interesting. I'll give you that," I said.

She leaned against the doorway and stared at me from across the room.

"Did you get the closure you were looking for, Doc?"

"Mission accomplished," I said softly. "And you?"

"Oh, I didn't need it," she said with a shrug. "Do yourself a favor, Doc."

"What's that?"

"Let that woman who works for you into your life. She looks like a keeper."

She gave me a small wave and left the office, closing the door tight behind her.

I got up and spent the next few minutes staring out the window at the view. The water looked calm, and I watched a speedboat charting a straight-line course to an unknown destination. Then I grabbed my phone.

"Jenkins," said the voice on the other end of the line.

"Hey, John. It's Doc."

"Doc White. Son of a gun. How the hell are you?"

"I'm great. It's been a long time. How are things at the IRS?"

"You know the drill, Doc," he said, laughing. "I just love being hated. What can I do for you?"

"I need you to start asset forfeiture on somebody."

"I thought you retired. Are you back working again?" John said, surprised.

"No, I'm out. I just wanted to give you a heads-up. And it's a big one. You're gonna be a hero."

"Now you're talking," he said. "Who is it?"

"Brewster Greedy."

"Greedy?" John said. "Man, we've been looking at him for years."

"Well, you can stop looking," I said. "He's about to go down hard."

"What's he up to?"

"He's running Fentanyl," I said. "A lot of it."

"Geez, that's some nasty stuff. You sure about this?"

"Positive. How long will it take you to freeze his accounts and make sure nobody has access to his properties?"

"Not long," John said. "When do you need it done?"

"Today, if possible."

"Geez, Doc," he said. "That's asking a lot. This better be worth my effort."

"Don't worry, John. You'll be thanking me."

"Okay, I can expedite it. But I probably won't be able to push it through until tomorrow. Does that work for you?"

"Yeah, tomorrow's fine," I said. "She won't have enough time."

"What?"

"Nothing."

"Okay, Doc. I'll keep you in the loop," he said. "Hey, next time you're back in D.C., give me a buzz. We'll grab a beer."

"Will do. Thanks, John."

I ended the call, took one more look through the picture window then headed outside. Just before I reached my vehicle, I heard the sound of splashing. I walked across the lawn and spotted Elle churning laps. I watched her effortlessly go up and down the pool for a few minutes and did my best to ignore the wave of sadness washing over me.

Maybe she thinks better in the pool.

"Yeah, I'd be trying to clear my head, too."

CHAPTER 31

When I arrived home, I found Felicia in the kitchen hovering over the stove. I pulled her in close, and we shared a long embrace until Samson decided he wanted in on the action. I knelt down to pet him then focused on the stove.

"You didn't have to make dinner," I said, sniffing a large pot that was simmering.

"No, I felt like doing it," she said, giving the pot a stir. "I was jonesing for some home cooking."

"What are we having?" I said, glancing around the stovetop.

"Well, that's fish soup," she said, pointing at the large pot.

"Smells great. What's it called?"

"Fish soup," she deadpanned.

"Funny."

"It's got wahoo and dumplings," Felicia said. "And we're having chicken with red beans and rice. And I made johnnycake for dessert."

"Fantastic," I said. "Can I get you a glass of wine?"

"Not a chance," she said, laughing. "Water's fine." She turned the heat down on the soup and leaned against the kitchen island. "How did it go?"

I gave her a short summary, and, as expected, received several frowns and scowls. When I finished, I sat down on a stool and waited for her questions.

"I'm going to need more, Doc."

"I know," I said, nodding.

"How do you justify doing that?"

"Which one?"

"Let's start with Dupree," she said, sitting down across from me.

"That was an easy call. He did all the work, right?"

"And rather than give the paintings back to the people who owned them, you gave them to him?"

"Most of them belonged to Greedy," I said.

"What about the others?" Felicia said, pressing the point.

"Nobody seems to be missing them," I said.

"Not yet," she said. "But what happens when the owners realize they're staring at a fake painting?"

"I imagine they'll file an insurance claim," I said with a shrug.

"Okay," Felicia said, then propped her elbows on the island and leaned forward. "What about Elle? How do you explain that?"

"Letting her go seemed like the best option."

"I can't wait to hear this one," she said.

"It's complicated."

"At a minimum," Felicia said, glancing over her shoulder at the stove. "She should be going to prison."

"The only thing prison would do is make her resentful," I said.

"Oh, the poor baby," she said with a laugh.

"I'd rather have her out on the street."

"Why?"

"To keep her focus on rebuilding her life rather than revenge," I said.

"You think she'll come after you?"

"No, Elle knows how big of a break I just gave her," I said. "She'll go away quietly."

"But if you sent her to prison, she might not?" Felicia said.

"Let's say it's not worth taking that chance," I said.

"And you had no compunction about having her husband's assets frozen?"

"None," I said, shaking my head. "Just because I couldn't send her to prison doesn't mean she should be rewarded for her behavior."

"But Dupree should?" she said, frowning.

"Yeah, I suppose that does sound a bit strange," I said. "I don't know, Felicia. It just seemed like a nice thing to do for the guy."

"Unbelievable," she said, getting up to stir the soup. She sat back down and sipped water, deep in thought. "And Greedy and Willy's shooter?"

"What about them?"

"You have any moral dilemmas about your plans for them?"

"Absolutely not," I said, shaking my head.

"Buddha will be disappointed, Doc," she said with a grin.

"It won't be the first time."

"You can justify it?"

"Let's say I can understand and accept it. How does that work for you?"

"Close enough, I suppose," Felicia said. "I do like how the Buddhists deal with good versus evil."

"Do you now?" I said, surprised.

"Yeah, I've been reading up on it," she said. "Since I'm now involved with you, I thought some tenets about patience and self-awareness might come in handy."

I laughed.

"Instead of dealing with the battle between good and evil, focus on ignorance and enlightenment," she continued.

"The three poisons of evil," I said, nodding. "Greed, ill will, and delusion."

"Greedy has all three in spades."

"They both do," I said, staring into her eyes.

"You've never even met the shooter, Doc."

"I don't need to meet him," I said. "I know hundreds just like him. And they never go away. They lurk, shed their skins, then return with a vengeance."

"Okay, Doc," Felicia said. "But I have to say, your approach doesn't sound very *enlightened*."

"I'm obviously still struggling with it, Felicia."

"Yes, I can see that. But I suppose the whole situation makes some sense to you," she said softly.

"I don't know," I said with a sigh. "There are just so many..."

"Layered shades of grey?"

"Yeah," I said, then took a deep breath and exhaled. "How long before we eat dinner?"

"About half an hour. Why?"

"I need to pack for Miami," I said, hopping off the stool.

CHAPTER 32

Miami International was its usual chaotic zoo, and I eventually made my way outside to the taxi stand.

"Hey," the driver said, hopping out of the car. "Do you have any bags?"

"No, just my carry on," I said, climbing into the backseat.

"Where you headed?"

"Downtown Hyatt, please," I said, sitting back and draping an arm over the top of the seat.

"What are you in town for?" the driver said, glancing at me through the mirror.

"Just tying up a loose end," I said, staring out the window.

"Let me guess," the driver said with a grin. "It's a woman, right?"

"Actually, no," I said, smiling back. "For the first time in ages, it's not."

**

Dupree sat quietly with a leg draped over his knee as he waited for the old man wearing a jeweler's eyepiece to finish his inspection. Eventually, the man removed the eyepiece and sat down across from Dupree with a confused frown fixed in place.

"What's the matter?" Dupree said.

"They're all originals," he said.

"Yeah, I know," Dupree said, scowling. "Isn't that what I told you three hours ago?"

The old man lit a cigar and puffed until he was happy with the way it was burning.

"Should I even ask how you got your hands on them?"

"Sure, you can ask," Dupree said with a shrug.

The old man stared back until a small grin appeared.

"How do I know people aren't going to come looking for them?"

"Let's call it an educated guess," Dupree said. "Like I said, nobody is going to be looking for them. At least, not in the foreseeable future."

"Okay," the old man said. "You're obviously a man with considerable talents. You interested in doing some work for me?"

"Nah," Dupree said, shaking his head. "This is my last one. Actually, I'm about to start a new job."

"Doing what?"

"I'm not exactly sure," Dupree said.

"Too bad," the old man said. "I could use somebody with your skills."

Dupree merely shrugged.

"How much do you want for them?"

"Eleven," Dupree said.

"Eleven? That's all?" the old man said, raising an eyebrow.

"That's the number."

The old man stared hard at Dupree.

"You must know what these are worth."

"To me, they're worth eleven. That's all that matters."

"Okay," the old man said, nodding. "I think you're nuts, but we got a deal."

"I thought we might," Dupree said, sliding a slip of paper across the desk. "I want a million in cash and the rest deposited into that account. By tomorrow."

"I can do that," the old man said, extending his hand. "I need to thank you. You just accelerated my retirement plans."

"Glad I could help."

**

Just before nine, I made the short walk from my hotel and spotted the Russian already waiting for me. He was leaning against a pastel-colored wall smoking a cigarette and watching the traffic and women going past. I came to a stop directly in front of him.

"Mr. White?" he said in a thick accent.

"Yes, Nikolai."

"Nice to meet you. Let's walk," he said, heading for a nearby alley.

I walked next to him in silence until he came to a stop. He glanced around until he was sure we were alone then rocked on his heels as he studied my expression.

"I've got a question for you, Nikolai."

"I've found that the fewer questions we ask each other, the better off we'll both be," the Russian said.

"No, this is an easy one," I said, forcing a smile.

"Okay," he said, nodding.

"You used to be in the circus, right?"

"How did you know that?" he said, stunned.

"The stilts," I said. "That was very clever."

"Yes, I thought so," he said. "Who was he?"

"Just a kid who did something stupid," I said.

"It happens a lot," he said, shrugging it off.

"How are you going to handle the hit?"

"I'm not sure," he said. "Each one is different. But my signature is two in the back of the head."

"It probably makes the cops think the shooter was Italian, right?" I said with a grin.

"Yes, it must have been the evil Mafia," the Russian said, laughing.

"How much is this going to cost me?" I said.

"Two hundred. In advance."

"I can do that," I said, reaching inside my sport coat. "I have it with me."

"Good. Who would you like shot?"

"You," I said, firing a single round into his forehead.

He dropped to the ground, a look of shock permanently etched on his face. I wiped the weapon clean, removed the silencer then tossed it into a nearby trash bin. I crossed to the other side of the alley then dropped the gun into the storm drain and strolled back to my hotel.

I called room service, then Felicia.

"Good evening," I said.

"Good evening. What are you up to?"

"I'm settling in with room service and a movie," I said, kicking off my shoes and stretching out on the bed. "I wish you were here."

"Me too," Felicia said. "But Samson and I are keeping each other company. Is it done?"

"It is," I said.

"And?"

"And it's done," I said.

"Any problems?"

"No. At least, not for me."

"Got it. Oh, the hospital called earlier. Sebastian is coming home tomorrow," she said.

"I'll get back as soon as I can."

"Did you order a hospital bed for him?" she said.

"I did. I'm sorry I forgot to mention it," I said. "Just have them set it up on his gallery. He likes to sit outside and look out at the harbor."

"You are something else," she said with a soft chuckle. "When will you be back?"

"The day after tomorrow. I'm heading to Nashville in the morning."

"Nashville?"

"Yeah, Dupree invited me to a showcase Harry is doing. An evening of country music."

"Have fun with that. Not my thing."

"Yeah, I know. Me either," I said. "Okay, enjoy your evening. I'll call you tomorrow."

"Be careful, Doc."

"No worries there. The hard part is done."

"So, it *was* hard?"

"Actually, if I'm being honest, it was way too easy."

CHAPTER 33

I waved to a small group of smokers huddled
outside the club and walked inside where I spotted Dupree
sitting at a table near the stage. Harry was on stage leading
the band through a raucous tune featuring fiddle and
mandolin laid over Harry's intricate guitar work. Dupree
spotted me, got up to give me a fist bump then sat back
down.

"What are you having?" he said over the music.

"Whatever you're drinking," I said, listening closely to
the lyrics. I grinned at Dupree.

"Yeah, I know," Dupree said. "The man is funny."

The chorus repeated and I laughed as I listened to
Harry's cynical drawl.

Me and Art both got a list, but we ain't got a bucket.
Art likes to complain, but I say...the heck with it.
Do this, do that, work the list, be all you can be.
Now, Art's a total mess, but it still works for me.
Life imitates art, or so the saying goes.
I think it's true, but he don't agree.
But when art mimics life, Art.
You're often forced to see it from your knees.

The band finished to enormous applause and Harry approached the microphone.

"Thanks so much, folks. We're gonna take a short break. But we'll be back for one more set. Make sure you tip your servers," Harry said, then flashed a big grin at one of the band members. "And if you can spare it, our drummer could probably use a little help, too."

I couldn't miss the hand gesture the drummer gave Harry as he climbed off the stage. Harry sat down between us and glanced back and forth.

"What do you think?" Harry said to Dupree.

"Good stuff, man. Really good."

"Thanks. Hey, Doc," Harry said. "You a country fan?"

"Actually, no," I said. "But you guys can cook."

"Yeah, I think it's working," Harry said, then spotted the backpack Dupree was holding. "What's that?"

"Your cut," Dupree said.

Harry accepted the backpack, set it on his lap and opened it to take a look. He flinched then stared at Dupree.

"How much is in here?"

"A million," Dupree said, then caught the nervous look in Harry's eyes. "Relax, man. Doc's cool. He's the reason you're getting it."

"Geez, a million," Harry whispered, then a deep frown appeared. "Hang on. A million out of what?"

"You believe this guy?" Dupree said, turning to me. "I give the man a million bucks, and the first thought that pops into his head is that I'm somehow screwing him over."

"I know how you work, Dupree. How much did you get?"

"Enough to give you a million, you ingrate," Dupree said. "I can't believe you, Harry."

"All right, Dupree," Harry said, shaking his head at his friend. "Okay, we're cool."

"Damn straight, we're cool," Dupree said. "Next time, I'll just buy you a new truck and a case of Bud."

"You sure you want this guy working for you?" Harry said to me.

"I guess we're going to find out, huh?" I said, laughing.

"You guys sticking around for the next set?"

"Yeah," Dupree said, nodding. "But while you guys are on break, I'm gonna step outside for a smoke."

"Okay, I'll see you guys after the show," Harry said, getting up, surprised by the weight of the backpack. "It's heavy."

"Man, try to do a guy a favor," Dupree said, watching him head backstage. "You want to join me?"

"Yeah," I said, getting up and following Dupree to the exit.

Outside, Dupree kept walking until we reached a deserted part of the street. He lit a joint, inhaled deeply then offered it to me.

"No, thanks," I said, waving it off. "It doesn't agree with me."

"That's strange," Dupree said through a cloud of smoke. "All these years, I've never heard it complain once."

CHAPTER 34

I was greeted by Samson when I reached the bottom step. We spent a few minutes getting reacquainted then climbed the stairs to the gallery. Sebastian was in bed, propped up on an angle, staring out at the water. He beamed when he saw me.

"Good afternoon, Doc. Welcome home."

"Good afternoon. How are you doing, Sebastian?"

"Never felt better," he said.

I turned to his nurse who was sitting next to him.

"Good afternoon, Mary."

"Good afternoon, Doc. I hope you had a nice trip," she said, getting to her feet. "I'll leave you two alone. I'm going to heat up some soup for you, Sebastian."

"Thank you," he said, watching her leave. "She's taking great care of me."

"Glad to hear it," I said, sitting down.

"Tell me all about your trip."

"Well, first I had something to take care of in Miami," I said.

"Did it have anything to do with Willy's murder?" Sebastian said.

"It had everything to do with it," I said.

"And?"

"He's gone."

He studied my expression until he was sure he understood what I was saying.

"Good."

"Then I went to Nashville."

"Nashville? What for?"

"To watch a musician doing a showcase," I said.

"Country music?"

"Yes. Not my favorite, but he was great."

"I like country music," Sebastian said. "Simple, yet strong, messages."

"Sure, I get that," I said, nodding. "The guy's got this one song about the difference between a bucket list and a to-do list that's funny as hell."

"Ah, the desire to do what one wishes versus what one has to do," Sebastian said. "I'm sure that troubles most people."

"Yes, it certainly does. What about you, Sebastian?"

"Me? I've never had to worry about that, Doc. The list has always been the same for me."

"You're a lucky man."

"I am," Sebastian said, doing his best to get more comfortable. "But right now, I'm thirsty. Do me a favor and go pack a big glass with ice then fill her up."

"You got it," I said, heading inside where I found Mary stirring a pot on the stove. "Is he still eating?"

"This is chicken broth with some vitamins dissolved in it," she said. "It's about all he can get down."

"Has he been much trouble?" I said, preparing Sebastian's drink.

"He's remarkably consistent," she said. "And a delightful man. Even when he drinks," she said, nodding at the glass of Jameson I was holding.

"This probably isn't good for him," I said.

"It makes him happy, Doc. And who are we to judge, right?"

"Yeah," I said, immediately putting the question out of my mind. "Thanks for all your help, Mary."

"It's the least I can do for him," she said, gently stirring the pot.

I headed back outside and held the glass close to his mouth. He grabbed it with both hands and shakily raised it. He got a mouthful down without spilling too much, then took a smaller sip. I set the glass down on the table and wiped his mouth with a tissue.

"Ah, thank you," Sebastian said with a contented sigh as he settled back into bed. "Nectar of the gods, Doc. Nectar of the gods. I hope they serve it where I'm going."

"I'm sure they will, Sebastian," I said with a chuckle. "Look, I need to run. Willy's mom is stopping by the house. But I'll be back for the sunset."

"It should be a good one," he said, then pointed at the glass. "One more for the road, if you don't mind."

**

Willy's mother was already at the house when I arrived. She and Felicia were sitting on the gallery chatting. I gave Felicia a small kiss then extended my hand to Mrs. Johnson.

"I'm sorry I'm a bit late," I said, sitting down at the table. "I had to check in on Sebastian."

"How's he doing today?" Felicia said.

"All things considered, pretty good," I said, then focused on the woman who was a wearing a floral-print dress and an expectant look. "Thanks for stopping by, Mrs. Johnson."

"Felicia said you have an update for me," she said, clutching her purse.

"I do," I said, nodding. "We found the man who killed your son."

"And?" she said, leaning forward.

"He's gone."

"Will he be coming back?" she whispered.

"No."

She studied my face, eventually understood my message then nodded.

"Why did he kill my Willy?"

"Because somebody paid him a lot of money to do it," I said.

"But why?" she said, her eyes begging for an explanation.

"I'm afraid Willy did the wrong thing to the wrong man," I said.

"But what on earth could he have done to cause that?" she said.

"He stole something very valuable."

"Was it drugs?" she said, giving me a look that made it clear she was afraid of my answer.

"Yes, it was. It's a drug called Fentanyl. It's very dangerous. Actually, I consider it poison."

"Was Willy using this drug?" she said.

"I don't know the answer to that question, Mrs. Johnson," I said, then decided to offer her a lifeline that might enable her memories to not be completely crushed.

"But I'm willing to bet he did it primarily for the money. He probably wanted to buy you something nice."

"He liked to talk about how someday he was going to buy me a new house," she whispered.

"That was probably it," I said, then glanced at Felicia.

"Yes," Felicia said, nodding. "That sounds like something Willy would do."

"And the man who paid the other man to kill my Willy. Have you found him?"

"We have," I said softly.

"And?"

"He'll also be gone soon," I said.

"Good," she said, wiping her eyes with a handful of tissues. "Thank you. Both of you."

"You're very welcome, Mrs. Johnson," I said. "I just wish there was something else we could do."

"Me too," she said, her shoulders trembling. "Are you sure I can't give you some money?"

"We're positive," I said. "That won't be necessary, Mrs. Johnson."

"It doesn't seem right," she said, shaking her head.

"Neither was Willy's murder," I said, patting her hand. "Let us know if there's anything else you need."

"Just take care of the monster who had my son killed," she said, slowly working her way out of the chair.

"You can count on that, Mrs. Johnson."

"I'll walk you to your car," Felicia said, holding one of her arms and leading her toward the steps.

"Goodbye, Mr. White," she said, glancing back at me.

"I hope you have a nice evening."

"Hah," she grunted as she grabbed the railing and slowly made her way down the stairs.

My phone buzzed and I checked the number and answered immediately.

"Hey, Merlin."

"What's up, Doc?"

"You tell me."

"I just got a call from our guy. Greedy is anchored offshore near Turks and Caicos."

"Good. How far offshore?"

"Far enough. Our guy wants to know if he should go in tonight or wait until morning."

I gave it some thought before answering.

"Tell him to wait until morning. Let Greedy enjoy his last night. And it'll make it easier for the cleanup crew."

"Okay. I'll have him call you as soon as he's ready."

"Perfect. Thanks, Merlin," I said, then had another thought. "How deep is the water where Greedy's anchored?"

"Who do I look like? Jacques Cousteau?"

"Never mind."

"Hey, I almost forgot to ask. Have you talked to Elle?"

"I have. I let her go."

"I knew you were going to do that," he said, laughing.

"You did, huh?" I said, annoyed by both his tone and prescience. "But I cleaned her out first."

"Ouch," Merlin said. "But I'm sure she'll survive it. How did things go in Miami?"

"Quickly."

"Glad to hear it. Another one bites the dust, huh?"

"Yeah, one down, several million to go. Talk to you later."

I set my phone down just as Felicia returned. She stood next to me slowly shaking her head.

"That was a tough conversation," she said.

"They don't get any tougher. She's such a nice woman."

"She's a sweetheart. But left to deal with a huge hole in her heart. Who was on the phone?"

"Merlin. Greedy has landed. We'll need to get an early start in the morning."

"Okay," she said, sitting down at the table. She wiped the sweat off her brow then used two fingers to pull her tee shirt away from her skin. "Geez, it's so hot and sticky today." She glanced around the gallery then looked back at me. "You feel like taking a shower?"

"Right now?"

"Yeah, I really need to do something a little more life-affirming."

CHAPTER 35

Brewster Greedy looked up from his phone to ogle the three women sunbathing on the bow. He refocused on the phone, scrolled through his unopened emails then set the phone down and stretched his arms over his head. He spotted the captain heading his way.

"Hey, Mr. Greedy."

"Hey, Skip," Greedy said, sitting up and draping a leg over his knee. "What's up?"

"I was just wondering if you want to come with me today," Skipper Kurt said. "I thought I might do a little exploring onshore."

"No, thanks. I'm just gonna hang out here," Greedy said, nodding and grinning at the sunbathers.

"Got it," Skipper Kurt said with a chuckle as he studied the women. "Which one?"

"I'm not sure," Greedy said with a shrug. "Maybe all three."

"I want your life."

"Good luck with that," Greedy said. "I thought we'd head out tomorrow morning."

"No problem," Skipper Kurt said, then spotted a boat heading straight for them. "I think we've got company."

Greedy sat up and grabbed his binoculars.

"Coast Guard?" Greedy said with a frown. "What the hell are they doing down here?"

"They've got some sort of cooperation agreement with the government," Skipper Kurt said. "Keeping an eye on the people running drugs, primarily."

"And they've got nothing better to do than bother people like me?" Greedy said, lowering the glasses.

Skipper Kurt shrugged as he kept a close eye on the vessel that was getting closer.

"Go see what they want," Greedy said.

He watched as the skipper headed for the stern and leaned over the railing. Greedy heard their muffled conversation, but couldn't decipher the content. A few minutes later, Skipper Kurt returned and spread his arms, obviously confused.

"They want to come aboard, Mr. Greedy."

"What on earth for?" Greedy said, getting to his feet.

"They didn't say."

"Damn it," Greedy snapped, then gave it some thought. "Well, I guess we don't have much choice, huh? Tell them to come aboard." Greedy glanced around the boat then his eyes settled on the sunbathers who were sitting up, confused by the intrusion. "You ladies might want to put your tops on."

Greedy strolled to the stern and watched as a uniformed man reached the top step of the ladder then hopped onto the deck. He glanced down at the Coast Guard boat and spotted two other men staring up at him. Greedy gave them a small wave then focused on the officer now standing directly in front of him.

"Are you Brewster Greedy?" the man said.

"That's me," Greedy chirped as he extended his hand. "And you are?"

"Captain Steel," he said, returning the handshake before looking around. "Man, what a boat."

"Thank you," Greedy said, then cleared his throat.

"Of course. Let me get right to it. I'm sorry to interrupt."

"Not a problem, Captain," Greedy said, studying the man's face closely. "How can I help you?"

"I'm afraid we have a bit of a problem, sir," Captain Steel said, spotting the women who were heading in his direction.

"What kind of problem?" Greedy said through a cold stare.

"These ladies are part of your crew?"

"They are," Greedy said.

"Are there others?" Captain Steel said, smiling at the blonde.

"There are two more. Why do you ask?" Greedy said.

"Could you please ask them to come up on deck?" Captain Steel said.

Greedy continued to stare at the Coast Guard officer then nodded at his skipper who immediately headed down a set of stairs.

"What's this all about, Captain?" Greedy said.

"We received an anonymous call this morning, sir."

"What about?"

"According to our tip, one of your crew members is wanted," Captain Steel said.

"Wanted for what?"

"The caller didn't go into a lot of detail, sir. But there are apparently some immigration issues along with several outstanding warrants."

All three of the sunbathers glanced at each other and began a hushed conversation. Skipper Kurt returned, trailed by the two bodyguards. They stood next to Greedy, confused.

"An immigration problem?" Greedy said, now completely relaxed. "I'm sure there's been some sort of mistake, Captain."

"I'm sure you're right, sir. But we do need to follow up on the tip."

"Of course," Greedy said, then grinned as he glanced around at his crew. "Okay, fess up. Which one of you has been naughty?"

All six members of the crew laughed.

"Go right ahead, Captain," Greedy said, sweeping an arm out in invitation. "Check their passports. Do whatever you need to do."

"I'm afraid I'm going to have to ask all of you to come with us to shore," Captain Steel said.

"What?" Greedy said, scowling.

"We'll need to coordinate with the local police on the island," Captain Steel said.

"Really?" Greedy said, his temper flaring. "You really need to ruin our day like that?"

"I'm sorry, sir," Captain Steel said. "I'm afraid I must insist."

"And if I don't feel like cooperating with this total invasion of our privacy?" Greedy said.

"Well, I suppose we could impound your boat until all this gets sorted out," Captain Steel said through a crocodile smile.

Greedy gnawed on his bottom lip as he gave the threat some thought. Then he shrugged it off.

"No, there's no need to do that, Captain," he said, glancing around at his crew. "Okay, let's get this over with." He turned back to Captain Steel. "Do you need me to come along?"

"No, sir," Captain Steel said. "We know who you are. You're welcome to stay here. In fact, I'd recommend that."

"You would?" Greedy said, immediately suspicious. "Why?"

"Oh, you know, just so no one gets any ideas about coming aboard while you're gone. You never know what might happen, right?"

"Yeah, you can't trust anybody these days," Greedy said, then nodded to himself. "This has got my wife's name written all over it. She just had to ruin my trip."

"If you'll all grab your identification and phones, we'll get going," Captain Steel said, addressing the crew. "Hopefully, it won't take long to clear this up."

All six went below deck.

"Where are you headed, Mr. Greedy?"

"Miami," Greedy said. "I'm surprised to see the Coast Guard down here."

"Well, we do a lot of work with the local police," Captain Steel.

"Trying to stop the scourge of drugs being smuggled into the country, right?" Greedy said.

"Yes, sir. It's a major problem."

"Are you having much success?" Greedy said.

"Ah, good days, bad days. You know the drill," Captain Steel said.

"Well, thank you for your service, Captain," Greedy said, rocking back and forth on his heels.

"I appreciate it, sir," Captain Steel said. "These traffickers can be very clever and tough to catch."

"I'm sure they are," Greedy said with a grin.

"Fortunately, they're not as smart as they think they are," Captain Steel said, returning the smile.

"Well, I'm sure you'll figure it out, Captain."

"There's no doubt about it, sir. In fact, I'm anticipating a major breakthrough any moment."

**

After dropping everyone off onshore, Carl drove off, headed for another section of the island then pulled into another dock and tied the boat off. He strolled to the other end and hopped into the boat waiting for him.

"How did it go?"

"Like clockwork," Carl said, putting on a different shirt before reaching for his phone. He made the call.

"This is Doc."

"Hey, Doc. It's Carl."

"Hey, man. How have you been?"

"Great. You?"

"No complaints," Doc said. "How did it go?"

"You're all set," Carl said. "When we left, Greedy was alone and pouting. I think I ruined his day."

"He hasn't seen anything yet," Doc said. "What did you do with the crew?"

"I had my guys walk them into the police station," Carl said. "Then they left them there."

"I imagine they're pretty confused by now," Doc said, laughing.

"Yeah, but at least they're alive, right?"

"Thanks for doing this, Carl. I appreciate it."

"No problem," Carl said. "I lost a cousin last year to that crap."

"Sorry to hear that," Doc said. "So, I'm good to go?"

"Whenever you're ready."

"Good. Hey, where did you get the boat?"

"I stole it," Carl said.

"You stole a Coast Guard cutter?"

"What am I, an idiot? Nah, I stole a boat that looks like a cutter then painted it. Merlin tells me you're working as a PI."

"I am," Doc said.

"Whatever floats your boat, Doc," Carl said with a laugh. "Okay, if you need anything else, Merlin knows where to find me."

"Thanks again, Carl."

"Happy trails," Carl said, ending the call. He looked over at the driver and pointed out to sea.

"Where to?" the driver said.

"The opposite direction from where we just came."

**

I set my phone down and took a sip of coffee. Felicia looked up from her computer screen.

"Was that the guy?"

"It was. We're all set," I said.

"Who is he?"

"Just a guy we've done some work with in the past," I said.

"Another ex-spy?"

"Sort of," I said with a shrug. "His situation is a little complicated to explain. You want to hear the story?"

"Thanks, but I'll pass," Felicia said. "I think I might need as much plausible deniability as I can muster."

"You worry too much," I said, reaching for my phone.

"You sure you want to do this?" she said, getting up to sit down next to me.

"I'm positive," I said, making solid eye contact with her.

"Okay," she said, nodding.

I scrolled through my phone, located the number then made the call.

**

Greedy scowled up at the sun that was covering his iPad screen with glare then headed for the stern. He stretched out, sipped his scotch and water then glanced at his phone when it buzzed. He checked the number then answered.

"Hey, Sweetie," Greedy said, sitting up. "What's going on?"

"I don't have a clue," the woman said. "The Coast Guard guys dropped us off at the police station then disappeared."

"They probably decided to let the cops handle things," Greedy said.

"That's what we thought. At first," she said.

"What do you mean?"

"The cops saw us sitting in the waiting room and asked what the heck we were doing there."

"What?" Greedy said, frowning.

"Yeah, it's totally weird," she said. "So, we were wondering if you could hop in the runabout and come get us."

"You're sure the cops don't want to talk to you?" Greedy said as his mind raced in several directions.

"Positive," she said. "They don't know anything about an immigration problem."

"Okay," Greedy said softly. "Hang on, I'll meet you at the main dock as soon as I can get there."

"Thanks, Brew," she said. "Remind me to thank you later."

"Yeah, I'll do that," Greedy said, his head preoccupied with other thoughts.

He ended the call without saying goodbye and began pacing back and forth on the deck. His phone buzzed again, and he answered it on the first ring.

"Brewster Greedy."

"Hey, Brewster."

"Who is this?"

"It's Doc White."

"Doc?" Brewster said, frowning. "How can I help you?"

"I just wanted to say goodbye."

"What?" Greedy said. "You're leaving the island?"

"No, actually I just got back," he said.

"My wife is right," Greedy said. "You are an odd duck."

"Guilty."

"What's on your mind, Doc? You have questions about ways to win the Dragon Lady back?"

"No, that door is officially closed. We've both moved on."

"Smart choice," Greedy said. "Have you seen her lately?"

"I think she headed off island," Doc said.

"Interesting. Why are you calling?"

"Like I said, Brewster, to say goodbye."

"You must specialize in circular conversations," Greedy said, sitting down.

"I wish I could say I was going to miss you."

"Oh, I see," Greedy said, laughing. "So, I'm the one who's leaving?"

"You are."

"And where am I going, Doc?"

"Naraka."

"Naraka? Is that somewhere in the Caribbean?" Greedy said, scratching his head.

"Yeah, I suppose you could say that," Doc said, laughing. "I hear it's one of those places that is everywhere, yet nowhere."

"As long as it's warm, right?" Greedy said. "Is there a point to this conversation, Doc?"

"Not really. Like I said, I just called to say goodbye."

"I'm afraid I have better things to do with my time, Doc."

"Really?" Doc said. "Given the fact that your crew is onshore, I thought you'd have tons of time to chat."

Greedy stared at the phone before continuing.

"How the hell did you know that?"

"The same way I know there's a special surprise waiting for you below deck," Doc said.

"What are you talking about?"

"The extra case," Doc said. "Three hundred is such a round number."

360

"Extra case?" Greedy said, his eyes growing wide. "What's in it?"

"Boom-boom. And I'm not talking about a dirty diaper."

"What?" Greedy whispered.

"Goodbye, Brewster. You've got thirty seconds."

The call ended and a wave of panic washed over him. Greedy tore down the steps that led to the lower deck, then another smaller flight that led to the hold. He came to a stop and glanced at the rows of boxes that were neatly stacked and secured in place by a mesh netting. Then he heard a loud, distinct click.

"No," he whispered.

It was the last word that ever passed his lips.

CHAPTER 36

I stretched out on the new double-lounger and draped an arm over Felicia's shoulders. She snuggled in tight and stared out at the harbor.

"Beautiful day," I said.

"Yeah, this is nice," she said, trailing her fingers up and down my arm.

We sat up when we saw the police cruiser heading up the driveway.

"There he is," I said. "Right on time."

We got up and watched the police chief as he walked toward the gallery. He climbed the stairs then shook hands and exchanged greetings with both of us.

"Have a seat, Chief," I said, gesturing at the table. "Would you like something to drink?"

"No, I'm good, thanks," he said, glancing back and forth at us. "You needed to see me?"

"Yes. We wanted to let you know that you can close the case on Willy's murder," I said.

"I see," he said, raising an eyebrow. "Why can I do that?"

"Because the guy who shot Willy is dead."

"Can I ask how you know that?" the chief said.

"Sure," I said. "He got shot."

"Where?" the chief said.

"Right between the eyes," I said.

"Actually, I was referring to the location, but thanks for the detail," the chief said, chuckling.

"It happened in Miami," I said.

"You were in Miami?" the chief said.

"I was."

"Doing what?"

"Looking for the shooter," I said with a shrug. "Unfortunately, he was already dead by the time I got there."

"Yes, I'm sure it was tragic for you," the chief said, again glancing back and forth at us. "Who was he?"

"A contract hitter," I said. "Turns out, he used to be a member of the Moscow Circus."

"Let me guess, a stilt-walker."

"Yes."

"Did the shooter tell you that?" the chief deadpanned.

"Nice try, Chief," I said with a laugh. "No, one of our associates uncovered that little nugget."

"An associate. Who might that be?"

"It might be any number of people, Chief," I said.

He stared at me for several moments before nodding.

"Fair enough," he said. "Have you had a chance to update Willy's mom?"

"We have," Felicia said.

"Such a stupid and tragic loss," he said softly, then shook it off. "You have a wonderful view from up here."

"Thanks. Yes, we like it," I said.

"You know, I had an interesting phone call this morning from a colleague on Turks and Caicos," the chief said.

"I've never been there," I said. "But I hear it's nice."

"It is," the chief said. "Yes, a most interesting call indeed."

"Well, don't keep us in suspense, Chief," I said.

"Brewster Greedy's sailboat blew up yesterday afternoon," he said, again glancing back and forth at us, gauging our reaction.

"Blew up?" Felicia said. "Where?"

"It was anchored about a half mile offshore," the chief said.

"Wow," I said. "Was Greedy on the boat?"

"He was," the chief said. "And oddly, he was by himself."

364

"His crew was probably onshore buying tee shirts," I said. "I guess they were lucky, huh?"

"Yes, I suppose they were," the chief said.

"Did they find Greedy's body?" Felicia said.

"They found a few pieces."

"Yuk," Felicia said, scowling.

"And the boat?" I said.

"My colleague said he'd never seen anything quite like it before," the chief said. "Millions of tiny shards of fiberglass."

"It must have been a huge explosion," I said, glancing at Felicia.

"Yeah, enormous," she said, nodding.

"I wonder if Fentanyl is flammable," I said, looking at the chief.

"I believe it is," the chief said. "Especially at high temperatures."

"There you go," I said. "It probably served as an accelerant."

"I can't think of a better use for that stuff," Felicia said.

"And the Fentanyl?" I said.

"It's all gone," the chief said. "But I'm sure it's doing some damage to the fish."

"That's too bad," I said, frowning. "Still better than having thousands of kids eating that crap."

"You're right," the chief said. "And you knew nothing about this?"

"What? About Greedy's boat blowing up?" I said, scowling at him. "Geez, Chief. Who the heck do you think I am?"

"I'm still trying to figure that out, Doc," he said.

"Well, I guess someone saved the FBI a ton of work," I said.

"I never bothered to call them," the chief said.

"Why not?" I said, surprised.

"I didn't want to waste their time on a false alarm," the chief said with a shrug.

"You're a man of great insight, Chief," I said, then looked at Felicia. "We never got around to calling them either, did we?"

"No, it must have slipped our minds," she said.

"Okay," the chief said, nodding. "This conversation went pretty much the way I thought it would."

"You sound disappointed, Chief," I said.

"No," he said, shaking his head. "I'm not."

"Thanks for stopping by," I said.

"I do have one more thing to discuss," he said.

"Okay," I said.

He turned to Felicia.

"Since the incident out on the water, I find myself with an opening," the chief said.

"So?" she said, sitting back in her chair.

"I was wondering if you'd like to come back to work."

"Not a chance," Felicia said without hesitation. "Sorry, Chief. Not gonna happen."

"Another conversation that plays out as expected," he said, nodding. "I understand, Felicia. But I felt compelled to ask." He pushed his chair back and stood up. "I suppose I should be thanking both of you."

"For what?" I said.

"I think we all know the answer to that question, Doc."

"I'm not following you, Chief. I'm afraid you lost me." I glanced at Felicia. "Do you know what he's talking about?"

"Not a clue," she said, shaking her head.

"I'll show myself out," the chief said. "I take it you plan on staying on the island, Doc."

"Absolutely," I said. "At least for the foreseeable future."

"Then I suppose I'll be seeing you around," the chief said.

"It is a small island," I said.

"Indeed. Not a lot of places to hide."

"You know where to find me, Chief."

We exchanged a handshake then he headed off with a small wave. We stretched back out on the lounger and resumed our previous position.

"You think he believed us?" Felicia said, nestling her head against my chest.

"Not a chance," I said. "He's too good of a cop."

"Yeah, I suppose he is," she said. "Do you think we'll be working with him in the future?"

"Only when we have to."

EPILOGUE

Sebastian's funeral was held on a steamy,
hot afternoon under a cloudless cobalt sky. Attendance was
sparse. A soft breeze out of the west did its best to
minimize the heat, but beads of sweat formed on my face
and arms as soon as I left the air-conditioned comfort of my
car. I made the short walk to the gravesite where Pastor
Samuelson, a young, imported priest was shuffling back
and forth on his feet surreptitiously checking his watch.
Surrounding him were four somber people who remained
silent as they looked at the casket then down into the
freshly dug hole.

Makes you wonder, doesn't it?

I shook my head at the voice. I would deal with the
implications of my own mortality later. Today was for
Sebastian.

I came to a stop and looked around and nodded at the
other mourners. My eyes landed on a woman and stayed
there. She nodded back in recognition, and a small smile
formed then disappeared. I didn't know the three elderly
men who gave me the once-over, apparently surprised to
see me here.

"Good afternoon," the priest whispered when he caught my eye.

"Good afternoon, Pastor."

The priest finally gave in and stared at his watch. Then he cleared his throat and announced to no one in particular, "I suppose we should get started."

He began with a short prayer then spoke in vague generalities about God's will and the well-lived life of a man he obviously hadn't known. When he finished, he glanced around and asked if anyone wanted to say anything. We all shook our heads, and the priest shrugged and concluded with a short, final prayer.

"Thank you all for coming," the priest said as he resumed his shuffle. "I'm sure Sebastian is looking down and thanking you."

This guy can't wait to get out of here. Or he needs to pee.

I stifled a smile as I focused on the priest who was organizing himself for departure.

"Feel free to remain as long as you wish," he said. "The workers will wait to…well, you know, until you have finished paying your final respects."

I gave the priest a small wave as he headed for his car. Then I approached Felicia's grandmother who remained at the edge of the grave staring down into the darkness.

"Good afternoon, Mrs. Smith."

"Good afternoon, Doc," she said without looking up.

"I didn't know you were friends with Sebastian."

"We were acquaintances," she said softly. "We both grew up on the island. I've known him…forever." She stared off into the distance as the breeze kicked up. "He was a nice man. Odd, but a gentle soul."

"He was nice. I'm not qualified to be the judge of odd."

"But you recognize it in yourself and others when you see it, right?" she said, her eyes twinkling as she finally made eye contact.

"You've been talking to Felicia, haven't you?" I said, grinning at her.

"All the time. And I need to thank you for what you've done. She's finally come out of the blackness."

"I didn't really do much," I said. "Apart from giving her a job."

"Don't be modest, Doc. And it's a meaningful job," she said, squeezing my hand to emphasize her point. "She's very fond of you."

371

"The feeling is mutual, Mrs. Smith."

"I know. But please promise me you'll keep treating her well.

"That's certainly my plan. Do you need a ride home?"

"No, Felicia is picking me up," she said, reaching into her purse for her phone. "She said she was coming to the funeral. I hope nothing has happened. Stop by the restaurant, Doc. I'll make you something special."

"You always do, Mrs. Smith," I said, accepting her hug. "I'll see you soon."

She broke our embrace and took another long look down into the grave. Then she seemed to shudder as if chilled.

"Do you ever think about death, Doc?"

"Far too often."

"At my age, I must admit to being a bit preoccupied with the notion. I should have been a Rastafarian," she said, again glancing down. Then she noticed my confused expression. "They believe in reincarnation. As such, there's never a need for funerals. Are you a religious man, Doc?"

"I'm a Buddhist."

"Another believer in reincarnation," she said, nodding. "Good for you. There's never enough time to get everything done in one lifetime."

"I can't argue with that, Mrs. Smith."

"What would you like to come back as?"

"A jazz pianist," I said with a shrug. "Or maybe a Golden Retriever."

She gave it some thought then chuckled. "Well, good luck with that." She headed off with a small wave.

I watched her depart, then noticed one of the three old men still standing next to Sebastian's grave. I slowly approached and cleared my throat to get his attention.

"Good afternoon."

"Good afternoon," he said, making solid eye contact.

"You were one of Sebastian's friends?"

"Yes, I was. From a very young age," he said, nodding. "I'm Wilbur."

"Doc. Doc White," I said, accepting his outstretched hand.

"The neighbor?" he said, raising an eyebrow.

"Yes, he lived next door. I'd only known him a few months."

"The soup man," Wilbur said. "He mentioned you the last time we spoke."

"I did bring him soup," I said. "Near the end, it was about all he could eat. I don't think I've ever seen you around."

"I live with my daughter in Miami," he said with a shrug. "She worries about me. And she wouldn't stop nagging until I finally agreed to move off island. Says this is not the place to be when you get old and sick." He glanced around and sighed. "I do miss the place."

"So, you're just here for the funeral?"

"I am," Wilbur said. "When we last spoke, Sebastian said it wouldn't be long. Unfortunately, I didn't get here in time."

As was often the case, unable to come up with anything better, I merely mumbled, "I'm sorry."

"It's okay," he said, exhaling emotion. "We had a nice long talk on the phone."

"Who are the other men?"

"Probably old drinking buddies. I don't know them."

"Sebastian didn't like to talk too much about himself," I said. "He really didn't have any family?"

"No."

Then he fixed a hard stare on me that made me uncomfortable.

"I drove by his house yesterday," Wilbur said. "I couldn't resist taking a trip down…what is it called, memory lane?"

"That's it."

"The house is a wreck."

"It does need some work," I said.

"When we talked, Sebastian told me the soup man was buying it."

"Yes. I am."

"So, you can knock it down and add some extra lawn? Or maybe put in a pool?"

"No, I won't be doing that," I whispered.

"I'm sorry. That sounded harsh. Judgmental," Wilbur said. "Over the years, I became a bit mistrustful of people such as yourself who move here."

"You mean, white people?"

His eyes flared briefly then immediately softened as a small smile emerged.

"Yes. Again, I'm sorry," he said softly.

"Don't worry about it. I often share the same thoughts."

"I see," he said, studying my face. "So, what will you do with the house?"

"I'm giving it to a friend."

"Just like that?"

"Pretty much," I said. "Can I ask you a question?"

"I can't imagine that could do any harm."

"What was Sebastian like when he was young?"

"Oh, he was remarkable," Wilbur said, his eyes wide and bright. "We called him the Lobster Man."

"Okay," I said, confused.

"We used to dive for lobsters when we were kids. That was so long ago," Wilbur said, his eyes fixed on the casket. "Sebastian could dive deeper than any of us. I still don't know how he managed to hold his breath that long. And he always came up with at least one lobster."

"And then he started fishing commercially, right?"

"He did," Wilbur said. "And drinking."

"He said he stopped when he turned eighty," I said.

"He tried. And had some success. His doctor told him he didn't have a choice. But quitting bought him an extra ten years."

"Sebastian said that if he'd known he was going to live to ninety, he probably wouldn't have ever stopped."

"Yes. He called it the longest decade. It was one of his constant complaints," Wilbur said, brushing a willowy strand of hair away from his face. "But he lived long and well. In my book, that says everything. Tell me, Doc. What brought you to St. Croix?"

"I thought I was looking for a woman."

"Thought? I take it you were wrong?"

"I was."

"But you still bought property here. Do you enjoy the water?"

"Only in my scotch," I said. "Over the years, I've discovered I have enough trouble surviving on dry land."

"I see," he said with a chuckle. "Will you be staying on the island?"

"I think so. I guess it depends."

"Be careful, Doc," Wilbur said with a grin. "The place sneaks up on you. It gets in your blood." He took one final look at the casket and the grave then sighed. "I need to run. My flight back to Miami leaves soon."

"It was nice meeting you, Wilbur."

"You as well, Doc. And thank you for taking such good care of my friend."

"I just wish I could have done more."

"I'm sure you did everything possible," Wilbur said. "Leave the regrets to others. Just live long and well, Doc. It's the best revenge."

"I'll try to remember that."

I walked next to him as we headed for our vehicles. Felicia's car came to a stop next to a large tree where her grandmother was waiting in the shade. Felicia got out and helped her into the passenger seat. Then she placed her hands on her hips and smiled as she watched me approach.

"I'm sorry I'm late," she said. "The lawyer didn't have the paperwork ready when I got there."

"Did you get everything signed?" I said.

"I did," she said, giving me a hug. "I'm now a homeowner with a mortgage."

"Pay me back when you can," I said, waving it off.

"Let's save that conversation for another time, Doc," she said, glancing at the gravesite. "I can't believe I missed the funeral."

"Don't worry about it. You said your goodbyes the other night."

"How did it go?" she said.

"It was pretty uneventful," I said. "He must have outlived all his friends."

"Ninety will do that," she said with a shrug. "What are you doing tonight?"

"No plans."

"Good. Then you're coming with me," Felicia said. "Follow me to Gram's place."

"Where are we going?"

"I thought we'd go for a boat ride," she said, opening the driver's side door.

"At night?"

"Don't tell me you're afraid of the dark, Doc."

"It's not the dark," I said. "It's all the creatures that can eat me if I fall in."

"You're such a baby. C'mon. You're going to like this."

I followed her as she made the short drive to the house. After getting her grandmother settled in, she climbed into the passenger seat and glanced over at me.

"You remember how to get to my boat?"

"I do," I said, backing out of the driveway.

We drove in silence until Felicia spoke without looking at me.

"I think Grams felt forced to take a good look at her own mortality today."

"She's got years left."

"We can only hope," Felicia said softly, then brightened. "This is going to be so much fun."

"Where are we going?"

"Buck Island," she said, glancing over. "We're going to count baby turtles."

"We are?"

"Actually, we'll be watching the people who are doing the counting."

"I thought access was limited during the hatch season," I said.

"I got a visitor pass," she said. "From a friend."

"Well, look at you. I guess it helps to be a local, huh?"

"It certainly doesn't hurt," she said with a shrug.

I turned onto the road that led to a dock where her boat sat gently bobbing in the breeze. We climbed out and made our way down the small incline. She untied the lines then hopped onto the boat and waved me on. Then she fired up the engine, and we slowly made our way out to sea. I forced myself to relax and did my best to enjoy the onset of the sunset turning the sky a darker blue tinged with wispy orange and yellow streaks.

"Have you done this before?" I said. "You know, counting turtles?"

"Many times," she said, glancing over briefly before focusing on the water directly in front of us. "I used to volunteer when I was a kid. Now, every time I see an adult turtle in the water, it takes me back."

"How's that?"

"It's hard to explain," Felicia said as she eased the throttle back. "I guess it's because all the adult turtles have managed to survive against some very long odds. For some reason, I find hope in that."

"Most of the babies don't make it to adulthood?"

"Probably less than one percent," she said.

380

"Not good."

"Indeed. Mother Nature presents some difficult challenges. To all of us. But I don't have to explain the concept of predators to you."

"No, I've got that one pretty well worked out," I said. "What goes after the baby turtles?"

"Birds. Mongoose," she said, glancing over with a shrug. "And that's before they even make it to the water. I need to go over a few things with you."

"Why's that?"

"Because you're a rescuer."

"Is that what I am?" I said, laughing.

"Very much so. Among other things," she said as a statement of fact. "Rule number one, don't try to help the turtles. They need to be left alone. Except if you see one heading the wrong way. Then you can pick it up and point it in the right direction a few feet from the water. Other than that, it's hands off. And no bright lights or flash photography. It disorients the turtles. So, no selfies."

"I can handle that."

"We'll see," she said, putting the boat in neutral. "I'm going to anchor offshore. We'll wade in from here."

"If I get eaten by a shark, it's on you," I said, glancing over the side.

"I'll take my chances," Felicia said, tossing the anchor into the water. She removed her sandals then hoisted herself out of the boat. "Are you coming or not?"

I followed her and felt the warm water envelop my legs. As I trudged through the shallow sea, I glanced out at the final vestiges of the sunset. The shadows were long and stretched out over the beach. When I reached solid ground, I noticed a man walking toward us with a huge smile. He came to a stop and gave Felicia a warm embrace.

"Good evening. You made it."

"Good evening. We did," she said. "How are you, Jimmy?"

"Just great," he said, glancing at me. "Good evening. I'm Jimmy."

"Good evening. I'm Doc. It's nice to meet you."

"Jimmy works with Parks and Wildlife and runs the turtle program," Felicia said. "How is it going this year?"

"So far, so good," he said, glancing up and down the long stretch of sand. "Did you go over the rules with Doc?"

"I did," she said. "Hands off. Unless."

"Perfect," Jimmy said. "Look, I have a couple of new folks I need to go over some stuff with before we get started tonight. Maybe I'll see you guys before you leave. Have fun."

"Thanks, Jimmy," Felicia said, watching him as he turned and headed off. "He's so good."

"Interesting work," I said, then spotted several small objects doing their best to scoot across the sand. "Is that them?"

"That's them," Felicia said, staring at the approaching parade of baby turtles. "Cute, huh?"

"It's amazing," I said, continuing to study their journey toward the water. "Shouldn't someone be counting them?"

"They'll count the tracks in the sand," she said.

I nodded as I continued to watch the turtles' progress in the fading light. One of the babies left behind by the others caught my eye, and I nudged Felicia's shoulder to get her attention.

"Is that normal?" I said, studying the struggling turtle. "It keeps veering off to the right."

"It looks like one of his front flippers is deformed," she said. "Poor little guy. I don't like his chances."

Then I spotted a large bird gliding in low just above the sand.

"That pelican is making a beeline for him," I said.

"I hate this part," she whispered.

I checked the position of the fading sun then took a few steps toward the baby turtle.

"Doc. What are you doing?"

"Just stretching my legs."

"Why don't I believe you?"

The baby turtle was only a few feet from the water as it continued to veer right. The pelican sunk even lower and spread its wings to the max. I took a few more steps then waved my arms over my head. The sweep of my shadow caught the pelican's attention, and the bird turned and soared skyward. But it immediately began a circling pattern.

"You're not much of a rule follower, are you?"

"I didn't touch him."

"I guess we can let it slide this time," she said with a laugh. "What is it with you and damaged things?"

She does ask good questions.

I looked back and forth from the turtle who was nearing the water's edge to the pelican that was again bearing down on its prey. I focused on the tiny, struggling creature and willed it into the water.

"Run, you little bugger. Run."

I hope you enjoyed *Getting Greedy*, the first installment in my new mystery/crime series, **Doc White Adventures**. Stay tuned for the next book in the series.

For those of you who haven't come across my popular, **The Thousand Islands Doggy Inn Mysteries**, I thought I'd give you a sneak preview at the first book in the series, *The Case of the Abandoned Aussie.* It's a terrific series and if you love dogs, good food, and smart, funny women, you're going to love the books. But I'm already twenty-three books into the series, so you have some catching up to do.

Thanks again for all your ongoing support, and I continue to be blessed with a wonderful group of readers. You guys are the best!

Bernie

The Case of the

Abandoned Aussie

A Thousand Islands Doggy Inn Mystery

CHAPTER 1

Oh, hi.

You caught me by surprise. I was right in the middle of trying to land this smallmouth bass and didn't see you right away.

But I'm delighted you decided to drop in for a visit. And as we like to tell everyone who chooses to stop by our little slice of heaven; thanks for coming and we hope you enjoy your stay.

And since it looks like we're going to be spending some time together, I suppose the best place to start is with me telling you a bit about myself.

First, let's get some of the easy stuff out of the way. My name is Suzy Chandler, and I live in one of the most beautiful locations in the world. It's a magical place called the Thousand Islands that's located on the St. Lawrence River. Now that I think about it, the islands are actually located *in* the River.

But that's probably a distinction without a real difference.

For some of the more geographically challenged, the St. Lawrence connects the Great Lakes to the Atlantic Ocean, a distance about 750 miles and it forms a large portion of the U.S. and Canadian border. But for us who live on either side of the River, when you're out on your boat, the border between our two countries is another one of those distinctions without a real difference.

But just trying telling that to the Coast Guard or Immigration if you happen to get stopped.

The town I live in is, like most small towns, friendly, relatively close-knit, and prone to gossip. During the summer months, the population of Clay Bay, our little town of about 2,000 people often triples due to the influx of tourists and island residents. But when winter arrives, and they can be long and brutal, only the heartiest of our residents remain.

Many people head south to escape the snow and cold, but I, and I'm not alone here, love the winter. I also appreciate where the River is located. If our region were in a climate that was warm year round, the place would be ruined and probably dominated by high-rise condos and a preponderance of umbrella drinks.

Not that I've got anything against umbrella drinks. Or even high rise condos. They both have their place. But that place isn't here.

The long winter that dominates the River with snow and ice gives it a chance to renew and refresh itself. So it can be ready for the arrival of spring and the annual onslaught of people eager for another summer on the River. I consider the winter renewal essential to the long-term future of the St. Lawrence. Winter also does the same thing for me. Coming out of winter, I am battle-tested and ready for whatever life decides to throw at me.

Regarding the question of how I put food on the table, along with my best friend and business partner, Josie, I run the Thousand Islands Doggy Inn, a place we created to provide dogs with the things they deserve; which is the best of everything. And I should also mention that spending one's workday surrounded by boundless, unconditional love isn't a bad way to go. And I know for a fact that it sure beats accounting. Or being a lawyer.

I'm sure you know that my comment about unconditional love was about dogs. Regarding my personal relationship status, I'm single. In fact, at the moment, I'm not even dating. I'm not particularly happy about that, but not torn up about it either. By now, I thought I'd be settled down, but I haven't had the privilege of meeting Mr. Right. Or if I have, I somehow missed it. I try not to think about that possibility too often. But I remain quietly confident. He's out there somewhere.

At the risk of sounding immodest, I think it's fair to say that other people would consider me good looking. Not drop dead gorgeous like Josie who makes men tend to forget their names just by looking at them, but I can hold my own in mixed company.

What's that? How old am I?

Nice try.

Only my mother knows how old I am, and she isn't talking. Revealing her daughter's age would divulge too much information about her own math problem.

I'm fluent in French, can cook a bit, enjoy good wine and conversation, and I love bad TV, especially any show that deals with solving a mystery.

Oh yeah, as you probably already figured out, I also like to fish.

And since it's the opening day of the bass season that's exactly what I'm doing at the moment.

I cast towards the edge of shallows and immediately saw the tip of my fishing rod begin to bend. The line tightened, I set the hook with a gentle flick of my wrist and began reeling the fish back towards the boat. Josie placed her rod in a holder attached to the transom, grabbed a net, then scooped the smallmouth bass out of the water.

That's one of the things I love about Josie. She's always there to help me out even when she'd rather be doing something else. Like not fishing.

I grabbed the fish, removed the hook, and gently slid it back into the water. It wiggled its tail for traction then disappeared beneath the water.

"That's nine," Josie said. "What's your secret?"

"I always catch what I'm after," I said, winking at her as I cast my line back into the shallows.

"Except men," Josie said, flashing me a small smile.

"Yeah, well, there is that," I said, checking my bait. "Besides, it's opening day. If you can't catch anything today, you don't deserve to call yourself a fisherman."

"Don't you mean fisherwoman?"

"I tried that," I said, shaking my head. "But it sounds weird."

"Fisherperson?"

I laughed.

"That's even worse."

"Well, this fisher-whatever is going back to trolling for muskie."

I watched Josie head to the stern and cast her line off the back of the boat.

"How many times do I have to tell you?" I said. "October and November are the best months to fish for muskie."

"Hey, they have to eat, right?"

I nodded. If there's one thing I don't argue with Josie about; it's eating.

"I'm pretty sure the muskie aren't waiting until October to grab a snack," she continued. "And the idea of catching a fifty-pound fish is more appealing than messing around with bass, no matter how many you catch. Besides, I love a challenge."

"Knock yourself out," I said, reeling in another bass.

"Nice one," Josie said, scooping the fish out of the water with the net. "Oh, I forgot to tell you. Your mother called this morning and said she was going to stop by later this afternoon."

"Great," I said, frowning.

"Another blind date?"

"Undoubtedly," I said.

"Who's up in the rotation?"

"Well, let's see. Recently Mom's gone lawyer, entrepreneur, doctor, executive. So I'm going to guess lawyer."

"You want to do our usual routine?" Josie said, stretching out to enjoy the early morning sun.

"If you're not busy," I said, casting towards the shallows.

"I'm never too busy to watch your love life crash and burn with my own eyes," Josie said, laughing.

"You're one to talk."

"At least I haven't needed any help," Josie said. "My lack of a love life is totally self-inflicted."

"I can ask my mother to fix you up if you like," I said, grinning.

Josie laughed.

"Thanks, but I'll pass. I've seen enough of her taste in men."

My mother.

Just wait until you meet her.

I reeled another bass towards the boat. Again, Josie grabbed the net and scooped the fish out of the water. I removed the hook and gently returned the bass to the water. By now, you've probably figured out that while I'm pretty good at catching fish, I'm even better at letting them go.

My catch and release philosophy stems from one simple fact: I hate the taste of fish.

I know. I've heard it all. Fish is good for me. I should eat more of it. They're packed with protein and nutrients. They keep your brain sharp. Eating fish can help cure depression.

Truth be told, about the only thing I find depressing these days is the prospect of having to eat fish.

Don't even get me started on sushi.

"I'm done," I said, putting my rod away.

I stared out at the open water of the St. Lawrence River. After a few false starts, summer had finally arrived, and I knew that the next five months would be glorious before another long winter arrived. A few hundred feet from the boat something caught my eye, and I grabbed the set of binoculars that went everywhere with me. Josie noticed and followed my eyes.

"What is it?" Josie said.

"I'm not sure," I said, staring through the binoculars. "Whatever it is, it's swimming. Probably a muskrat. Or maybe a mink."

Josie grabbed her pair of binoculars and trained them on the object.

"It's heading right towards us."

"Yeah," I said. "And it's making good time."

"That's not a muskrat, Suzy. It's a dog."

"You're right. It's a puppy. The poor thing looks frantic."

"And very focused on us."

We both watched the puppy continue to paddle its way towards the boat.

"Should we go get him?" Josie said.

"No, let's stay put and let it come to us. If we move the boat, it might freak out even more."

"Okay," Josie said. "It's a good swimmer. I'll grab a towel."

Josie headed to the bow and returned with two large beach towels. I knelt over the edge of the boat, and the puppy swam directly into my arms. I lifted the puppy out of the water and held it against my chest as Josie began toweling its head. The puppy licked both our hands, then sneezed.

"What a gorgeous dog."

"Have you ever see one that wasn't?" Josie said, laughing.

"Well, this one is especially gorgeous. Australian Shepherd, right? Look at those beautiful green eyes. How old do you think it is?"

Josie took the dog and held it up in the air. She removed the towel and examined the tag attached to the elaborate collar it wore.

"Probably around three months. And she's a girl. Her name is Chloe. How are you, Chloe?" Josie looked at me. "She's scared, but she seems fine. We'll get her back to the Inn, and I'll take a good look at her."

When Josie says she'll take a good look at the puppy, she means it. Like every veterinarian I've ever met, she's incredibly devoted to her work and loves dogs almost as much as I do.

And that's a lot of love.

Josie put the dog down, and we laughed as it shook vigorously, spraying water over both of us. I repositioned the towel and held the puppy against my chest. She licked my hand again then nestled its head under my arm.

"You poor thing," I said. "What were you doing all by yourself in the middle of the river?"

The boat jerked and stopped drifting. Josie looked off the stern and saw her fishing rod bending severely in its holder.

"How about that?" Josie said, racing off to grab her rod. "No chance of catching a muskie, huh?"

I watched Josie struggle against the weight of the fish on her line as she reeled it in. As she continued, it became apparent, if it was a muskie, it was of world record size.

"There's a phone number on the collar," I said. "The owner must be frantic."

I turned away from Josie's ongoing battle with the fish, and I grabbed my phone and dialed the number on the dog's collar.

"Uh-oh," Josie said.

"What is it?" I said, staring off into the distance as I waited for the call to connect.

"This ain't no muskie."

"Hang on. It's ringing."

"Need you over here, Suzy. Oh, my goodness."

"What is it?" I said, holding the puppy with one arm and the phone against my ear as I walked to the stern. "Dang, nobody is answering."

"Listen," Josie said.

"What is that?"

"Well, I can't be sure, but it sure sounds like a phone ringing," Josie said.

"Yeah, but where?"

"Down there. In the water."

I glanced over the back of the boat and saw the body floating face down.

"Wow. Poor guy. It is a guy, right?"

"Yes, it certainly is. We need to call Jackson."

"Hang on. Let me check something first."

I ended the call, then immediately pressed the redial button. The sound of a phone ringing under the water returned.

"Well," I said. "If there's any good news here, I think we found Chloe's owner."

"What is that stuff floating on the surface near his head?" Josie said.

"That's weird. Is that oil?" I said.

"I don't think it's oil," Josie said, peering down into the water.

"The bigger question is where did all these bees come from?"

www.ingramcontent.com/pod-product-compliance
Lightning Source LLC
Chambersburg PA
CBHW070618260626
47161CB00007B/2481